DATE DUE JAN 0 7

04/2007			
GAYLORD			PRINTED IN U.S.A.

STILL AS DEATH

This Large Print Book carries the
Seal of Approval of N.A.V.H.

STILL AS DEATH

SARAH STEWART TAYLOR

THORNDIKE PRESS

An imprint of Thomson Gale, a part of The Thomson Corporation

THOMSON

GALE

Detroit • New York • San Francisco • New Haven, Conn. • Waterville, Maine • London

THOMSON
™
GALE

Thorndike Press® Large Print Mystery.

The text of this Large Print edition is unabridged.

Other aspects of the book may vary from the original edition.

Set in 16 pt. Plantin.

> **LIBRARY OF CONGRESS CATALOGING-IN-PUBLICATION DATA**
>
> Taylor, Sarah Stewart.
>   Still as death / by Sarah Stewart Taylor.
>   p. cm. — (Thorndike Press large print mystery)
>   ISBN-13: 978-0-7862-9215-8 (alk. paper)
>   ISBN-10: 0-7862-9215-6 (alk. paper)
>   1. Saint George, Sweeney (Fictitious character) — Fiction. 2. Police —
> Massachusetts — Cambridge — Fiction. 3. Women art historians — Fiction.
> 4. Art, Egyptian — Fiction. 5. Theft from museums — Fiction. 6. Mas-
> sachusetts — Fiction. 7. Large type books. I. Title.
> PS3620.A97S75 2006
> 813'.6—dc22   2006031017

Published in 2007 by arrangement with St. Martin's Press, LLC.

Printed in the United States of America on permanent paper
10 9 8 7 6 5 4 3 2 1

For Lynn Whittaker

ACKNOWLEDGMENTS

Most readers will realize that the Hapner Museum is an entirely fictional creation. Still, I am very grateful to Bart Thurber, curator of European Art at the Hood Museum of Art at Dartmouth College, for showing me around a *real* college art museum and answering my many questions. Any mistakes or deviations from reality for the purposes of plot are mine and mine alone. Information available from Steven R. Keller and Associates and the Museum, Library and Cultural Property Protection Committee, American Society for Industrial Security was invaluable for my research into museum security.

I found a number of books helpful in my research into Egyptian burial items: *Jewels of the Pharaohs* by Cyril Aldred; *Howard Carter Before Tutankhamun* by Nicholas Reeves and John H. Taylor; *Ancient Egypt:*

7

Treasures from the Collection of the Oriental Institute University of Chicago by Emily Teeter; *The Complete Valley of the Kings* by Nicholas Reeves and Richard H. Wilkinson; *The British Museum Book of Ancient Egypt* edited by Stephen Quirke and Jeffrey Spencer; *The World of the Pharaohs* by Christine Hobson; *Tutankhamun: His Tomb and Its Treasures* by I. E. S. Edwards; *The Complete Tutankhamun* by Nicholas Reeves; and *Official Catalogue, The Egyptian Museum Cairo* by Mohamed Saleh and Hourig Sourouzian.

Finally, a huge thanks to Ryan Quinn at St. Martin's Minotaur and most of all to my editor, Kelley Ragland, for her patience and understanding during an intense time. I have been so lucky to work with Lynn Whittaker over the past few years. She is a great agent and a great friend. And a big thank-you to my family, especially to Susan and David Taylor for grandparenting beyond the call of duty, to Matt Dunne for his love and support, and, of course, to Judson Dunne.

PROLOGUE
1979

The room was silent as a crypt.

Karen Philips laid the jewelry out on her worktable and reflected on the aptness of the metaphor. The items spread out before her had, of course, come from crypts or, more accurately, tombs of ancient Egyptians who had been well outfitted for their passage to the afterlife. Under the bright fluorescent bulbs, the faience, glass, and metal amulets, the beaded necklaces and collars lost some of their appeal. But she knew that they would look beautiful in a display cabinet, their colors revealed under perfect, golden light.

She felt a little charge of excitement. She had seen wonderful pieces of gold and bead jewelry in Cairo and in New York and in Washington, DC, but this was the first time she had actually handled jewelry from an ancient Egyptian tomb. The collection was part of a recent donation to the university museum made by a wealthy alumnus with an interest in Egyptian antiquities, and everyone, including Karen, was riding the wave of excitement generated by the announcement.

The donation was the result of a carefully planned friendship between Willem Keane, the museum's curator of ancient Egyptian art, and Arthur Maloof, a financier with a huge personal fortune. Willem had convinced him to hand over a number of items from his excellent collections, and he was most excited about the donation of a stunning sheet-gold mummy mask that would make the museum's collection of antiquities the envy of most museums in the world. Because of laws forbidding antiquities from leaving Egypt, it was rare that important pieces like the mask came on the market anymore, Karen knew.

There were some other items of interest in the Maloof collection: canopic jars that had held the organs of a mummified king, game boxes, and a large number of little shabti figures that had acted as stand-ins for the dead in the next world, meant to do any work they might be called on to do. The jewelry had been kind of an afterthought. There weren't any especially rare or valuable pieces in the cache, and she assumed that Maloof wasn't interested in storing them anymore and had decided to let Willem have them along with the mask.

Willem hadn't been particularly excited about the jewelry, but when Karen had asked him if she could inspect it, he'd readily agreed. She was writing her thesis on women's funeral jewelry and thought she might find some additional material among the new acquisitions. In any case, she was probably the first scholar to really study them, and that gave her a little thrill.

She looked over the files to get some background before inspecting the pieces themselves. First was a series of little amulets in the shapes of animals and deities that had held various meanings for the ancient Egyptians. There were a huge number of scarabs and eyes of Horus, a few crocodiles, vultures, and baboons. The little charms had likely been found among the linen wrappings on a mummy, meant to protect the dead in the tomb. The amulets were common and Karen had seen them before. There was no need to pay them much attention. Next was a series of simple bracelets and necklaces made of gold and glass beads. She was able to date them pretty reliably to the New Kingdom, and she took some notes before moving on to the last piece, a beaded falcon collar featuring rows of gold and faience beads interspersed with amulets of many different kinds of stones. The falcon heads at either end of the thick necklace were made of gold, with accents of lapis and carnelian.

Karen sat up a little straighter in her chair. It was a beautiful collar and she hadn't expected to find it. The file on it said it was eighteenth dynasty, from a tomb in Giza, but she didn't think that could be right. It looked vaguely familiar to her. Not the necklace itself, but the style. She jotted some notes on a piece of paper and was about to go back to the files when she started at the sound of voices out in the basement gallery. It was against security regulations, but she had left the door to the study room propped open just a bit to let in some fresh air. She couldn't hear what they were saying, but she assumed they were looking at the displays of Egyptian antiquities, Willem's two sarcophagi and the exhibits of statuary and other items from the collection.

She turned back to the collar, knowing she was lucky that Willem had given her access to it before he'd even had a chance to look through the pieces himself. She was very, very fortunate. *Don't forget it, Karen.*

Don't let yourself forget how lucky you are.

Willem's recommendation would look good when she applied to graduate school, and experience with the jewelry would be helpful if she became a curator. *When,* she reminded herself, remembering what the speaker at the last meeting of the campus women's group had said about undermining one's own possibilities. *When* she became a curator.

She sifted through the papers in the file folder, trying to find a document that mentioned the beaded collar. According to the paperwork, the jewelry had been excavated in the Valley of the Kings in 1930 on a dig sponsored by a British collector named Harold Markham. The Markham collection was well-known, and much of it had gone to places like the Metropolitan Museum and the British Museum, so that was in order.

But she couldn't shake the feeling that the collar wasn't eighteenth dynasty. In any case, it was so well preserved it was hard to believe that it was three thousand years old. It was what she loved about Egyptology, the vibrancy of the works of art, the way they seemed so relevant, so modern so many years later. What it must have been like to be one of the first archaeologists to uncover

13

the entrance to a king's tomb, to stand there under the hot Egyptian sun, to hear the men shout suddenly that they had found something, a staircase! She had relived Howard Carter's discovery of the tomb of Tutankhamen so many times that she almost felt as though she'd been there.

Ever since she had seen the Tutankhamen exhibit at the Metropolitan Museum in New York on a school trip four years ago, she had known that this was what she wanted to do. She had begun learning about Egypt, about the strange burial customs and the cult of the afterlife that had so obsessed the ancient Egyptians. She had loved memorizing the names of the gods and goddesses, the strange-sounding words, and then the hieroglyphs, the code that unlocked the secrets of that ancient world. She had done research into which colleges and universities were the best for studying Egyptology, and then she had decided that she wanted to study here. After that, everything she had done was for the purpose of attaining this goal. It had been easy to keep her grades up, knowing that the prize for doing so was realizing her dream.

After she'd gotten to the university, the dream had become Egypt itself, and during her junior summer, she had finally been able to go, joining a dig at Giza for three months with an expedition from the Hapner Museum that included Willem Keane and some other faculty members, along with a number of graduate students.

She had been disillusioned, of course. There was no way she wouldn't have been disappointed by the reality of Egypt, the hot, dirty poverty of the cities obscuring the fantasy she'd created, the endless sand and drudgery of work on the dig. She had known enough about archaeology at that point to know that she wanted to be an art historian and not an archaeologist, that it wasn't all uncovering intact tombs and treasures, but still she'd been surprised that it had been so different from her expectations. They were digging for tiny pieces of ancient history now, shards and fragments instead of golden statues and alabaster unguent vases, all the things of Karen's dreams.

It had been a sort of relief to return to the university and the museum, with its lovely pieces of antiquity, already cleaned of dust and dirt and grime, already in place behind glass. But then she'd realized that the darkness she'd found in Egypt had followed her home.

It was while she was away that she'd

begun to question whether those beautiful things should be behind glass in an American museum at all. A young Egyptian graduate student working on the dig had told her that Egypt's history had been looted by rich white men, nothing more than "pirates," who had stolen his country's most valuable assets, leaving nothing behind but empty graves. "Why is it?" he asked, "that I should have to come to America or Britain to see the art of my own country? You Americans wouldn't stand for it. You'd buy it back or find a way to take it, just as you take everything you want. The white men are nothing more than rapists, taking what they wanted by force when they couldn't seduce my countrymen into giving it willingly."

Since coming home, she'd been different too. It was as though she'd awakened from a fog, she thought. She saw things so differently now. Everything she'd once taken for granted was now as uncertain as the history of the beaded collar.

As she was putting the collar into its box, she heard the voices again out in the gallery. This time, there was something about them that made her pay attention, something about the urgent low tones of the two men who seemed to be arguing.

"You're not doing it right," she heard one say. "Like this." *Museumgoers,* she told herself. *Looking for the sarcophagi.* And then there was a loud crack from outside the door, a violent sound, and then another one. She jumped up, surprised, overturning the metal stool she'd been sitting on, and she heard one of the voices say, "What the fuck?" and then the men were at the door, two of them, dressed in raincoats and carrying hatchets. She saw the hatchets before she took in the details of their plain, almost pleasant faces, and she must have screamed because the shorter of the men yelled, "Shut up!" and crossed the room to her, clapping a hand over her mouth and pushing her to the ground, grinding her face into the musty-smelling industrial carpet that lined the floor of the study room. Sitting on her back, he twisted her arm behind her. Her shoulder throbbed. She struggled to breathe against the carpet, gasping and choking, and tasted stomach acid in her mouth.

"Who the fuck are you?" the man near the door asked in a low, hissing whisper. Karen could hear her own breathing, ragged and uneven. She felt as though she'd run twenty miles. "You weren't supposed to be here, you bitch."

"Give me the tape," the one on top of her

said in a similarly low voice. *They're afraid of someone hearing,* she told herself. *They think someone can hear.*

There was a slapping sound and then the ripping sound of tape being pulled from a roll. "No one said anything about someone being down here," the guy near the door said.

The man turned her over. He took a strip of silver duct tape from the roll and severed it with his teeth, then slapped it over her mouth. She felt her lungs panic, forced herself to slow down and breathe through her nose.

He looked at her then and she knew, from the look on his masklike face, from the almost dreamy fixated look in his eyes, what he meant to do. She shook her head. *No. No!* She knew her fear would only excite him. His eyes were green and somehow dead. She could smell his breath, peppermint masking stale beer, and he was sweating. She could smell that too.

"Do her hands and feet," the other guy said.

"Why don't you get the stuff out and I'll be right there." He was still looking into her eyes.

"No, you asshole. Tape up her hands and feet and get out of here."

She saw the dreamy look leave his eyes, and then she was turned over again, and her shoulder screamed as he pulled her arms behind her and wrapped the tape around and around her wrists and ankles.

"Be good," he said, giving her a strange little pat, almost reassuring, as he stood, taking the duct tape with him.

"Okay. Let's go. We have to hurry now," the other one said, and she craned her neck around, trying to get a look at them, trying to burn those plain, very average faces on her brain. The guy near the door had eyes that were too close together. The other guy had a weak chin, a slight underbite.

She watched them flip the light switch and open the door, and before it swung shut, she saw the Plexiglas display cabinet, which must have been split with the hatchet, the statuary inside tipped over, their long noble faces lying facedown, in mockery of her own confinement.

The museum is being robbed, she said to herself before the door clicked shut and the storage room fell dark. *That's what they're doing. They're robbing the museum.*

ONE

Sweeney St. George awakened slowly, aware only of a sense of breathlessness, as though something was interfering with the air getting into her mouth and down into her lungs. She opened her eyes to darkness, darkness, she realized, of a specific texture, soft, and smelling faintly of . . . fish.

She rolled over and sat up, displacing the large black cat that had been sleeping nestled up next to her face, her prolific red, curly hair a comfy cat bed. The cat, now sitting up in the dignified iconic pose of his species, blinked a few times and looked indignantly at her as if to say, "I had just gotten comfortable, thank you very much."

Sweeney gently pushed him off the bed, and the cat stretched as he landed gracefully on the floor, then turned and sprang onto the windowsill and out the slightly open bedroom window onto the fire escape. He turned back, gave her a farewell glance through the window, and was gone.

"What?" the other inhabitant of the bed asked sleepily. "What's wrong?"

Sweeney curled herself against the long back and whispered into warm skin, faintly scented by the dark brown ovals of soap sent every month from London. "Nothing, just the General. It's okay. Go back to sleep."

She lay there for a few minutes, listening to his deep, even breathing, then got out of bed, slipped into the silk robe on the rocking chair in front of the window, and went into the kitchen. It was nearly six and the sun was rising above the Somerville skyline, giving everything a clean and optimistic aspect that Sweeney appreciated. She got the coffeemaker going and broke two eggs into a frying pan, flipping them onto a plate when they were just barely set. Two pieces of buttered toast and an orange completed her breakfast, and she sat happily munching as she watched her next-door neighbors enjoy their own breakfast on their second-story balcony. It was late August and al fresco dining offered a respite from the current heat wave. Through the open kitchen window, Sweeney felt a slight breeze and turned toward it for a moment. As she finished eating and got up to rinse her dishes in the sink, she heard a whoosh and turned to find the General sitting on the kitchen windowsill, watching her.

"What are you doing back here?" she asked him. "I thought you'd gone for the day." The cat, who had been living with Sweeney for ten months now, tended to leave through one of the windows in her apartment early in the morning and return at night for dinner and bed. What he did during the day she had no idea.

Sweeney had inherited the General, and every time she looked at him she thought of the young boy she had befriended the previous fall. Dying of leukemia, he had made her promise to care for the cat. When she had first brought him home the previous fall, she had tried to get him to use a litter box and be a proper indoor cat, but he had hated using the box as much as she had hated cleaning it, and when she accidentally left the bedroom window open one day, they both discovered a routine that suited them. Sweeney did not want to fuss over him too much. He, in turn, did not like being fussed over.

He looked meaningfully at her plate, still smeared with egg yolk, and she set it on the counter for him. In a few seconds, the plate was clean and shiny, and the General used one huge paw to wash his whiskers before disappearing again out the window. "Have a nice day," Sweeney called after him.

Once she'd washed up, put on jeans and a linen blouse and tied her hair up and out of her face against the heat, she leaned over the bed and brushed its occupant's dark fall of hair away from his forehead. "Ian?" she whispered. "I'm heading out to the museum. It's seven. I'll see you tonight, okay?"

He opened his eyes and looked up at her, squinting into the sunlight. His glasses were on the bedside table and she knew he saw only the vaguest outline of her face. "But it's early," he said. Ian didn't usually get to his office until nine or ten.

"I know, but the exhibition opens in three weeks and I still have so much to do. The catalogs are done and I have all this text to write. They're still painting the galleries and I need to make sure all the framing is right. I told Fred and Willem I'd get in early."

"Okay, okay, I can take a hint. However . . ." He reached up and pulled her back into bed. "I assert that I ought to be allowed to have a small memento of your existence, since I shall have to do without you all day."

"But I have so much to do . . ." She ran her hands over his bare chest, trying to decide if she wanted to be seduced. His skin

23

was as warm as sun-baked stone, his arms around her sure and familiar. It had been almost six months since he'd arrived in the states to open a Boston office of his London auction house, and Sweeney often found herself surprised at how quickly they'd settled into domesticity. They had known each other for nearly two years now, she supposed, so even though they'd been in the same city only since January, it made sense that there had been no need for prelude. But still . . . Sometimes when she came home at night and found him reading the papers on her couch or wrapped in his navy blue, monogrammed bathrobe and cooking dinner, she had the sense of having entered someone else's house. She sometimes thought to herself, *Who is this man?* for a moment before she remembered, *Oh, it's Ian.*

In any case, she thought, looking at him, he was a very handsome man and a very kind one and, at the moment, a very sexy one.

"Just one thing you have to do here, though," he murmured, unbuttoning her blouse. She thought about protesting, then relaxed into his arms.

"Okay," she whispered into his ear. "But only because you're so persuasive."

■ ■ ■ ■

Forty minutes later she was walking through the front door of the Hapner Museum of Art, holding a cardboard cup of coffee. The Hapner was arguably among the most distinguished college or university art museums in the country, and like most art museums connected with institutions of higher learning, the Hapner had a strange and eclectic collection, largely dependent on original holdings and gifts by alumni or benefactors. In addition to works of American, European, and Near Eastern art, the Hapner housed the university's well-rounded collection of ancient Egyptian antiquities — thanks to the interest of its director and Egyptologist Willem Keane and the proliferation of wealthy and well-connected alumni associated with the university through the years.

The grand gray stone façade of the museum presented a paternal and imposing aspect to passersby which, Sweeney had always thought, seemed singularly uninviting. She stopped for a moment to look up at the banner over the main entrance. STILL AS DEATH: THE ART OF THE END OF LIFE it read, announcing Sweeney's exhibition of funerary art from the museum's collection. It panicked her to see the words up there when she hadn't even finished putting everything in place.

"Hi, Denny," she called out as she climbed the ten stone steps to the main foyer. In contrast to the outside of the museum, the foyer was surprisingly welcoming, bathed in sunlight from the soaring skylights high above the marble floor. The antiquities were housed in the basement and on the main floor, with the European and American galleries on the second, third, and fourth levels. The museum was constructed around a central courtyard, open all the way to the ceiling, with wraparound balconies on each floor that led into the galleries. Standing in the courtyard, you could look all the way up to the balconies of the fourth floor high above you.

The security guard raised a hand and answered, "Hey, Mizz St. George." She had tried to get him to call her by her first name long ago, but Denny Keefe, who had been working at the museum for thirty years and apparently using the formal address for all that time, wouldn't budge. "Hot day, huh?"

"Yeah. Again." She smiled at him, glad as she always was that the museum administration hadn't let Denny go for someone

younger and spryer, but rather sup-
plemented his presence with a revolving collection of imposing-looking twenty-year-old
bodybuilders to safeguard the collection.
Denny himself wasn't a very convincing
security guard, but he was a cheerful presence and Sweeney liked him. He had always
reminded her a little of a frog, with his large,
egg-shaped eyes and his longish white hair,
which he kept smoothed to his head with
applications of a slippery substance that
smelled vaguely of sandalwood. His uniform
had never fit him properly and the loose
green fabric added to the effect. Sweeney
wasn't sure what he would do if he were
actually faced with a determined art thief,
but she liked the idea that he might just put
out his tongue and . . .

She headed up to the third floor, where a
series of connected galleries would soon
house her exhibition. It had long been a
dream of Sweeney's to plan an exhibit of
the things she studied: tombstones and
mourning jewelry, death masks and Victorian postmortem photographs, and Egyptian
burial items.

The pieces had all been chosen, and she
had spent the previous year working with
museum staff to create installations and
displays for the items. As she walked into

the first of the linked galleries, she saw that one of the Egyptian sarcophagi had already been carried up. Tomorrow they would be bringing up other Egyptian burial equipment from the basement galleries. Though they could no longer display the museum's mummy, they could display many of the items that would have been buried with it. The elaborate preparations of the bodies of the ancient Egyptians — first the nobility but eventually those on other levels of society as well — were great evidence for the overriding assertion of Sweeney's exhibition: that death and speculation about the afterlife were the motivating factor for much of the great art of the world. By choosing representative pieces of funerary art from different eras, she hoped to show the diversity of responses to human mortality.

Today she had to choose a piece of Egyptian funeral jewelry to replace one that the conservation department had determined wasn't in good enough shape to be displayed. The catalog was already completed, of course, but she and Willem had decided that they should just choose another piece. She hadn't found exactly what she wanted among the displayed items, so she went down to the storage areas located beneath the museum to browse the files.

The art and antiquities displayed in the Hapner's galleries represented only a tiny percentage of the museum's holdings. The rest of the items were stored in five large rooms beneath the museum. Banks of file cabinets flanked the large workspace where Harriet Tyler, the collections manager, had her office and controlled access to the rooms of priceless and not-so-priceless treasures.

Every piece in the museum's collection, no matter when it had been acquired or donated, no matter how insignificant it might be, had a file containing information about its history and connection to other pieces owned by the museum, and Sweeney went to the *E*s and found the files kept on examples of ancient Egyptian jewelry.

Her choices were very nearly endless. The museum had a huge number of Egyptian antiquities, most of them unimportant pieces that had been gifted to the university long ago. They were used for research, brought out for special exhibitions, or loaned to other museums, but for the most part, they remained in storage. Attacking the row of files, Sweeney felt a bit like a prospective dog owner at the pound. Who would the lucky antiquity be?

She had already included the more obvious examples of Egyptian funerary art, the sarcophagi and the canopic chests and jars that had held the internal organs of entombed ancient Egyptians. What she didn't have was an example of the elaborate jewelry that had been buried with the mummies, the amulets and collars and pectorals that archaeologists often found among the layers of linen wrapping the prepared bodies. Some jewelry from ancient Egypt would be a nice counterpoint to the Victorian mourning jewelry she was also including in the exhibition.

There were scores of insignificant pieces, scarab rings and gold hoop earrings that had been donated years ago and weren't seen by anyone but students anymore. Sweeney remembered coming down to the museum as a graduate student and looking at some New Kingdom amulets for a paper she was writing about funerary mythology.

Now she found listings for a number of amulets in the shape of various animals and flowers that had special meanings for the ancient Egyptians: hippos and flies and vultures and lotuses and fish. She put them aside, thinking it might be interesting to include a few, but quickly forgot about them when she opened the file folder labeled, "Beaded Collar. 18th Dynasty." On the outside was a little grid with a name and date scrawled in it. Sweeney assumed it was a record-keeping device to track everyone who had taken the piece out of storage. It appeared that the last person had been someone named Karen Philips.

There was a photograph of an absolutely magnificent piece of jewelry stapled to the inside of the folder, and Sweeney spread it out on one of the worktables to get a better look. The photo showed an intricately beaded collar made of gold and faience that would have covered the chest area of some very lucky mummy. It had falcon heads where the strings of beads gathered together on either side, and the eyes and beaks were accented with blue and amber-colored stone. The file was thick with paperwork, shipping labels and lists and receipts, and as Sweeney looked through the documents she decided they had to represent the object's provenance or history of ownership. Most pieces donated to the museum were accompanied by similar paperwork showing that the person who was donating it was the actual owner. From the paperwork she saw that Arthur Maloof had donated the collar in 1979. Well, well, well. The basement gallery had recently been renamed the Maloof Gallery, and she knew that Arthur Maloof had donated the gold funerary mask that was the crown jewel of Willem's collection.

She looked at the photograph again. Why wasn't the collar on display? It was as beautiful as anything Sweeney had seen from the period, almost as stunning as some of the collars found in the tomb of Tutankhamen, though the beadwork was finer and more delicate, stylistically different. She decided she'd ask Willem if he could have the collar brought out of storage.

The collar decided upon, Sweeney headed back up to the third-floor galleries. The next order of business was figuring out the placement of the twenty postmortem photographs in the exhibition. She'd always loved the haunting photographs of deceased loved ones that had been so important to the Victorians. Because of her desire to include them in the exhibit, she'd gotten important support from Fred Kauffman, the Hapner's curator of photography. All of the pieces depicted the deceased, most of them dressed in their finest clothes and posed in coffins or upright in chairs. Sweeney had always been fascinated by the oddly moving postmortem photographs that had been so popular during the nineteenth century. For many Victorians, the postmortem portrait was the only one they would ever sit for.

Families would spend what were then exorbitant sums in order to have a final image of a loved one.

She was starting to go through the framed photographs and daguerrotypes and tintypes stacked against one wall when Fred came into the gallery.

"Morning, Sweeney. How's it going?"

"Very well, thanks." He looked over her shoulder at a set of daguerrotypes of a young girl. She was dressed in what looked like a white christening dress and propped up in a fancy wing chair. To the unpracticed eye, she might have been a pale but lively six-year-old posing for the camera. But the static, staring eyes told a different story, and Sweeney shivered a little, the way she always did when looking at postmortem photos of children. There were a lot of them around. Epidemics felled so many infants and children. She always thought of those parents, left with a single image of the child who would never grow or change.

The process of choosing the photographs that would be included in the exhibit had been a push and pull between Sweeney's interests and Fred's. She had tried to be conscious of his opinions and expertise, but she kept remembering a report card she'd received in the third grade: "Sweeney does not work well as part of a team," the teacher had written. "She prefers to do group projects on her own and does not like to share credit or responsibility."

But she liked him enough to want to make it work, and she was proud of how the exhibition had turned out. Fred was a short, well-padded guy with curly gray hair who was passionate about photography. He wore unfashionably large glasses that reminded Sweeney of a camera's telephoto lens, and though she knew he had gotten his Ph.D. from the university in the late '70s and was a good twenty years her senior, he had always treated Sweeney as an equal. They had gotten to know each other fairly well over the last few months, and she and Ian had been out to dinner with Fred and his wife, Lacey.

Fred was giving his opinion about where to hang a particularly haunting daguerrotype of a young girl when Willem stuck his head in to see how they were doing. Every time she saw him, Sweeney couldn't help thinking about the first time she'd met Willem. She'd been an undergrad, doing an internship at the Hapner the spring semester of her junior year, and she'd been assigned to work with Willem. He'd been curator of ancient art then, and he'd had Sweeney doing research on an Egyptian sarcophagus that had been given to the university. She had been nervous, very much in awe of the good-looking man who was known around campus for being very brilliant and very icy, and when he'd said, "Well, have you gotten inside yet?" she hadn't realized he was making fun of her. She'd almost climbed into one of the stone vessels before he'd cracked a smile and let her off the hook.

She and Willem got along well now, and she knew he respected her work, but she always felt a little bit like a nineteen-year-old student around him. He was a tall, rangy man of sixty, with perfectly cut gray hair and a professorial mustache. Unless he had a meeting or event, he always wore a gray or tan cashmere sweater, jeans, and expensive running shoes.

"Sweeney, the catalog looks terrific," he said. "I'm really pleased." He was holding one of the paperbound catalogs, with the title of the exhibition superimposed over one of the postmortem photos. There had been a lot of talk about whether it was too macabre an image to put on the cover, but Sweeney had eventually gotten her way. It worked well, she saw now, the cover image literally confronting the viewer with the reality of death, and with the desire of the living to memorialize those who had passed, a desire that had led to a highly stylized mourning ritual. These were themes that Sweeney examined throughout the exhibition, from the funerary items from ancient Egypt to the modern-day mourning items she'd found — memorial tattoos and car decals as well as contemporary mourning jewelry.

Willem held up the catalog. "Good work. I wish I could say the same for her." He nodded toward the hallway, and Sweeney knew he was referring to Jeanne Ortiz, a professor of photography and women's studies who was curating an exhibit on depictions of women in American photography that would run sometime over the winter. Sweeney liked Jeanne and was interested to see the exhibit, but she knew that Willem couldn't stand her and found the somewhat radical premise of her show specious to boot. When he'd discovered that Jeanne was planning on including a series of photographs from *Hustler* and *Penthouse,* he'd raged for days.

Sweeney and Fred exchanged a look, neither one wanting to get Willem going on Jeanne's various transgressions.

"Well, I'm off," Willem said. "Tad has a pile of papers for me." Tad Moran, Willem's assistant, was always trying to get Willem to sit down and sign papers while Willem preferred to spend his time roaming his museum.

"Before you go," Sweeney said, jumping up and going over to her worktable to find the file containing the information about the collar, "I think I found another piece I want for the exhibition." She held out the folder.

"Great," Willem said, distracted. "I don't have time, but show it to Tad. He'll arrange everything and I'll have a look and see what I think. Good progress. I'm very, very pleased."

Fred stood up as Willem turned to go. "Do you have a minute, Willem? I just wanted to talk to you about the Potter Jennings exhibit. The book's out in December and I was thinking . . ." Fred's biography of the American photographer Potter Jennings was, in many senses, his life's work, and Sweeney knew he was hoping that Willem would agree to an exhibition that would help promote it. Willem, a singularly focused Egyptologist and antiquarian, didn't seem very excited about it. Sweeney knew that the only reason she'd been able to get Willem to be supportive of her exhibition was that she was including some of his favorite pieces of Egyptian burial items from the museum's collection.

"Okay, walk with me," Willem said, looking bored. "See you, Sweeney."

"I'll leave you to it, then," Fred said to Sweeney. Something came over his face suddenly. *He's ashamed,* Sweeney thought. She watched them walk out of the gallery and along the hallway, then went back to her work.

By four o'clock, she'd figured out the placement of all of the photographs and was feeling considerably more confident that the exhibition would be ready by the date of the opening. She headed over to the museum's administrative offices to ask Tad about the collar.

The museum staff's offices were on the second floor of the annex, a modern glass addition that had been built onto the museum in the '70s and provided office space for Hapner staff as well as members of the History of Art Department like Sweeney. She used her electronic passkey to cross over to the annex, knowing that the system was recording the time she passed through the doorway as well as her identity. The security was necessary, of course, but it always felt a little Big Brother to Sweeney.

Tad Moran was talking to Harriet out in

the reception area, and when he saw Sweeney he gave her a shy smile and said, "Hi, there. How are things coming along?" before glancing nervously behind him. Tad always seemed scared of something, Sweeney thought. Willem probably. Tad had been working for him for years, and she'd always wondered why he hadn't moved on to another job. Willem was brilliant but famously a tyrant to work for. Tad had been quite a gifted Egyptologist, apparently, and had chosen to be Willem's right-hand man rather than make a career of his own. She'd once asked Fred about it, and he'd said that he thought he'd heard that Tad had a sick wife at home, something like that. He wasn't a bad-looking guy, Sweeney thought, though he appeared not to have changed his haircut or clothes since he'd been in prep school. His dark brown hair was parted unfashion-ably on the side, and he always wore khakis and neatly pressed blue oxford cloth shirts with red and blue or yellow and blue striped ties. Though he must be in his early forties now, he looked far younger, his thin face nearly unlined and his short brown hair untouched by gray.

"Fine. Willem said to ask you about this piece. It's in storage, I guess. But I'd love to make a last-minute addition." She held out the file folder and added, "We know it's not in the catalog or anything. It's just to provide some more context," when she saw that Tad looked a little panicked. It was very late to be making additions.

He jotted down the numbers written on the outside and said he'd arrange for it to be brought up. "What are you going to do about displaying it?"

"I think there's room in the cabinet that's already there."

"Good. I don't know if you've got time to build something new."

"You definitely don't have time to build something new," Harriet offered. Sweeney resisted the urge to slap her. Harriet was a perfect collections manager, a hyperresponsible cataloger and record keeper. Her precision got on Sweeney's nerves. Her bobbed gray hair hardly moved when she shook her head, and her clothes were always perfectly matched, brown shoes with brown slacks, black shoes with black slacks. Sweeney always had the feeling Harriet didn't like her.

"Fine. I'm not going to." Sweeney turned to go, then remembered the file. "Hey, all these old documents in here, what are they for?" Sweeney showed him the documents, the inventories and shipping labels and lists.

"Probably someone was researching the provenance," he said.

"That's what I thought. Does every item in the collection get the same treatment?"

"Not always," Tad said vaguely.

But Harriet jumped in, pleased at an opportunity for didacticism. "You may have heard about museums having to search their collections for Nazi art. Well, we're also particularly concerned with antiquities. There was a 1970 UNESCO convention that prohibited the removal of any more antiquities from their countries of origin, and then a 1983 law passed here in the states that basically said the same thing. It had been a particular problem in Egypt, where you could buy antiquities right on the street. The UNESCO treaty meant that if you wanted to accept or buy a piece, you had to be able to prove that it was part of a legitimate collection that had been assembled before 1970. That's probably a piece that was given to the museum and someone was just checking to make sure everything was in order."

Tad turned to go. "I'll let you know when they can bring it up for you."

"Thanks. Do you know why it's not on display? It's really beautiful. I just thought Willem might have some reason."

41

"I couldn't say," Tad told her. "We have a lot of beautiful things that we can't display for whatever reason."

He was right, Sweeney reflected as she walked out into the humid afternoon air. She was just going to have to be satisfied with that.

Two

It was almost seven by the time Sweeney got home to the apartment on Russell Street. Walking past the newly renovated triple-decker next door, she felt a pang of nostalgia. Before a wealthy young couple with two kids had bought the old Victorian and turned it into something out of *Architectural Digest,* it had been the shabby home to a Russian couple who used to give Sweeney bottles of homemade wine at Christmastime; a Bulgarian poet who used to ask her out at three-month intervals, as though she might have forgotten she'd already said no; and an assortment of students whose lives Sweeney tracked by the romantic partners who came in and out of the building, the cars with out-of-state license plates bearing parents and grandparents at graduation time, the nods hello when they recognized Sweeney on the street or on the T.

It wasn't that the new people weren't nice.

In fact, Sweeney had had a pleasant conversation with them a couple of weeks before, during which the wife had promised to invite Sweeney and Ian over for dinner. But Sweeney hadn't felt like investing much time in the relationship since she knew she wouldn't be on Russell Street much longer. Her landlord had told her he was selling the building. She'd sold some of her father's paintings the previous winter, and the proceeds had swelled her bank account beyond any hope she'd ever had for it. She had thought briefly about buying the dilapidated triple-decker, but it was much more than she needed and she didn't really want to go into the rental business. Her landlord had said he was hoping to sell by the end of the year, but she'd avoided thinking about it too much.

And she'd avoided telling Ian about the conversation. When he'd first arrived in Boston, he'd taken a room at a hotel for the first few weeks, but it hadn't been long before he'd moved into Sweeney's apartment. She had found the whole idea of it somehow amusing: Urbane, English Ian, living in her shabby apartment with its noisy pipes and creaking floorboards. He claimed not to mind, but it had been only a month or two before he'd started dropping hints about the lack of closet space and bugging her about looking for a bigger place. Sweeney had chosen avoidance, changing the subject and trying just to go on as they were, ignoring the fact that Ian had planned to be in Boston for six months and he was now coming up on the eighth. He flew to Paris once a month to see his daughter, but Sweeney knew it bothered him being so far away.

As she climbed the stairs to her apartment, however, she felt a little wave of pleasure at the thought that he was there, waiting for her. She smelled something delicious as she opened the door and was greeted by the sight of her boyfriend — for lack of a better word — lighting a candle at her already-set dining room table.

"Hey," he said. "Steaks are almost done."

"Steaks? Mmmm." She dropped her bag in her office, stopped in the bathroom to splash cold water on her face, and went through to the kitchen, where Ian now had his head stuck out the window, checking the steaks on Sweeney's fire escape hibachi. She could smell them cooking, could smell something tangy and salty, probably his famous teriyaki-ginger marinade. He ducked back in and she hugged him from behind. "I could get used to this."

As soon as she'd said it, she wished she hadn't. She couldn't see the expression on his face, but his voice was amused as it said, "That's the point."

She pulled away and found two wineglasses, then filled them from the bottle of red on the table. "The General around?"

Ian took his glass. "He made an appearance when he smelled the steaks, but when he realized I wasn't going to give him any, he returned to his nightly perambulations."

"His nightly perambulations?"

"There's something about that animal that has me using words like 'perambulations'."

Sweeney smiled. Ian, who had grown up with dogs, didn't much like cats, but he'd been very understanding about the General. The cat had been rude after Ian moved in, carrying his socks into the bathroom and dropping them in puddles of water from the shower, and leaving mouse entrails in his perfectly polished shoes. Sweeney had tried to convince Ian that the mouse parts were proud offerings, but she knew as well as he did that it was an act of hostility.

"Good day?" he asked as they tucked into the steaks.

She swallowed. "Fruitful, anyway. I figured out where we're going to place most of the postmortem photographs. And the catalog looks great. I think it's coming together finally." She washed a piece of tender meat down with a swallow of red wine. "Oh, hey. What do you know about the UNESCO convention? Something like that. It's meant to stop people bringing Egyptian antiquities out of the country."

"Not just Egypt. The United Nations Educational, Scientific and Cultural Organization's 1970 Convention on the Means of Prohibiting and Preventing the Illicit Import, Export and Transfer of Ownership of Cultural Property. It's a mouthful, I know, but it basically said that member countries could take back illegally acquired antiquities if they could prove they'd been stolen. It was a really dreadful state of affairs, people bringing vases and things home in their suitcases. They realized they had to do something or Egypt was going to lose its entire cultural heritage. What there was left of it, of course. Why do you ask?"

"I told you Willem and I want to round out the Egyptian part of the exhibition with another piece of jewelry, right?" He nodded. "Well, I found the perfect piece today. It's in the museum's permanent collection but it isn't displayed right now. I can't imagine why because it looks fabulous in the picture, but anyway, there were all these documents showing everyone who had owned it."

Ian took a long sip of his wine and sat back in his chair. "There have been some high-profile cases recently of collectors who created fake documentation in order to pass off a stolen piece as legitimate. What you'd have to do is create a paper trail showing that the piece was excavated and legally acquired before 1970. There was a dealer in New York, someone I knew pretty well, good reputation and all that, who got indicted a couple of years ago for trafficking in stolen antiquities. Apparently he was knowingly buying statues from a British collector who had bought them on the black market in Egypt. They'd cooked up this whole thing where they said the statues were part of the collection of some earl who was an explorer. They forged documents and stained them with tea to make them look old. That kind of thing."

"I guess the stakes are high enough that it would be worth going through all that."

"Oh, yes. There was one piece, the head of a king, I believe, that was worth more than a million dollars."

Sweeney whistled.

"That's right. Would you like some ice cream?" He got up to clear their plates.

"Of course I would." She stood up half-heartedly to help him.

"Uh-uh. Sit. I'll do it." She did, gratefully.

"So how's the exhibition coming along, anyway," Ian asked once they'd finished their butter pecan and he'd told her about his day.

"Fine. I've got a lot to do still, but the catalog looks great and the Egyptian stuff is all ready to go now. Everything — or nearly everything — is framed at this point and I'm going to start some of the wall label text tomorrow. We open September tenth, so I need to get moving on it." She looked up at him. He was going to Paris on September 10. "Oh, no, I forgot you're going to Paris. You're going to miss the opening."

He looked away quickly, then said dismissively, "Well, I might be able to change it. We'll see." He cleared his throat and stood up, taking their ice cream dishes into the kitchen. "I talked to Peter today," he called back. Peter was Ian's partner in London.

"Yeah?"

"He thinks we need to figure out whether I'm coming back to London or not. The Boston office is doing very well, but he's feeling shorthanded over there."

"Oh." Sweeney poured herself another glass of wine, finishing the bottle.

"Sweeney." He came back into the room and sat down across from her. "We need to talk about this." His glasses made his eyes look a little bigger than they actually were, and in the candlelight she felt intensely scrutinized.

"Well, do you want to stay? What do you want to do? I mean, couldn't they hire someone in London to take over for you? Or if you want to go back, you could . . ." She was babbling, looking everywhere but at him.

"I would love to stay, but I can't. You know how hard it's been being apart from Eloise so much. I hate seeing her just once a month."

"So, what? You're just going to go back?" Suddenly she realized she didn't like the idea of that, either.

He reached across the table and took her hands. "No, I'm not going to just go back. I want you to go back with me."

She couldn't look at him. "But what about my work? What about my apartment? What about the General?"

"I have a lot of contacts at universities back home. So do you, for that matter. You could commute to Oxford a couple of days a week. There are universities in London, you know. And I have a very large house.

You could have an office. I don't know how it works with animals. There might be a quarantine or something, but the General can come too, if he's allowed."

She took a too-fast sip of her wine, sputtering and dribbling it on her blouse. She dabbed at the linen with a napkin and said, "I don't . . . I don't know. I don't want you to go back. But I haven't been here very long. I don't know if I could . . ."

"Is it London?"

She took a deep breath and considered. Was it London? Ian knew she hadn't been back since her fiancé had died in a terrorist bombing there three years before. She didn't say anything.

"So it's me."

"It's not. It's just . . . it's a big move. I don't know if I could just pick up and . . ." As she said the words, she felt the weight of everything she'd have to move, the second-hand couch she loved, her framed photographs of gravestones, the leather club chair that had belonged to her father and that her aunt Anna had given her. And then she felt the weight of everything she'd be leaving behind: her best friend, Toby, the university, her favorite bakery and pub and Chinese place. This was home.

"Sweeney, I know it's a big move, but I

don't know what alternative we have. If we want to be together . . . ?" It was a good question and one she didn't know how to answer.

"I know. I'm sorry." She took another long sip of her wine and felt better. There was time. He wasn't asking her to make a decision right now, was he? She reached out and took his hands. "We do want to be together. Of course we do." She was very conscious that she hadn't used "I." "You know that."

There was something sad and scared in his face as he dropped her hands. "Just think about it, okay? That's all I'm asking you to do."

THREE

Willem Keane poured two glasses of bourbon from the bottle on his desk and handed one to the man sitting across from him. "To the canopic chest," he said, raising his glass. He had to stop himself from grinning like a little kid. Cyrus Hutchinson was a stern, serious man, but he was very proud of his gift and Willem knew he needed to strike a perfect balance between excitement and professional decorum.

"To the canopic chest," said Hutchinson, with an elegant little gesture that matched Willem's. They each took a long sip and studied each other with mutual respect and a little bit of suspicion.

"Really, Hutch, we truly appreciate this gift to the museum. I hope you know what a meaningful thing you've done for generations of students and faculty. It's a stunning piece. It really is." Willem turned to the chest sitting on the table in a corner of his office. In the low, green-tinged light from his desk lamp, the rich alabaster glowed like milk suspended in the air. The eighteenth-dynasty chest was rectangular, about the size of a small suitcase, with four compartments that once contained the internal organs of a young Egyptian king. The spaces where the liver, lungs, stomach, and intestines had rested were topped by alabaster stoppers in the form of the heads of the deities Imsety, Hapy, Duamutef, and Qebehsenuef, a human, a baboon, a jackal, and a falcon. He felt a sudden surge of something like arousal, a speeding of his blood, and forced himself to calm down. It was always amazing to him that he could get so jazzed up about a new acquisition.

"Well, I'm very happy to do it," Hutchinson said, nodding his head, his long, droopy face and white eyebrows holding a bit of worry. "How long do you think it will be before you can complete the new exhibit?"

"We should be able to do the necessary work over the Christmas holidays. Perhaps we can have an official unveiling in January? We want to make sure that the university community, and of course the public, knows what a wonderful thing you and Susanna have done." Hutchinson lit up at that. He was, Willem thought, an essentially ego-driven man. In fact, his formidable ego was what Willem had used to get him to part with the canopic chest. He had begun courting the old man three years ago, seeking him out at an alumni event and then writing him a sickeningly sycophantic note about how much he would like to see the family collection of Egyptian antiquities. Hutchinson was the American grandson of a British explorer who had plundered sites in the Valley of the Kings for years before he died of a massive coronary in the arms of his Egyptian mistress in a Cairo hotel. His booty was housed in a number of museums, but an unknown number of pieces had remained in the family, a fact that had given Willem a small charge of illicit pleasure when he'd learned it.

He had seduced Hutchinson, he saw now, grooming him for the final outcome by making sure not to rush things, by giving the man time to come up on his own with the idea of a gift to the museum. By the time he'd suggested the gift of a small statue from his grandfather's collection, Willem had anticipated his move and was ready with his argument that the statue would disappear into the museum's other holdings, whereas something like a canopic chest, for example, would stand out. Perhaps they could even build a special exhibit for it . . . ? Something with a plaque indicating that it had been gifted to the museum by a famous and valued alumnus . . . ? Hutchinson hadn't known what hit him.

"Of course, we'd love to show it off even before the new exhibit's done," Willem said now. "We're having an opening in a couple of weeks. A young woman from the History of Art Department is curating an exhibit of funerary art from various times and places. She's chosen a number of pieces from the museum's collection. I hope you'll come up from New York and be our guest."

The door opened and Tad Moran came in holding three copies of the transfer papers. Willem met his eyes and indicated that he should put them down on the desk. He didn't want to rush Hutchinson, didn't want him to feel ambushed. Tad, who had been working for Willem for so long that he was able to read something as subtle as the tiny nod of a head toward the desk, smiled and put them down.

"Have you met my right-hand man, Hutch?" Willem asked. "This is Tad Moran, our assistant director here."

"Very pleased to meet you, sir," Tad said pleasantly, shaking the man's outstretched hand. He was good at this kind of thing.

"Anything else, Willem?"

"No, thanks very much." Tad closed the door behind him, leaving them alone.

"It will be safe, won't it? Until the exhibit's built?" Hutchinson asked, worry again creasing his forehead. His country house in Connecticut had been burgled a couple of years ago, and the burglars had made off with a Chagall and some important jewelry. He was a bit obsessive on the subject of security.

"Don't you worry. We'll have it locked up and alarmed and everything. The insurance company wouldn't have it any other way." Willem smiled reassuringly, though he knew it would be hard to get the necessary work done in the time before the opening.

"Excellent." Hutchinson finished his bourbon and put his glass down on the desk. "I should be going, Willem. I have to catch my train." The more time Willem spent with spectacularly wealthy men like Cyrus Hutchinson, the more he came to enjoy their range of funny affectations, such as Hutchinson's habit of taking the train everywhere. Of course, he'd agreed to be driven up yesterday because he was bringing the canopic chest. But he'd dismissed the driver, an employee of some secret security firm that catered to the rich, so he could take the train home today.

"Absolutely," Willem said. "And again, thank you so much." His eyes darted to the chest and he forced himself to level his gaze at Hutchinson's eyes. *Hang on,* he told himself. *Only a few more minutes and you can be alone with it.* "I'll be sending you an invitation to the opening. I think you'll enjoy it. A number of pieces from our Egyptian collection will be on display. With your formidable knowledge of antiquity, I know you'll be interested to see funerary art from other periods."

He'd gone too far. Hutchinson gave him a suspicious look.

Cursing himself, Willem waited a beat and went on. "Oh, and we just need to get your John Hancock on these," he said lightly, reaching for the transfer papers. "For the lawyers, I guess."

He showed Hutchinson where to sign and tried not to sigh when the other man put the pen down and said, "Thank you. Take good care of my prize." Hutchinson raised his eyebrows impishly, and for a moment Willem had the sense that he knew what turmoil he was in. *Don't show your hand, Willem. Casual, just be casual.*

He showed Hutchinson out to the elevator, then hurried back to his office, telling

Tad that he wasn't to be disturbed. He had an hour before they would put the chest into the museum's vault for safekeeping.

He shut his door and forced himself to finish his bourbon before he crossed the room to the chest. The alabaster was cold to the touch but smooth as human skin. He lifted one of the stoppers, feeling its unexpected weight, cupping his hands around the young king's almost feminine face.

And then, nearly at the point of tears, he replaced the stopper and kneeled down to embrace the chest. He was able to lift it without too much effort, his arms encircling its cold, hard weight.

It was absolutely beautiful. And it was all his.

FOUR

"Dinner in ten, hon," Lacey called out from the kitchen. "I'm putting the pasta in."

"Okay," Fred Kauffman called back. "I'm just cleaning up in here and I'll be right in." He took another sip from his glass of chilled Pinot Gris and continued stacking bills in the basket Lacey had bought for the purpose a couple of months ago when they'd decided to try to get control of the mail on their dining room table. The resolution for neatness had been prompted by a visit home from their twenty-year-old daughter. As they'd sat having breakfast, she'd looked around the house and proclaimed them slobs, regaling them with tales of visits to the homes of her college friends where, apparently the mail was always sorted and nobody ever got cat hair on their pants when they sat on the couch.

The amazing thing, Fred decided, was that it had affected them so deeply, or at least deeply enough that Lacey had bought the basket and he had started the little routine of sorting the mail when he got home every evening. But then both of them had always been a little afraid of Kyra. Even as a baby she'd had a way of looking at them and making them feel they were doing exactly the wrong thing.

As he looked around the dining room, though, he felt suddenly annoyed at his youngest child. This was her home. It was where they had raised her and her brother, and while he had to admit that it *was* usually cluttered to the point of messiness, it also had a comfortable charm that he'd wished for growing up in his parents' immaculately decorated Manhattan apartment. The downstairs rooms were dominated by his and Lacey's interests: framed black-and-white and color photographs hung on every wall, crammed together so that they almost looked like collages. Where there weren't photographs, there were textiles Lacey had bought in Japan or Latin America, as well as large pieces she had knit or woven herself. Fred looked up at a huge sea green panel made of distressed wool and scraps of fabric that hung over the sideboard. It had always reminded him of a fisherman's net, the pieces of fabric unlucky fish.

The rest of the mail was easy to sort. He pitched a couple of credit card offers, then piled the four or five remaining envelopes in the center of the dining room table and sat down, taking another long sip of his wine.

He'd had a long day, and a tough one, and coming home to the smell of frying onions and Lacey's tomato sauce simmering on the stove had been just what he'd needed.

He turned around and craned his neck so he could see her in the kitchen, standing at the stove, hoping that he'd feel a familiar rush of desire and affection. But all he felt was the same dull sadness he'd been feeling for weeks now. It had nothing to do with Lacey, of course, at least he didn't think it did, but Lacey was the barometer of how far he'd sunk. For most of their twenty-four-year marriage, the mere sight of Lacey had caused him to nearly overflow with gratitude. They had met at a friend's dinner party twenty-five years ago. Fred had been a graduate student then, working on his Ph.D. thesis on Potter Jennings and acting as a T.A. at the university.

He'd felt like chopped liver at the dinner party, everyone more accomplished, richer, better-looking than him. When the man to his right had asked him what he did and he said that he was a graduate student working on a thesis on Potter Jennings, the man had said, "Gosh, old Potter! How is he? Still taking drugs?" and Fred remembered feeling so angry at the man's easy condemnation of the man he'd come to love for his complicated impulses and brilliant eye that he'd almost gotten up and left the party.

But Lacey, who had been sitting across the table, had saved him. "I love Potter Jennings," she'd said in her Quebecois-accented English. "I have a print of that famous photograph of the Colorado Rockies. It must be such a privilege to know intimately the work of such a man."

He'd been charmed by her strange syntax and by her long reddish braid that she kept hanging over one shoulder like a scarf. She had been dressed in what he later learned were garments of her own creation, a woven knee-length dress and a tissue-thin sweater the color of new grass, and she'd looked utterly foreign to him. He'd fallen in love with her that night. Everything he'd achieved, he'd achieved for her, in a way.

Now, after twenty-five years, his book on Potter Jennings was finally going to be published. They'd sent him the jacket a few days ago, with the wonderful blurbs on the back, and a note from his editor telling him how excited she was. It was the book that could make his reputation. So why did he feel as though the world was ending?

He turned to the stack of personal letters. There was one addressed to both of them from Lacey's brother in Montreal. He'd let her open that. And there was one from some good friends in Sonoma, just a little thank-you note for a weekend they'd spent recently in Cambridge.

Then he opened the last one, a long, thin white envelope with a Boston postmark. He unfolded the expensive writing paper and felt his heart seize when he read the name at the bottom. Something clanged in the kitchen and he started, snatching up the letter and pushing it under one of the hand-woven place mats he and Lacey had brought back from last year's trip to Ecuador.

He took another sip of the wine, his heart pounding, and forced himself to turn slowly around. Lacey was still in front of the stove, and even though he knew there was no way she could see him from the kitchen, he turned so that his body blocked her view and took the letter out again. He had known what it was, of course. It was the letter he'd been expecting all these years, worded almost exactly the way it had been worded in his nightmares.

He sat back and thought about what to do. It wasn't the first time he'd thought about it, of course. If he was honest with himself, he'd always known that someday he would get this letter. He'd thought about coming forward, about offering some kind of deal. But it had all been theoretical. He hadn't actually *had* to do anything about it until now.

"Hon?"

He jumped up, covering the letter with a magazine and clutching the envelope to his leg. Lacey was standing behind him, holding the half-empty bottle of Pinot Gris.

"Yes? Dinner?" He tried to pretend he was just straightening up the catalogs on the table.

"I just drained the pasta." She topped off his glass, but in his nervousness he reached for it too quickly and knocked it over, sending white wine across the table and soaking the place mats and mail. "Are you okay?"

"Fine," he said, grabbing a dish towel that was sitting on the sideboard and mopping up the wine. "Fine. Sorry about that. I was just reading an article and you surprised me."

"Okay. Let's eat. I have some work to do

after dinner." She kissed his forehead, and he could smell the fresh, spicy floral scent of her soap. Carnation, he thought, letting the familiar aroma fill him with calm.

He watched her as she disappeared into the kitchen. Lacey. Lacey. It was the most beautiful name in the world. Suddenly the dull, listless sense of plodding was gone. His limbs felt alive again. He loved her so much. She couldn't find out about the letter. He would do anything to make sure she didn't.

FIVE

Jeanne Ortiz hit you like a tropical storm, sudden and lush, generating energy as she went. When Sweeney ran into her on the stairs to the third-floor galleries the next morning, she had the sense that she'd been overtaken by something as inescapable and overbearing as the weather.

"Sweeney, I was looking for you. I have a favor to ask." In Sweeney's experience, Jeanne always had a favor to ask, or a favor she thought she could do for you but that always ended up being more like a favor for her. She had been teaching at the university for only a couple of years, though she seemed to know everybody and everybody seemed to know her. She was officially a member of the Women's Studies Depart-ment, but she was always forming partner-ships and "creating opportunities for com-munication across the disciplines," as she liked to say. The show she was in the initial stages of planning was the result of just such a partnership among the History of Art Department, the museum, and Jeanne. How Willem had been convinced to allow the show was beyond Sweeney. She assumed it was the result of some kind of political tit for tat that would make sense only years down the line when it became apparent what Willem was getting out of the deal. In the meantime, though, Jeanne was doing everything she could to drive him crazy.

Sweeney, however, actually quite liked Jeanne. She was a bit of a study in contradictions and Sweeney found she was always surprised by her. Ortiz, for example, was the surname of one of her ex-husbands, and Jeanne herself was a Norwegian-American farm girl from northern Minnesota. She had bright blond, extremely curly hair that gave her round face a look of eternal youth. And she had huge breasts, which she refused to contain in a bra and which bounced almost independently of her body underneath the thin fabric of her Guatemalan embroidered dresses or too-young printed T-shirts. She loved wine and traveled once a year to the Loire Valley or Tuscany or Emilia-Romagna or southeastern Australia or somewhere to tour vineyards. But she was not as particular about her food and often ate Cheetos or pasta out of a can for lunch. Above all, she was a dedicated teacher and a serious scholar, and though Sweeney found her brand of feminism a little overbearing, she agreed with her on pretty much everything. Now she was looking expectantly at Sweeney, as though she might agree to the favor without having to be told what it was.

"A favor? Well, do you think we could talk about it later? I'm in kind of a rush. I think Willem wants to see what I've —"

"Willem!" Jeanne snorted. "You just tell him that you're the curator and you're offended by his paternalism. If you were a man, he wouldn't be looking over your shoulder all the time, wanting to know how things are going. He'd let the exhibit speak for itself."

"You think so? Well, I'd better get going. But e-mail me and we'll figure out a time to —"

Jeanne cut her off again. "Do you know, he tried to cancel my exhibition after he found out I was including examples of pornography? If you asked someone on the street whether there was academic freedom at the university, they would tell you there was. But there isn't! You know there isn't, and you can help me stand up to him." She pushed a few blond corkscrews behind her ear. "We'll get together a group of women faculty members to protest his treatment of us. Then he won't dare cancel the show and he won't dare ask for oversight of your exhibit. Imagine!"

"Well, he didn't exactly ask for oversight," Sweeney said. "I think he just wants to know how things are going."

"Oh, there's Tad. I have to talk to him," Jeanne shouted out, her voice echoing through the third floor. Sweeney looked down to see Tad Moran hurrying across the courtyard in his scared rodent way, his dark head bent to the floor. The poor guy, he was probably trying to stay out of Jeanne's path.

Sweeney thought she'd escaped when Jeanne said, "Oh, and about the favor. The WAWAs need a faculty adviser. I was thinking you'd be perfect. They need someone young, you know. They think I'm an old fogey, out of another era. I make them feel like feminism isn't relevant anymore. But someone young, well, I think you could really get them excited again about all the work we have to do on this campus." Jeanne was walking backward down the stairs as she talked in an increasingly loud voice. Sweeney held her breath, afraid she was going to fall.

The WAWAs were a campus women's

group and Sweeney couldn't remember what the acronym stood for. Women Angry, Women Active, something like that. She'd gone to a few meetings when she was an undergraduate, and she'd attended a rally where women stood up and shouted the names of men who had date-raped them. It had made her uncomfortable, though she hadn't told anyone but her best friend, Toby, that at the time.

"So, can I put you down?" Jeanne called up as she disappeared around the corner.

"I'll have to think about it," Sweeney called back, not at all sure that Jeanne had heard her.

Exhibition prep staff were in the galleries, putting the finishing touches on the display cabinets and temporary walls. The paint had dried and Sweeney was pleased with the creamy ecru color she'd chosen. She had a list of things she needed to check with Tad, so she went over to the annex and found Fred and Tad in the main office, standing outside Willem's office door, obviously eavesdropping. From behind the door, Sweeney could hear Jeanne's voice rising in anger.

"Poor Willem," Sweeney whispered. Tad raised his eyebrows and Fred tried not to laugh.

They all turned away as Willem and Jeanne came out of Willem's office, Willem looking annoyed and Jeanne vaguely triumphant.

"There a party I don't know about?" Willem asked them.

"Hmmmm?" Tad had a good way with Willem. He knew when to engage and when to ignore him. "Sweeney, did you need something?"

"Couple of things. The proofs of the wall labels for the postmortem photos look ever so slight blurry to me. Is that possible?"

Tad looked annoyed. "Yes. We've been having some problems with the printer. I'll take care of it. What else?"

"Any word on the collar? I can't wait to see it. And we'll have to get a wall label for it. I thought Willem might want to write it."

Tad looked slightly uncomfortable. "It may be a little while. It wasn't where it was supposed to be in storage when I went to get it this morning. The numbers must have been wrong or something. It happens. I'll let you know."

"But we have it, right?" Sweeney panicked all of a sudden. She had gotten excited about the collar, and she wanted to make sure she'd be able to show it.

"Have you gone and lost a piece of art

again, Tad?" Jeanne asked loudly.

Tad noticed the two interns who were making copies at the other end of the office and gave Jeanne a severe glance. "No, Jeanne. It's just been mislabeled is all. We've revamped the directory and . . ."

Sweeney exchanged a glance with Fred, who raised his eyebrows. If someone didn't kill Jeanne by the time she had finished with her show, it would be a miracle. She laughed and disappeared into the staff kitchen in a cloud of victorious energy. Whatever she'd gotten Willem to agree to, it had ruined his day. His face looked like the prairie just before a thunderstorm.

Sweeney returned to the galleries and got back to work on the exhibition. She made good progress, and by the time she decided to break for lunch at one, she was feeling like it might actually be possible that she would be ready for the opening in three weeks' time. She treated herself to the moo shu pork luncheon special at the grimy Chinese restaurant around the corner from the museum, then stopped for some wine to take home for dinner, bringing the bottles with her so they wouldn't get too hot in the back of her car.

At least it was cool inside the museum, she thought, as she climbed the stairs back up to the third floor. The museum felt very quiet and very empty, and outside the galleries she stood at the balcony for a moment looking down on the courtyard. It was a good forty feet down, and staring at the swirling marble floor below she felt dizzy all of a sudden and stepped away from the railing. She wondered suddenly if anyone had ever fallen. The railings weren't that high. A child could easily climb over. But she supposed that children didn't often run around the museum unattended. She entered the gallery again.

"Okay, Sweeney," she said out loud in the empty space. "Back to work." She followed her own admonition and sat down at the table, resolving to finish at least five labels before getting up again.

Six

Had we but world enough, and time,
This coyness, lady, were no crime.

Tim Quinn skipped ahead to the end again.

Let us roll all our strength and all
Our sweetness up into one ball,
And tear our pleasures with rough strife
Through the iron gates of life:
Thus, though we cannot make our sun
Stand still, yet we will make him run.

He grinned. Now he got it. This guy, the guy who was narrating the poem, was trying to get his girlfriend to sleep with him, and he was telling her that time was passing and they'd better hurry up before they were dead. He wasn't sure what the guy meant by "sweetness," but there was kind of an interesting image there, tearing through the "iron gates of life." It was like the gates were protecting the woman. Or the gates . . . maybe the gates *were* the woman. . . . That Marvell was a dirty bastard. It sounded like some kind of flowery language that you'd use only to say beautiful, romantic things, but he was just putting the moves on a woman.

He put the book aside. This was something he'd noticed about the class already. A lot of the poems they read seemed complicated, but all they were saying was stuff that regular people said all the time. It was the way they said it that made it literature rather than just some guy talking to his girlfriend.

Tim Quinn had been enrolled in his beginning English literature class for a couple of weeks now, and it still gave him a thrill to open up the textbook and see all those words covering the thin pages. It was like they had crammed as much literature into that book as they could, and somehow it made him feel that anything was possible, that he had all these words at his disposal and that he could read them all, if he wanted. It was the same . . . what was the word? *Openness,* maybe, the same openness he felt when he walked into class on Tuesday nights, assuming he wasn't out on a case and Patience, his daughter's babysitter, was available that night. He came in and sat down and felt the bigness of the future. Of his future.

"So what, are you going to be an English teacher now?" Havrilek had asked him when Quinn had told him about the class. Quinn didn't think he wanted to be an English teacher, but even the possibility of it was exciting to him. It made him think about all the other things he could be: a chef, a lawyer, a ship's captain. He wasn't sure why he was thinking this way. He loved being a cop. But there was something about considering other possibilities that made you feel free, he decided. That was how his class made him feel: free.

The door of his Honda opened and Detective Ellie Lindquist poked her head in. "You ready?" she asked. She and Quinn had been taking a lunch break, Quinn getting homework done in the car and Ellie reading the papers at a Starbucks in Central Square. But lunchtime was over and they were back on duty. Quinn tossed his textbook into the backseat, and Ellie got in and stuck a huge paper cup into Quinn's cup holder. She liked the Starbucks concoctions that tasted more like candy than coffee, and he could smell the sweetness steaming out of the cup, vanilla and caramel and milk. It was hot out, too hot for coffee, and he wanted to ask her how she could stand to drink it, but she saw him looking at it and smiled. "Hey, you want me to go get you one?"

Quinn suppressed the urge to snap at her. "No, no. That's okay. We should get back." She pushed a strand of dirty blond hair behind her ear and looked away as though he'd hurt her feelings. Ellie had a sharp little face that emotions couldn't hide on, happiness and anger and discomfort broadcasting across her wide blue eyes and thin lips as though she didn't have any control over them.

He wasn't sure why she irritated him so much. Ever since Marino had wrecked his back and taken early retirement, he'd been without a partner, and he'd happily worked with a bunch of different guys while they did some kind of internal restructuring of the department. When Havrilek had told him that Ellie was going to be his new partner, he'd had to stop himself from protesting. She was about twelve years old, for Christ's sake, or at least she looked it, and she'd been a detective for only a couple of months, since coming to Boston from somewhere out in Ohio. Even her accent irritated him, with its nasally vowels, "kyen" instead of "can." It drove him crazy.

"That's the point, Quinny," Havrilek had said when Quinn politely mentioned that she seemed awfully young. "You're a more experienced detective and she's a less experienced detective. She's smart as shit, though, and I want you to help her out."

Quinn pulled out and was heading back to headquarters when the radio in the car came to life and the dispatcher's voice came on. "We've got a suspected homicide. Young female." The voice gave a location in east Cambridge. "Quinn and Lindquist? You there?" Quinn looked over at Ellie, who suddenly looked a little scared. She'd never been first on the scene for a homicide before. For the month they'd been partners, they'd been working outstanding cases back at headquarters, on the phones, on the computers, in the interview rooms. But this was the real thing and he found himself worrying about how she was going to do.

"Yup, Sylvia, we've got it." She gave them the cross streets. "We're on our way."

Quinn knew this part of east Cambridge well. It was the part of the city that didn't make it onto the walking tours or calendars, a neighborhood where many Cambridge residents had never been and one they probably didn't know even existed, though, like

79

every neighborhood in the city, it was gentrifying by the day. As a patrolman, he'd frequently responded to domestics and brawls over here, and he knew there had been an increasing amount of gang activity, but there were also young couples moving in and fixing up houses and more and more Saabs on the streets. The dispatcher hadn't given them much to go on, assuming they'd get what they'd need from the guys on the scene.

He parked in front of a liquor store and followed the line of uniforms to an alley between an empty storefront and a 7-11. "That's where she is," he said, pointing.

"What should I do?" she asked quietly, in a way that bugged him.

"Don't do anything," he said, too harshly, then added, "Wait 'til I say."

The small body appeared to be that of a young girl, though on his second look, noticing her hips and rounded backside, Quinn realized she was more likely to be a young woman. She had been dumped — Quinn knew immediately by the way she was lying and because there was a black plastic bag underneath her — at the end of a dismal little alley filled with overflowing trash cans and piles of garbage. She was facedown, wearing black pants that had been pulled down around her thighs and a flowered pink blouse that was bunched up under her arms. Her back was smooth and brown, a small, perfect mole in the very center, between her shoulder blades. The outfit struck him. It wasn't the kind of thing he'd expected to find, more like what you'd wear to a job interview than . . . than what? *Face it, Quinn,* he said to himself. *You were thinking she was going to be a hooker, weren't you?* Because of the neighborhood. He hated it when his prejudices crept up on him like that.

He and Ellie checked in with the young sergeant who was guarding the scene and went to work. Once the crime scene technicians arrived, it was a matter of getting all of the information they could from the people who were still here. She'd been found by a guy who lived on the street and had happened to glance into the alley as he walked by. From the brown bag in his hand, Quinn figured he had gone out for his first drink of the day, but to his credit he'd called it in from the only working pay phone on the block and waited until the cops arrived. Usually you looked at the person who'd reported finding a body, but Quinn knew there was nothing here. This guy was too straightforward, just a sad, out-of-work guy who was now itching for whatever he had in his bag. Quinn was tempted to tell him to go ahead, but he couldn't very well encourage his best witness to get plastered before they'd had a chance to question him.

Once they were ready to turn her, he told Ellie to join him. "You can see she wasn't killed here, can't you?" he said offhandedly.

"Yeah, the bag kind of tipped me off." It wasn't sarcastic, just sort of matter-of-fact, but it annoyed him anyway.

"Good." He brushed past her and knelt by the body, looking at the girl's face staring up at the hot gray sky. She had light brown skin, and in life she had been pretty, dark haired, dark eyed, small and round. She was wearing quite a lot of makeup, a too-dark foundation that showed along her jawline, apple-red blusher on her cheekbones, pink eye shadow that matched the blouse, and bright pink lipstick that had smeared along one side of her face.

After the body, the first thing crime-scene services would look at would be the trash bag. They would hope to find something on it that might tell them how it — and the girl — got there. If they had been carried in a car, there might be fibers from the carpet, or traces of oil. If a man, or men, had carried the load, there might be hairs or microscopic pieces of skin on the bag. Then, of course, if the girl had been raped, as it appeared she had, there would be a treasure trove of evidence there, semen, hair, maybe DNA under her fingernails.

The truth was, though, that the crime might be prosecuted with all the forensic evidence in the world, but it was much more likely it would be solved from finding out who the girl was, what she had been like, who she had hung out with, what she had liked to do on the weekends. You didn't find your killer with the scientific stuff, Quinn had learned. You just used it to pin it on him. It was the regular old cop work that got you into court in the first place.

And that would start with finding out what her name was. He called his witness over and asked him if he knew her. The guy looked like he was going to throw up, but he choked out, "Luz Ramirez. Her family lives over there." He pointed to a dismal-looking brick apartment building across the way.

"Okay." He turned to Ellie. "That's our first thing. We gotta talk to the family, find out where she was going, then we'll want to start doing door-to-doors, that kind of thing, see if anybody saw her last night." He looked again at the victim's face. She looked younger and younger the more he stared at her. "She's dressed up like she was going somewhere. We gotta figure out who the hell she was going to meet."

SEVEN

Olga Levitch poured the steaming water into her teapot and waited a few minutes for the tea to steep. While she waited, she planned her day, mentally traveling through the rooms of the museum, starting her cleaning at the top of each room and working her way toward the bottom and out the door. When the tea was ready, she poured it into her thermos and went to get her cleaning cart. Though it was only five A.M., she could tell that it was going to be another hot day, and she craved something cool and relaxing. The Impressionists, she decided — she would take her tea break with the Impressionists.

It was her favorite part of the day, when she put aside her cleaning supplies and sat down for those delicious twenty minutes to drink tea and look at the art. After twenty-seven years, she knew every painting in the museum as well as her own face in the mirror. It was why she had kept the job, despite the low pay and the early starting hour. Actually, she liked getting to work at five. In those dark hours before the staff started arriving, before the museum's doors opened to the public, she could pretend that she was at home in her grand palace, that all the art was hers, to be looked at as she pleased. As she dusted, she could make believe that she was caring for her own collection, that the paintings all belonged to her. It was something about America that she found interesting, this idea that you might be able to own a painting yourself, that you might be rich enough to live in a house that looked like a museum. Of course, she had gone to the Hermitage when she lived in Moscow, and she remembered feeling proud that her country owned such beautiful things, but she had never wanted to actually own them herself. That was what America did to you. It made you want things. And when you couldn't have them, it made you sad, sad about something you never should have wanted in the first place.

She started out in the basement, in the cavernous stone room that housed the museum's collection of Egyptian antiquities. The room gave her the creeps, and she tried to clean it as quickly as possible. She hated the stone arches that were big enough for someone to hide behind, the recessed corners that lay in shadow even when all the lights were on. And a number of the pieces had been taken upstairs for the exhibition so it seemed even emptier than usual.

She vaccumed and swept, then went around quickly, dusting display boxes and glass. The art down here had never made much sense to her. It was interesting, of course, and very old, but it wasn't beautiful. It didn't make her happy or sad or relaxed or energetic or any of the things that the works in the upper galleries did.

Olga would never take her tea break down here.

It was now nearly seven and the museum was coming alive for the day. She took the elevator up to the first of the second-floor galleries and started cleaning, stealing only cursory glances at the Flemish paintings housed in that room.

She had just finished and was packing up the cart so she could start on the special galleries when she heard footsteps in the hallway below. She crept over to the balcony and looked down to find Harriet Tyler, the collections manager, walking quickly toward the staircase.

Olga maneuvered the cart out into the hall just as Harriet came up the stairs. She started when she saw Olga, one hand flying to her hair, and she gasped out loud.

"Oh, hi, Olga. I'm sorry, you startled me."

"Hello," Olga said, pushing the cart past her. It had been kind of fun scaring her, seeing the look on her face. She allowed herself a brief moment of anger in the elevator. Staff members sometimes did come into the museum before seven when they opened the main entrance, but it hadn't happened in a while and today she had been looking forward to being alone for her tea break. With everything she had on her mind, why couldn't she have had the morning to herself, just for once? It was always the way, just when she really wanted to be alone, someone came in early and foiled her. Of course, they usually seemed surprised to see her too.

The one person whom she didn't mind seeing when she came in was Mr. Keane. She and Mr. Keane understood each other, she decided. She could tell he liked being alone too, and when he came in early, he made a point of not talking to her, as though he knew that just hearing words from another human's mouth was enough to ruin those quiet, perfect mornings. If she happened to pass him on her way to the supply closet or on the stairs, he would nod to her but never say a word. It was like they had an understanding, though neither of them had ever spoken of it, and if they ran into each other during the day, he was always very polite and would say, "Good morning, Olga" or "Good afternoon, Olga." She liked Mr. Keane.

As she started on the top-floor gallery that housed the museum's collection of twentieth-century art, she tried to put aside her anger but found it hard with the Picasso and those other strange paintings staring at her. Those awful faces reminded her of the secret police, they way their eyes looked when they questioned you. "Where were you last weekend, Mrs. Levitch?" "What has happened to your husband, Mrs. Levitch?"

She sat down for a second to get her breath. She had been happy, and now she was thinking about the bad times, about the time before she had come to America. She took a deep breath and tried to calm down, but there was no way around it, her morning had been ruined.

For the next hour, she went about her work, trying to lose herself in the familiar routine, and it was nearly eight by the time she was ready to go over to the annex. She moved quickly through the staff offices, vacuuming and emptying the wastebaskets. Sometimes, she liked to look through the staff members' desks. It was interesting what she had found on occasion: photographs of people Olga knew weren't their spouses, bottles of liquor, letters that had been hidden at the backs of drawers. Olga never took these things; she didn't want anyone to know that she went through the desks. But she liked knowing about them, liked holding the information, as though it were a valuable and perfect coin she could decide when to spend.

At nine, she decided to take her break. She got her thermos and went into the cleaning supply closet to get her biscuits. Ever since she'd worked at the museum, she'd kept a tin of shortbread hidden in the closet for her morning tea break. The buttery Danish cookies were one of her only extravagances, and she lived in fear of one of the other staff members taking them, thinking they were for public consumption. So she kept the tin hidden behind the extra rolls of toilet paper, her delicious little secret, a spot of luxury in her working day.

She got her three cookies out of the tin and was just about to go back to the galleries when she heard someone out in the hall by the entrance to the storage areas. Not wanting to have to engage in small talk, she opened the closet door a little so she could see into the hall and waited, standing against the door so she couldn't be seen.

It was a couple of minutes before she heard footsteps coming out of the storage area and stopping by Harriet's desk. She watched the hallway, being careful not to make any noise, until the footsteps had receded again and the hallway was empty once more.

Olga took her cookies and thermos into the gallery. It was very interesting the things you saw early in the morning, she thought. It was really very interesting indeed.

EIGHT

Jeanne Ortiz lay back on the couch and studied the nude body of Trevor Ferigni as he bent over the stereo, putting on a new CD he said he wanted her to hear. Personally, she hated his music — odd, clanging metallic stuff by bands with ridiculously surreal names — but he was so excited about it that she couldn't deny him the pleasure of playing it.

Trevor — or Trev, as his friends called him — was a nineteen-year-old sophomore from California who wanted to be a musicologist and had taken a women's studies course from her last spring because his mother wanted him to. Jeanne tried not to think about that too much.

She hadn't planned on anything happening, not with this one, but he had started it. Of course, if anyone found out, that fact wouldn't matter in the least, but she knew it to be true. He'd made an appointment to see her and when she'd asked him how he was doing, he'd acted really upset and told her about his family, the Berkeley professor parents who were divorced but lived three blocks from each other so that the kids could go back and forth, his six-year-old stepsister, Electra. He'd wanted to come east for college, he'd told her, but he'd never realized he would be this homesick.

That first time she had just listened, then given him the name of the health center and told him to ask to see a counselor there. The next time he came to see her, in tears again, she had told him to come to her house for dinner that weekend. She had made chicken with rice, given him a few glasses of wine, and assumed she would send him on his way feeling a bit better, feeling as though he had a surrogate parent in Cambridge. But as it turned out, he'd been fun to talk to, and they had had more than a few glasses and ended up in bed together. He had kept drinking wine, and at some point she had realized he was flirting with her. Feeling the old buzz at the idea of an illicit encounter, she had asked him whether he had a girlfriend or — she'd hesitated, giving the question an edge — someone he was "seeing."

He'd smiled and said no, then added, as

she'd known he would, that he did have a crush on someone . . . older. His blush was what had made her take the next step. She had been expecting to be his educator, a role she usually relished, but it turned out that Trevor had taken advantage of the lax rules of his Berkeley households and had been sexually active since he was fourteen. His various partners, he'd told her, had included some of his mother's friends. He'd stayed in town over the summer, partly because of her, Jeanne feared, and they'd gotten lazy, going out to dinner once or twice and even walking through the yard on a Sunday morning.

"You know, now that school's starting again, we have to be more careful," she said, almost shouting over the music.

"What?" He was bopping around, un-ashamed of his young body, which was a little on the skinny side, his tan legs slightly bowed. Jeanne found it incredible that he was so immodest. She'd been brought up to believe that bodies and windows were to be covered at all times, and her own adult practice of nudity was a completely self-conscious thing. She dressed the way she did and paraded nude in front of her lovers to make a point. But to Trevor, it came very naturally, something that both delighted and intimidated her.

"I said, we have to start being careful again."

"I don't want to be careful. I'm not in your class anymore."

"That doesn't matter. You still are a student, even if you're not *my* student."

He kept dancing around but didn't answer her.

"Trevor?" Her voice sounded a tad shrill, much too maternal for her taste. "Did you hear me?"

"Yeah." He closed his eyes, waving his arms in the air like a cheerleader. The music raged behind him.

"I have to get going," Jeanne called out as he pretended to play the drums. What she really meant was, "You have to get going."

"Come on, not yet." He stopped dancing. "Let's smoke a joint first." He went over to his backpack, which was leaning up against her front door, and took out a baggie and some rolling papers.

"No, I have a meeting." She'd smoked with him only once, but she knew it had been a huge mistake. "Besides, I don't really smoke pot. That one time was just, you know, because you were."

"Is that right?" He raised his eyebrows at her. "And the sex is the same thing, huh?"

There wasn't any menace in his words, but something about the way he said them made her wince. She stood up and wrapped a chenille blanket from the couch around her naked body.

"No," she said weakly, "it's not like that. You know that."

"I guess," he said. But he looked hurt.

"Come on. I really have to get going."

"So, can't I hang out and listen to the rest of the album? It's so rocking." He flashed her a smile, and she had a sudden vision of what he must have looked like as a five-year-old boy.

"No. I need to lock up and it's not a good idea for you to stay here."

" 'Not a good idea'? We're not committing a crime or anything."

"I know, but . . . I could get in trouble."

"Only if they find out." He raised his eyebrows at her and she felt suddenly afraid. This one was different. There was something about him that was just too confident in bed and at the same time too emotionally involved. Was he in love with her? She didn't think so. But there was something he was getting from this relationship that he was going to want to keep on getting, and she felt her stomach buzz a little with uneasiness.

"All right," she said, giving in, looking forward to the feeling of checking out, of not worrying about Trevor and his intentions for a little while.

Jeanne's mother had always told her that she had no discipline, that she'd never get anywhere because she couldn't make herself do things she didn't want to do and couldn't stop herself from doing things she did. She'd always considered that she'd proved her mother wrong. She had gotten somewhere, made a success of her life. Obviously she had overcome what her mother had called "the devil" in her. But as she watched Trevor roll the joint, then light it, she reflected that perhaps her mother had been right.

NINE

Sweeney woke in the night, wide awake, alert to the sounds of the bedroom, the deep even breathing coming from Ian's side of the bed, the low, intermittent rumble of traffic, the indeterminate sounds of the city. Between the light coming in the window from the nearly full moon and the streetlights outside, she could see nearly all the details of her bedroom. Washed of color, her belongings looked both familiar and strange, different versions of themselves. She sat up, and the General, who had been curled up next to her head, rose too, blinked twice, and rubbed against her, asking to have his ears scratched.

She had been dreaming, and something in her dream had startled her awake. Searching her memory and not coming up with anything, she swung her legs around, sat on the edge of the bed for a moment, and then got up and padded into the kitchen, the

General at her heels. He sprang onto the counter, rubbing against the half-empty bottle of red wine next to the sink and looking expectantly at the bag of cat food against the wall.

"It's the middle of the night," Sweeney whispered to him. "It's not time for breakfast yet." She sat down at the kitchen table and felt the cool breeze coming through the open window. It was three A.M., and Sweeney reflected that it was probably the only time of day or night she'd feel the cool air until the heat wave was over.

She stood and reached for the unfinished bottle of wine, then poured herself a half glass, listening to make sure Ian was still asleep. Sipping it, she wandered around the apartment and finally climbed through the open window in the kitchen to sit on the fire escape.

It was the stairs that made her remember her dream. She had been standing at the top of a long stone staircase, disappearing into the earth. The stairs had terrified her, but still she had decided to descend, to find out what was at the bottom. She remembered the loose soil beneath her feet, the way she had kicked up little stones that had plunk-plunked to the bottom of the staircase. What had been at the bottom? She must have awakened before she reached it because she couldn't remember anything other than her slow, terrified descent.

She finished her wine, thinking that the staircase had seemed vaguely familiar to her, but where was it? She told herself that it was just a dream and that it probably didn't exist.

"What's wrong?" Ian asked as she crawled back into bed.

"Nothing," Sweeney whispered. "Just a bad dream." And she let him pull her into the circle of his arms, her head resting on his chest, his heart beating away as she fell asleep again.

Sweeney had been hoping that she'd arrive at the museum the next morning to the news that the collar had been located and was being transferred up to the gallery, but when she found Tad in his office, he looked up at her apprehensively from behind his glasses. He knew why she was there.

"Sweeney, we haven't found the collar. Willem's furious, can't understand how this happened. We know it's in there somewhere, but they changed the cataloging twenty years ago and he thinks maybe it's just stored under the wrong number. I don't have time to really investigate right now, though, so I think you may have to do without it." It struck her that though he was trying to seem nonchalant, he was in fact pretty worried about it.

"Can I help? I'm in pretty good shape workwise, for today, anyway. I'd be happy to look around."

He gave her an exasperated glance. "Fine. Okay. Sign a key out with Harriet and see what you can find. My theory is that it's in with the African jewelry. It all got recategorized as Willem acquired more Egyptian items. But if you can't find it, don't come back and ask me to look for it again. I'm not going to have time until the end of the week. And Willem's already all up in arms about us misplacing something, so please don't go to him and complain when you can't find it." He gave her what was meant to be a serious look. "Okay?" He looked more harried than she'd ever seen him, and she almost felt bad about pressing the issue.

"Okay. Thanks, Tad." She tried not to grin as she went back out into the main office and stopped by Harriet's desk to sign out a storeroom key.

Harriet handed it over and entered Sweeney's name in the log of everyone who went in and out of the storage areas. She pushed it forward for Sweeney to sign. "You have to sign now," she explained. "New policy. Willem read some article about a student impersonating a professor or something."

"Seems like a good idea," Sweeney said, signing her name. "Thanks."

As always when she entered the storage rooms, Sweeney felt like she'd entered the ultimate junk shop. The mobile storage units that lined the three walls of the first room could be spun open to reveal shelves full of treasures, row upon row of small carved items from various corners of the world: jewelry, musical instruments, pipes, and other artifacts. Storage cabinets and bureaus held textiles and more valuable pieces, and open shelving against the fourth wall held statuary and ceramics. There were a few racks — ceiling-high metal grates where paintings could be hung — but most of the paintings in the museum's collection were housed in other storage rooms.

Sweeney went to the area where the museum's collection of Egyptian antiquities was held. Most of the really good pieces were displayed, so those back here were either less important, redundancies, or in poor condition. There were a few plain canopic jars and some broken statuary. And then there was the jewelry, kept in the drawers of a closed storage unit. Sweeney put on a pair of gloves and opened the first drawer.

Willem had about twenty gold amulets displayed out in the Egyptian galleries, but there had to be another fifty or so in here and Sweeney looked through them carefully. The next drawer held the larger pieces of jewelry, and this was where the collar should have been, according to the reference numbers on the file. But while there were some nice beaded necklaces and tons of amulets, the falcon collar wasn't there. Tad was right.

Next she decided to check among the African jewelry, but when she finished searching the shelves and drawers, she realized that it wasn't there either. She tried the rest of the drawers in the jewelry cabinet and finally decided to search through all of the jewelry collections in storage. This took a while, and although she had fun looking through pieces from Europe and China and Iran, she was frustrated when she'd gotten all the way through without any success. And the problem was that she really had no idea when it had been misplaced. When had it been acquired? She checked the file. Maloof had given it in 1979, along with some other jewelry. There was a note, signed by Willem, about how it rounded out the museum's collection of eighteenth-dynasty funerary equipment and provided a nice counterpoint to another piece the museum already owned. Sweeney knew that curators at museums like the Hapner had to be able to make an argument for why a certain piece should be acquired. Even if a donor was giving a gift outright, the museum would be responsible for the upkeep of the item for all eternity. In any case, Willem's argument must have been successful. But Sweeney still didn't have a clue as to when the piece might have gone missing.

All she really knew, Sweeney reflected, was that someone named Karen Philips had studied the piece at some point. She checked the date on the front of the folder. November 1979. Maybe she could ask Karen Philips.

Sweeney removed her gloves and went back out to Harriet's desk. She handed in her key and signed out on the storage room log. "Hey, Harriet, does the name Karen Philips ring a bell? Apparently she studied this piece I'm looking for, and I'm wondering if I can get in touch with her somehow."

Harriet took the log back and looked nervously up at Sweeney. "She was a student intern," she said. "She was here a long time ago. I don't remember exactly when. But I've been here almost thirty years and it was during the first five or so years I was at the museum."

It was remarkable that Harriet could remember the name of a student from more than twenty-five years ago. "You don't know where she went after college, do you?" Sweeney knew she could probably get some information from the alumni office. They tried to keep track of every graduate of the university.

"No." Harriet glanced quickly down at her desk, where a framed photo showed her husband and two young sons playing on a beach, and then said very quietly, as though she were passing on a shameful secret, "She died. It was terrible. Everyone at the museum liked her."

Something in the way she said it made Sweeney ask, "What happened?"

Harriet looked around as though she didn't want anyone to hear, then leaned forward and whispered, "She committed suicide. They said she was depressed and she hanged herself in her residence house."

Harriet didn't know much else about the untimely death of Karen Philips, so Sweeney decided to do a little research at the library. The yearbooks were kept in an out-of-the-way bookcase on the second floor, and

Sweeney took a stack of them — 1979 to 1985, just for good measure — and settled down on a couch she had often fallen asleep on as an undergrad.

She was going back through the yearbooks and looking at the sections separate from the class pictures just to make sure she hadn't missed anything when she came across a page toward the end of the 1980 book with a picture of a young woman and the words, "In Memoriam. Karen Philips. 1960 to 1980."

The picture was a candid snapshot of a young woman standing in front of a brick wall. She was pretty, with bowl-cut brown hair feathered back and away from her face. Her rather large, dark eyes were cast away from the camera. Harriet was right. Karen Philips was dead.

After a few phone calls to the alumni records office, Sweeney had some more information. Karen Philips had entered the university as a freshman in 1977. She was from Greenfield, had graduated from the local public high school and, during her sophomore year, had declared her major as the history of art. She had been a student intern at the Hapner Musuem and had gone to Egypt with a group from the museum the summer before her senior year. The next

March, she had been found hanging from a belt in her single room. That was the bare bones of her career at the university. As an afterthought, the secretary at the alumni office added that Karen had been a Lorcan Fellow.

Sweeney had also been a Lorcan Fellow during her undergraduate career. The fellowship offered money for travel to students particularly interested in art history.

Beyond that, there wasn't much information. Suicides were not unknown at competitive colleges and universities, after all, and the secretary who had read the file to Sweeney over the phone said that as far as she remembered, the police had been satisfied that Karen Philips had committed suicide. Sweeney, hearing impatience creep into her voice, knew she wasn't going to get anything more there.

She decided to try to put her mind somewhere else for a little while and spent the rest of the day going over the exhibit. She was happy with the way it was turning out, and the more she thought about it, the more convinced she was that she was telling the story she wanted to tell, the story of how throughout recorded history, human beings had responded to the recognition of mortality by creating art, art that helped them process the idea of death, art that gave them a kind of immortality, art that would serve the dead in the afterlife and serve the living in the here and now.

Funerary art fascinated Sweeney because it danced on the subtle line between form and function. Gravestones were needed to mark the site of a burial, but they had become canvases for the stone carver's hopes and dreams for his own death. The ancient Egyptians had believed it necessary to entomb their kings with all of the things needed in the afterlife, but these common household items had been made glorious with gold leaf and carnelian, paint and beads.

Sweeney's exhibit would start with a room of artifacts that spoke to the elaborate preparations the ancient Egyptians had made for death. Alongside a sampling of sarcophagi from the museum's collection, she had included information about the elaborate process of mummifying bodies and a variety of canopic chests and jars used to hold the internal organs once they had been removed.

The exhibit then took a look at grave markers, including photographs of very early stone dolmens, and moving on to the American gravestones that were Sweeney's specialty, including rubbings, photographs, and castings of cemetery art from the earliest days of the American colonies.

Then came the postmortem photography, as well as other mourning items from the death-obsessed Victorian period. Sweeney had included a whole cabinet of hairwork mourning jewelry, and looking at the delicate pieces arrayed on green velvet, she couldn't help but think of Brad Putnam, her student and friend, whose murder she had gotten involved in investigating because of its connection with a collection of mourning jewelry. It was how she'd met Quinn, and as she thought of Brad now, she felt an overwhelming sadness at the pointlessness of his death.

The last room of the exhibit would include contemporary funerary art, loosely defined. Sweeney had lately become interested in impromptu memorial displays, the piles of flowers and teddy bears, liquor bottles and candles that appeared on the sites of highway accidents or murders. She still had to finish choosing the pieces for this final installment of the exhibit, but she was hoping to include some modern examples of mourning jewelry she'd heard about, pieces of plastic into which ashes were pressed, as well as some examples of memorial decals, the stickers that some teenagers had started putting on their cars to honor friends dead to gang violence or suicide.

She was finished for the day, but she didn't feel quite ready to go home, so she decided to go back to the library to see what more she could find out about Karen Philips. She left her things at the museum and walked over in the late-afternoon heat. The heat wave had gone on for nearly three weeks and the city felt permanently steamy. Sweeney, who hated the heat, nevertheless tried to take the long view. It wouldn't be long before she was complaining about the fourth snowstorm of the season.

The library kept bound copies of the university's student-run daily newspaper going back thirty or forty years, and Sweeney thought these archives might be a good bet for further information about Karen Philips's death. She knew the university tended to keep a stranglehold on information about anything as ignominious as a student suicide. But the student paper would have been able to interview Karen's friends and classmates.

She found the four papers for the month of March 1980, and quickly found the front-page story on Karen's suicide. She had been found by a friend named Deirdre

Holt who had stopped by Karen's room to pick her up for lunch. Deirdre Holt had entered the room — the door had been left unlocked — when she didn't get any answer to her knock, thinking she would wait for Karen. She had found Karen dead, and the Cambridge police had been called in. The official verdict was that she had hanged herself sometime the night before.

Karen Philips had been an art history major with a special interest in Egyptology, the article said, and she had worked at the Hapner Museum as a student intern during both her sophomore and junior years.

Sweeney read on. There were some nice comments about Karen from friends and fellow members of something called the Women's Arts Collective. As far as Sweeney knew, the organization no longer existed, but the article told her that WAC published a monthly women's arts magazine and Karen had been one of the editors. There was one quote that interested Sweeney, from another *WAC* editor with the improbable and wonderful name of Sharonna McClure. "Nobody really understands the pressures women face here," Sharonna McClure had offered. "Karen was a victim of a corrupt and unequal system."

Beyond that, there wasn't much more.

Karen's parents had come from Greenfield to get their daughter's body, and a memorial service was scheduled in her hometown in a week's time. There was the de rigueur statement about the pressures of college and living on one's own, and health services stated that any student who needed counseling should drop by or call the number below.

Sweeney wrote down all of the names included in the article. She was closing the binder containing the 1980 editions when she caught sight of a newspaper headline from the November before Karen's death. "Art Heist at University Museum."

Sweeney read on. "Unknown thieves carried out a daring daylight heist of valuable Egyptian antiquities from the Hapner Museum. Authorities say the theft may be the most significant in the history of the university." Sweeney knew there had been a major theft at the Hapner in the late seventies or early eighties, but she had forgotten the details.

"The thieves posed as museumgoers," the article continued, "and managed to subdue a museum security guard and Karen Philips, a student intern who was working at the museum, and to remove the items from displays during a time when the museum

112

was quiet and nearly empty because of a weekly meeting of staff members. Among the stolen artifacts are important relics of the eighteenth dynasty, though the museum's most recent acquisition, a gold funerary mask that is perhaps the Hapner's most valuable antiquity, was safe in a storage vault at the time of the robbery. Dr. Willem Keane, curator of Egyptian antiquities for the Hapner Museum, said that the recent exhibit of artifacts from the tomb of King Tutankhamen has raised interest in Egyptian artifacts and perhaps led to the theft."

Sweeney looked for other references to the theft and found a few subsequent articles that confirmed what she remembered of the case, that the pieces had never been recovered and the thieves never caught, but that police believed the heist had been carried out by professional thieves, possibly working for figures connected to organized crime in Boston.

Sweeney felt a familiar little buzz of excitement. So Karen Philips had been working at the museum during the heist and had been tied up by the thieves. She seemed to have been the last person to see the falcon collar. And then she had hanged herself a few months later.

Slow down, she told herself. One thing

doesn't necessarily have to do with the other. She would have to find out a lot more about the robbery, about Karen Philips's death. And the collar might show up at any moment. Tad had said that it was probably just misplaced.

Sweeney had been so pleased when she'd been named a Lorcan Fellow. It had been very prestigious and she assumed had been a much sought-after prize in Karen's time as well.

There probably wasn't anything in it, but it couldn't hurt to get a little more information. And there was one person she knew who could get her the police reports from the robbery and Karen's death.

She could ask Quinn to look into it.

Back at the museum, she gathered her things together and was heading toward the main entrance to her car when Tad came up the stairs, carrying the dark leather briefcase he seemed to take everywhere.

"Hi, Tad," she called out. "Are you heading home?"

"Yeah. Though I have to say, the idea of leaving the air-conditioning here doesn't sound very attractive right now." He smiled, then looked shyly down at the ground.

"I know what you mean." They waved

good night to Denny and walked out into the furnace of the late afternoon. Students walking by them on the yard seemed to be moving in slow motion, trying not to exert themselves too much. Even the rush-hour traffic seemed languorous and sludgy.

"Hey, Tad, can I ask you something?" Sweeney said suddenly. "You were working at the museum in 1979, when there was that big heist of all of the Egyptian pieces, right?"

He nodded. "I was a grad student, but I was working part-time for Willem. Why?"

"What happened? A student was asking me about it today and I realized I didn't really know the details."

"I wasn't at the museum. We were having a staff meeting off-site, but I guess these guys came in and posed as members of the public. They pulled guns on Denny, tied him up, roughed him up a bit, and then took their time breaking into the display cabinets. The cabinets weren't alarmed in those days. The whole thing took about a half hour. When we all came back from the meeting, we found Denny and called the police."

"Denny? Was he okay?"

"He was in the hospital for a bit. I've always thought that's why Willem keeps him on. Denny had some troubles after the thefts. Took him a while to get back on his feet, and his wife left him. I think Willem feels guilty about what happened. Though he's been talking recently about firing him. He said, 'God forbid someone tries to break in.' " He looked panicked all of a sudden. "Don't repeat that."

"No, I won't. There was a student intern who was there too, right?"

Tad looked up. "Yeah. Karen. She was working in one of the study rooms and she'd left the door open. They didn't hurt her the way they hurt Denny, but they tied her up and she was pretty scared. She . . ." He stopped and left whatever else he'd been about to say unsaid.

"She had done some research on the collar, right?" Sweeney wanted to see what he would say.

"I have no idea." His voice was neutral. "That was a long time ago."

"The pieces have never been recovered?"

"From the heist? Nope. The university hired a private detective a few years ago, and we got some information indicating that it was connected to organized crime. Maybe the same guys that did the Gardner." The 1990 theft of more than $250 million worth of paintings, among them famous pieces by Rembrandt and Vermeer, from the Isabella

Stewart Gardner Museum was the largest art heist in history. Sweeney had been in college then, and she remembered what a huge story it had been in Boston.

The Gardner heist had been carried out by two men wearing Boston Police uniforms who had convinced security guards to open up the museum. Sweeney knew that it had long been rumored that the Gardner heist was the work of mobsters with links to the IRA, but the FBI had never found anything definitive and no one had ever seen the paintings again.

"Did anyone around the museum have any theories about who it was?"

"Not really. For a while, the police seemed to think that someone inside the museum had tipped them off, because they pulled it off during the staff meeting, but then it came out that quite a few people outside the museum knew about the meeting too, so I think they let that go." He started to edge away from her. "My car's over there so I'll just . . ."

"Oh, yeah, thanks." She had a sudden urge to ask him whether he had known Karen Philips well, but instead she watched him go and decided that there was something about Tad that made you feel sorry for him. He was too eager to please, somehow, too willing to put aside his own needs for everyone else. She wondered if Fred was right about the sick wife at home, and she wondered if that was why he'd given up on his own academic career.

But then she thought about how her own choices might look to someone who didn't know what she had been through. We really are mysteries to each other, she thought. We really are.

TEN

Denny Keefe flipped the long row of switches controlling the lights in the basement galleries and watched as the fluorescent bulbs flickered and then died, leaving everything in darkness except for the small lights on the security cameras, telling him that they were on duty, ready to catch a thief if that thief tried to come into his museum and take something.

When his girls were little, they'd loved a book about a boy who got flattened in some kind of accident and then volunteered to hide inside a painting in a museum to catch a thief who was stealing the museum's art. He thought of the cameras that way. It was like he could be there, watching and waiting to make sure nothing happened to the museum he'd come to think of as his own home. It was his mission, his burden, to protect what was in these walls at any cost. He was going to do whatever he had to do to make sure nothing happened, ever again, to any of these beautiful things.

He moved up to the third floor, taking a moment to look at a row of framed photographs leaning against a wall. This was where the red-haired girl was putting on her show. He looked at a black-and-white photograph of a little girl lying on a bed and staring up at the ceiling. Another one showed an older woman lying in her coffin.

They were photos of dead people — he'd figured out that much from the title of the show. He studied a few more, moving into the next gallery, where the walls were covered with photographs of gravestones. He'd always liked gravestones, personally, and when he and April had been together, they'd sometimes gone and walked around in the cemeteries out near her mother's house in Waltham. It had given April the creeps sometimes, but he liked reading the names on the stones.

Sometimes he could relate to the people in those photographs, he thought. Sometimes he felt like he looked alive, but was really dead inside.

He'd felt that way ever since April had left. Dead inside. A few times, the girls had asked him why he didn't want to date anybody, why he didn't go to places where he might meet a nice woman his age, have someone to cook for him again, someone to love. And what he told them was that he was okay on his own, that he liked living by himself. But the truth was that he didn't think he had enough inside for a woman. He didn't think he had anything left.

He hit the lights on the third floor. He went down to the second floor and got the lights there too, then made his way back to the main floor and started the closing procedure, setting the alarms and methodically checking every gallery, every restroom, every place someone could hide. Someone had hidden in the men's room once. Maybe fifteen years ago. He'd waited until everyone was gone, then taken his time cutting a painting out of its frame. He'd been caught on his way out, though, when he'd tripped one of the silent alarms by the main entrance.

In the almost thirty years he'd been working as a security guard, Denny had seen a lot of changes in the way they did things around here. When he'd first been here, the security had consisted mostly of the people who watched over the museum's works of art. He and the other security guards had been just about the only line of defense — aside from the locks on the doors and the alarm system — and they had stopped a lot of attempted crimes. Not the big thefts, necessarily, but other stuff, college kids trying to draw graffiti on paintings, a few minor thefts of small pieces.

All that had changed in 1979, of course. Denny went down to do a final sweep of the basement and stood for a minute in the darkness, listening to the hum and rattles of the machines under the museum, the furnaces and water heaters and everything. And he thought about lying on the cold stone floor that day in November, tied up, injured from the beating the men had given him, waiting for someone to come back and find him. For some reason, those memories had been coming back with more frequency lately, the way the ropes had burned against his skin until his wrist had gone numb. He remembered the way it had hurt to breathe, because of his broken ribs, and the way he kept looking down to find blood running from his broken nose. Only he hadn't known it was from his nose and he'd wondered if it was coming from his mouth, if he was dying. That's what always happened before people died in films, wasn't it? Blood came out of their mouth.

It was strange, the memories coming back now, after all this time. Over the last few weeks, as he'd been walking around the museum, things had come back to him, the way the thieves' voices had sounded, the jacket one of them had worn, with a tear at the elbow. What had the guy been thinking, trying to pass himself off as a regular museumgoer, with that big tear on his elbow? Denny hadn't noticed it that day. It was only later that it seemed burned on his brain.

When he was finished doing the evening security procedures, he entered his name in the logbook and handed it to David, the guy who was on overnight. They didn't have him work nights anymore, and he found he kind of missed it. There was something about being all alone in the museum, with no one else there, that made you feel like maybe it was yours. He used to wander slowly through the rooms, thinking to himself that he was lord of a big estate, that he was showing off his paintings. His father had told him that the Keefes had once been kings of Ireland, and as a child, Denny had dreamed of going back to claim his castle, to restore the Keefes to their rightful place on the throne. He remembered being bitterly disappointed when some other kid had told him Ireland didn't have kings and queens anymore.

"You okay?" David asked him, writing his own name in the book and tucking it beneath the desk.

"Yeah, sorry. Just thinking about something."

"Okay. Have a good night."

"Yeah. You too. Hey, keep an extra eye out tonight. There was a weird guy in here before, dressed in this long coat. He didn't have anything on him, but it just seemed kind of strange, being so hot and all."

David nodded, looking at Denny as though he was a little bit crazy. The new guys trusted the machines, the alarms and buzzers and motion detectors and all, to the point that they sometimes forgot they were guards and not damn secretaries. Ah, well, there wasn't a lot he could do.

It was still hot when he came out into the evening, and he stood for a moment breathing the thick, not-very-fresh air. A pretty girl in a tank top walked by, and Denny watched her breasts bounce under the pink fabric without feeling much of anything. He was numb. About the museum, about his children, about everything. He got up every day and did what he had to do to get himself through to the evening, when he could go home and have a drink and fall asleep in his chair listening to sports radio.

But he didn't have emotions anymore, he decided. And it wasn't just since April'd left that he'd felt this way. It was since that day when the museum had been robbed, when, lying on the cold floor wondering if he was going to die, he'd thought he'd lost a little bit of his soul. As it turned out, he'd lost it all.

ELEVEN

More than thirty years after the car accident that had claimed her mobility — as well as the life of her husband — Cecelia Moran still owned the same colonial where Tad had grown up, and as he pulled up in front of the house, he felt a little surge of pride, as he always did, that they had managed to hang on to it through the years. It hadn't been easy. The house was in a part of Newton where real estate values had soared and the taxes seemed to just keep going up and up. It would have been easy to sell so many times, but Cecilia loved the house, and there was a part of Tad that knew she couldn't survive without her familiar things, her art and furniture and knickknacks, and the view out her back window into the little garden that Tad spent nearly every weekend tending.

It was all about choices, he told himself. He had made so many choices in order to keep the house, and at moments like this, he knew it was worth it. There were other moments, when he considered where his career might be if he had gone on to teach rather than staying with Willem at the museum, moments when he realized that he was a forty-nine-year-old man who was still living with his mother. And in these moments, he thought about the choices he had made of which he was not so proud, and he thought about the things he had done of which he was ashamed, and he wondered whether it was all worth it.

His mother was in her wheelchair in the living room when he came in, watching one of her recorded nature shows on television. Tad kissed her on the cheek and watched the screen for a minute as a grizzly bear caught salmon in some Alaskan stream.

"Look at that," she said, watching the bear dip its paws clumsily into the water and come out with a flailing fish. "You wouldn't think he would be able to do that with his big hands, but he can!" She was wearing one of her purple bathrobes, the belt cinched around her large middle. Her face had changed over the last year, aged and gotten both looser and puffier due to her medication, and he searched for the beauty that he'd always found there as a boy. He found it in her eyes, wide and browny-green, still intelligent and just a little coy.

"Paws, Mom."

"What?" She was rapt, staring at the screen.

"Nothing."

In the last year, ever since her heart troubles had started, she had lived more and more in this room, watching television, living, he thought, vicariously through the wild animals hunting on the Serengeti or somewhere near the Arctic circle. She especially liked shows about birds and could sit for hours watching hawks and eagles and tropical parrots wheeling against a clear blue sky. If Tad thought too much about the symbolism of her television habit, he got horribly sad. He had done everything else for her, but the one thing he couldn't do was to free her from her imprisoning chair.

"Good day, Mom?" he asked, dropping his briefcase on the hall table and checking to make sure the nurses had shut off the gas on the stove. A couple of weeks ago he had come home to find the gas turned on and pilot light off. He had yelled at the nurse responsible, but he was now very careful to check.

"Oh, yes. Gloria was here today. I like Gloria the best. She was telling me about

128

Jamaica, where she's from. She said that the breeze itself, coming off the ocean, is so sweet you just want to open your mouth and eat it up. Isn't that a beautiful way of describing it? It made me think of that trip your father and I took to Bermuda that time. Do you remember? You were about five and you stayed with Auntie Carol?"

Tad did not remember, but he said, "Oh, yeah. Was Bermuda like that, Mom? Was the breeze sweet there too?"

"Oh, yes. That's exactly what I remember about it. It was funny how Gloria saying that brought it all back, you know?" She was engrossed in the program again, watching as a mother grizzly bear ambled across a desolate brown landscape with two cubs.

"Yeah." He picked up the stack of bills on the hall table and gave it a quick look. There was a long envelope that he recognized as coming from his mother's insurance company. He had been fighting them for months on a series of bills related to her last hospitalization. It was all stuff that Medicare should have covered, but they were telling him that it was his responsibility and he didn't understand why. He tore open the envelope and saw the new balance listed at the bottom of the bill: $34,246. It didn't seem possible. It had been half that six months ago, but there had been the latest hospitalization and she had wanted a private room, even though Medicare had warned it might not pay for it. He put it back down and tried to forget about the number. There wasn't much else of interest, some more bills and a huge stack of the catalogs his mother loved to look through. At the bottom of the pile was a long envelope with the return address of a local roofing company. He opened it and took out a sheet of paper, reading the words on it with growing horror.

"What shall we have for dinner, darling?" his mother called out to him. He looked through to see the credits rolling at the end of the grizzly program. What she really meant, he knew, was, *What are you going to cook for us?* He pushed down resentment and cleared his throat.

"What are you in the mood for?"

"I don't know. What about those chicken cordon bleu things we had last week. Are there any more of those?"

"No," he called back, "but I can go out and get some."

"That would be lovely," she said. "If it's not too much trouble. And we can watch the rest of the show about the flamingos. Don't you love flamingos?"

He came through to the living room. "Sounds good," he said.

"What's that letter you're holding?"

"Oh." He held it up. "It's from that guy I asked to come look at the roof. He finished his quote. He says we have a lot of rot in the northeast corner and that it all needs to be ripped up and replaced."

"Oh, dear, how much is that going to cost?"

"He says fourteen thousand dollars."

"Oh." She looked concerned and her eyes sought his. "That's so much. Will it be okay, Tad? Can we . . . can we afford it?"

The short answer, of course, was no they couldn't. Tad had gone to the bank last week to see if they could get another line of credit on the house. That was the only good thing about property values going up. He'd been turned down and had gone home and made a list of all their debts, trying to get a handle on exactly what they owed. The numbers lined up on the page in his mind: $12,450 on the credit cards, the other medical bills, $19,000, plus the bill that had come today. Then there was the roof. What was he going to do? When the bank's loan officer had broken the news that they had tapped out the equity in the house, he'd suggested that Tad ask a friend, a family member, maybe. But there wasn't anyone. He didn't have any friends. There was just Willem.

Willem. He hadn't thought before of asking Willem. Suddenly there was a small light of hope. Willem could lend him some money.

He found his car keys and wallet.

"I'll find a way, Mom. Don't worry about it. I'll find a way."

TWELVE

Sweeney pulled up in front of Quinn's house around six-thirty, still not convinced her impromptu visit was a good idea. At the very least she should have called first, to make sure he was even home. She didn't know if the missing collar had anything to do with Karen Philips's suicide and the robbery, but she wanted to know more about them. And Quinn was the only person she knew who had access to that kind of information.

She and Quinn had had coffee a couple of times, before Ian had arrived, just to catch up. They had gone together to the memorial service of a child who had been connected to their experiences in Concord the previous fall, and she remembered looking over at him during the service and thinking that at some point during the weeks they'd been together in Concord, he'd become someone she really cared about, a friend rather than a business associate or a mere acquaintance.

Sweeney had thought they would stay in touch. But somehow, once Ian was there, she hadn't called him, and the last time he'd left her a message, she hadn't called back. She wasn't sure why, but it had just seemed easier, simpler. She had told Ian about Quinn, of course, and about what had happened in Concord, and she didn't think he would have minded if she had met Quinn for a cup of coffee or a meal. But for some reason, she hadn't gotten in touch until now.

She parked in the narrow little driveway and knocked on the front door. All of the windows in the house were open and Sweeney could hear a voice singing somewhere in the house. It sang a melodious, accented French, and Sweeney made out a few words here and there, something about a rabbit and a turtle. She waited a minute, listening, and then knocked again.

The voice belonged to a tall woman with very dark skin and a fall of shimmering cornrows. Through the screen, Sweeney was at first struck by her loveliness and then, when she turned, by the long scar that ran down one side of her face. It was still partly open, as though it had not been stitched but had just healed the way it was. The inside of the scar was pink, like the interior of a seashell, and Sweeney had to keep from cringing.

"Hello?" the young woman said, opening the door. Megan was hugging her legs, and she looked up at Sweeney and gave her a toothy grin.

"Hi," Sweeney said. "I'm looking for Tim. Is he here?" She waved at Megan. "Hi, Megan. You're so big. I don't think you remember me, but I took care of you for a little while last fall." The little girl grinned up at her. She wasn't a baby anymore, but a toddler. Her reddish blond hair was secured in two pigtails. She looked like Quinn. She had his eyes: very round, very blue, with thick lashes much darker than her hair.

"He's working, but he will be home soon." She smiled a little. "Are you a friend of Tim's?"

"Yes. I guess I'll try to catch up with him later."

The woman hesitated and then gave a little smile. "He just called. He's on his way. Do you want to come in and wait?"

"Oh, okay, sure. That would be great. Thank you." She followed the woman inside, Megan toddling behind them. "I'm Sweeney, by the way."

"Oh, yes. I think I have heard about you,"

135

the woman said. Sweeney wondered what Quinn had said. The woman hesitated again and then, in a quiet voice, she said, "I am Patience."

Sweeney misunderstood at first, thinking she meant to say that she was patient. When she realized it was the woman's name, she smiled. "It's nice to meet you."

Megan climbed up into Patience's lap and put her arms around her neck, then twisted her head around to look shyly at Sweeney. Sweeney smiled and waved again and Megan turned to Patience and murmured something in her ear.

"Yes?" Patience asked and Megan murmured it again. This time Patience laughed out loud. "Rouge! She said rouge. For your hairs. *Oui, ma cherie.* Rouge!" Megan smiled up at Sweeney.

Sweeney got down on the floor and played with Megan while Patience cleaned up the living room, and ten minutes later they heard a car pull up in front of the house and then Quinn's voice through the screen. "Patience? Who's . . . ?" When he saw Sweeney on the floor, he looked first apprehensive, then pleased. "Hey. I didn't recognize the car."

"I got a new one," she said. She looked out the window at her gleaming, pale blue

Volkswagen Jetta. She'd hated giving up her decades-old Rabbit, but it had finally not so much broken down as disintegrated into a pile of rust. She still hadn't quite got used to being the owner of a fancy new car.

He grinned. "It's about time. Did you meet?" He gestured to Patience, and they both nodded. He was very tan and his hair looked lighter. There were little white lines at the sides of his eyes, as though he'd been squinting into the sun. Sweeney thought maybe he'd put on a little bit of weight. Either that or he had started working out. She wasn't sure what it was, but he seemed more solid than she remembered. When she'd first met him, she'd thought him only conventionally good-looking, but now that she knew him better, she could see there was more to his face than that. His eyes weren't just blue, but a couple different shades of blue, darker at the centers around the pupils, and he had a tiny round scar over one cheekbone, from chicken pox, she'd decided, though she'd never asked. His eyes narrowed a bit in a smile, erasing the squint lines.

"Yes, she shows Megan how to, what did you call it?" Patience put her hands in the air. "Pat-a-cake?"

"Oh, I don't know what you call it. Just

. . ." She put her hands up and clapped them to Megan's again. "Miss Mary Mack, Mack, Mack, all dressed in black, black, black. With silver buttons, buttons, buttons, all down her back, back, back." Megan squealed with delight.

Quinn laughed. "I remember the girls doing that in elementary school."

Patience took a pale blue cotton cardigan sweater from the couch and smiled at them. "I'll see you tomorrow. Tim." She said his name very deliberately, as though she was trying to prove something.

"It was nice to meet you," Sweeney told her.

"Yes." She smiled in a sly sort of way that involved her eyebrows. "You as well."

Sweeney shot him an inquiring look once Patience was gone.

"I've been trying to get her to stop calling me Mr. Quinn," he explained. "But now she calls me Tim in this way that makes me wish I'd never brought it up."

"She seems great, though. She's amazing with Megan."

"Oh, yeah. I couldn't ask for anyone better."

There was an awkward silence that was filled by Megan asking to be picked up. Quinn lifted her into his lap and sat her on the end of his knee, bouncing her up and down.

"So, have you had a good summer?" Sweeney asked, not quite ready to get to the point.

"Yeah. Busy. I took a week off, though, and Megan and I went to the Cape. It was nice, kinda weird being there by myself with her with all the families around, but it was okay. She loved the beach."

"Good." Sweeney looked around the room. He'd changed it since the last time she'd been here, but she wasn't sure how. It seemed neater, less cluttered, toys and books piled into baskets next to the couch. The wall over the fireplace was nearly filled by a large picture of Megan, posed smiling in front of an obviously fake background of bright flowers. "You're probably wondering why I'm here," she said finally.

He looked embarrassed, then stood up and said, "Kinda. Hey, you want to go for a walk? It's hot in here."

"It's hotter outside." She looked up and found that he was nervous, so she stood up. "Okay. We might as well."

He got Megan strapped into her stroller and they headed out into the humid evening. A couple of boys were playing soccer in one of the postage stamp front yards along the street. As they passed, the ball shot out at them and Sweeney stopped to toss it back. The air smelled of summer, of rotting fruit, of Popsicles, of grass. Quinn was wearing khakis and a navy polo shirt, but he'd changed into flip-flops and she could see the tan lines along his feet. Looking at him in profile, it struck her that he was tired.

"Okay," Sweeney said. "So there's something I want to ask you about. It may be nothing. I don't know." As they walked, she told him about her exhibit and the missing collar, and then about Karen Philips and the art heist.

When she was done, he just looked confused.

"So . . . ?" He raised his eyebrows skeptically at her.

"So . . ." Now that she had to explain her suspicions to him, she realized she couldn't put them into words. "So doesn't it seem strange to you that, I don't know, that all these things happened around the same time? That she worked on this collar, that she was there when the museum was robbed, that the collar has disappeared from the museum, and that she killed herself? Doesn't that seem strange to you, when I say it like that?"

Quinn looked pained. "Sweeney, I was at the scene of a murder yesterday, then I came home and discovered one of my knives missing, then when I went out to my car today, someone had keyed the passenger side door. Does that seem strange to you, when I put it all together like that? What do you think? That she had something to do with the robbery at the museum? That she took the necklace herself?"

Sweeney hadn't thought that, but now she considered it. Quinn took a deep breath as though he was going to make a speech, and again she realized how tired he looked. But she had never known him not tired.

"Sweeney, there are still people working on the thefts at the Hapner. I'm sure they know everything about everyone who was working there at the time and I'm sure they've looked into this girl's death."

Woman, Sweeney thought. *She was twenty years old.*

"But what if they didn't?"

"It's the FBI that's handling this now," he said. "They have manpower, they have resources, unlike me. I'm sure they did." They had reached the end of the block, and he turned the stroller around, starting for home.

She felt as though she'd lost him, so she

141

came right out with what she wanted. "I was thinking you could just kind of look at the case again, see if they really did look at all the angles."

"Sweeney, I'm sorry, but I've got enough on my plate right now without opening up old suicides. I'm sure they looked at it pretty carefully at the time. I highly doubt she had anything to do with a multimillion-dollar art heist. She was a student, right?" He seemed annoyed, and all of a sudden she wondered if it was because she had never called him back.

"I didn't say she had anything to do with it. Maybe she knew something about it."

"Whatever." He stopped to pick up a stuffed hippo Megan had thrown out of the stroller, and as he stood up again, Sweeney saw annoyance flash across his face. "Look, I'm breaking in a new partner and I've got a girl who was brutally sodomized and dumped in an alley and I can't get anyone to talk about her because I don't speak Spanish. I don't have time to open up a case that's been taken over by someone else anyway, okay?"

"Fine." They were back at his house, and Sweeney fumbled in her pocket for her car keys. "I'm sorry I bothered you."

"You're not bothering me. I just . . .

Megan, don't keep throwing that out of there." The hippo was on the ground again and Megan started screaming when she heard the hardness in his voice. He undid the stroller straps and picked her up, saying, "I really don't have time for this, Sweeney. You can't just drop by after all this time and not calling and expect me to be your personal cold case squad." They looked at each other for a moment, both surprised at his words. His mouth was set in anger, but his eyes weren't cold, only sad.

You know it's not like that, she wanted to say.

Instead, she turned and headed for her car, feeling as though she might burst into tears. What was wrong with her? If he was going to be a jerk, then fine, let him be a jerk.

As she got in, she heard him curse and then heard Megan scream again. When she looked back as she pulled out of the driveway, she saw him holding his flailing daughter and she hung on to her anger, not making any excuses for him, and she watched as Megan's legs knocked the stroller over, spilling toys out onto the sidewalk. She screamed even louder.

Served him right.

Sweeney stopped at the supermarket on her way home and got premade gazpacho and some hot Italian sausages to do on the grill. By the time Ian got home at eight, she had dinner almost ready and was setting the table.

"Smells good," he said, coming up behind her and kissing the side of her neck. She turned around and kissed him on the lips, leaning into it and pressing her body against his. He responded, pulling her closer and cupping her face in his hands. "Tastes good too."

"I'm happy to see you," she said, meaning it more than she'd meant anything she'd said all day. She'd had a few glasses of wine while she got dinner ready, and now she found herself pleasingly buzzed, the memory of Quinn's words dulled by the wine. "I'm really happy to see you."

"How nice." He leaned back and looked at her, pushing her hair away from her shoulders. "Shall we eat and then you can show me how very happy you are?" She nodded and smiled, bringing the bowls of gazpacho and plate of sausages into the dining room and opening another bottle of red

Spanish wine.

"What do you remember about the art heist at the Hapner back in 1979?" she asked once they were sitting down with their food. "Was there ever any buzz about the stolen works in the art world?"

"The Hapner? Oh, yes, it was all that Egyptian stuff, is that right?" She nodded. "I don't think so, though I remember something about an underworld figure coming forward to claim that he knew where the works were. Is that right? Or was that the Gardner?"

"That was the Gardner, but apparently some people thought it was the same people. The Irish mob, links to the IRA and all that."

He watched her face for a minute. It was because she'd mentioned the IRA, she realized, and she went on lightly, to show him she wasn't thinking of Colm. "I was talking to someone at the museum about it today. I just wondered if you'd ever heard anything."

"I can't say I have, but we're a pretty reputable house. There are others that aren't quite so, how do I say it, persnickety. Lovely gazpacho."

"You mean there are other auction houses that would sell stolen paintings or artifacts, knowing they were stolen?"

"They wouldn't advertise it, but there are places that have acted as a go-between, places that might privately broker a deal."

"I've never understood that. What's the benefit in having, say, a stolen Vermeer? You can't really display it, you can never sell it. Why go to all that trouble?"

"There are collectors who just like knowing they own the piece. Possession is enough." He speared a sausage and split it in half on his plate, spreading Dijon mustard on the inside. "I did hear something interesting about your museum," he said. "Willem Keane just got a gift of a canopic chest from a graduate of the university. It's supposed to be a very nice little piece."

"I know. He's been so excited about it. They're building a new exhibit for it and everything. I think he's going to have it on display during the opening of my exhibition." She looked up. They still hadn't talked about whether Ian would be there.

"I've been thinking about something," he said, picking up on her thought. "What if I don't go to Paris in September so I can go to your opening, and then we go over together in early November and stay for a few weeks? Maybe through Thanksgiving. I really want you to meet Eloise, and we could get out of the city for a few days, do some traveling. How does that sound to you?"

"Early November? I was thinking of going to Mexico, actually. For the Day of the Dead. I've never been, and I want to write something about it. It's supposed to be . . ." She trailed off as she saw the look on his face. "What?"

"Nothing." He stood abruptly and went into the kitchen. She heard him fiddling with the hibachi out on the fire escape and felt like a disobedient child waiting to hear about her punishment.

"Were you going to invite me to come?" he asked when he came back into the room.

"I don't know. I hadn't really thought about it. I mean, it's for work." That wasn't strictly true, of course. She had thought about it. She just hadn't decided whether she wanted him to come along and now she knew she'd bungled it. "Why, do you want to come?"

He did something strange with his mouth and got up again and took his plate into the kitchen. She heard him banging around in there, unloading the dishwasher and clanging pots together in the sink. She waited a minute and then followed him in, taking her wineglass and the half-empty bottle with her.

"Are you mad? Do you want to come to Mexico?"

He watched her for a moment and she kept talking, in order to fill up the silence. "Of course you can come. I just wasn't sure you wanted to. I mean, I thought I'd stay in hostels and stuff and do some hiking and maybe visit some archaeological sites. I know you would rather stay in hotels is all, and I was kind of thinking it might be easier to do on my own, but of course . . ."

He turned to look at her. "Is this about your father?"

"My father?" She had no idea what he was talking about.

"Is this about your father? Your going to Mexico?"

She leaned back against the counter and reached for her wine, stumbling a little as she did so, and she was very conscious of him watching her, of him staring at her hand as she lifted the glass to her lips.

"How many glasses of wine have you had tonight?"

"Excuse me?"

"You heard me," he said again, but gently, not in anger. "Was that five or six?"

"I've had as many as you've had," she said, going back into the dining room for the rest of the dishes.

"No, you haven't," he said when she came back to the kitchen, again very quietly and gently, as though he were talking to a child. "You've had six. And what scares me a little is that you're not even really drunk."

"Ian, can we please not talk about this? I'm fine." Showing him how little she needed the wine, she took her glass over to the sink and dumped the slippery liquid down the drain.

"You've been drinking a lot lately," he said very quietly. "I'd started to notice, but I've only just realized how much it's been."

"Ian, I'm fine." She steadied her gaze on him, showing him how sober she was, though in fact the light above his head was a little blurry and she had the feeling of floating just a few inches off the ground. She gripped the side of the counter, then let go when she saw Ian glance down at her hand.

His face was hard to read. She saw anger there, then sympathy, and finally something soft and sad that sent panic clanging through her body.

"What did you mean about my father?" she said, trying to change the subject and realizing what he'd meant as she said the words. "Oh, you mean because of Mexico?"

He nodded, his head tilted just a bit, still

gazing intently at her in that way that made her want to run.

"Well, yeah, I mean . . . I guess I always wanted to go because that's where he lived at the end of his life. But I've also never been there for Day of the Dead. And for someone in my profession, that's pretty unacceptable."

"Are you still in touch with any of his friends?"

She wasn't sure how the conversation had turned pleasant again, but she was grateful that it had. "God, no. There was a woman he lived with. She was the one who called my mother and told her he'd killed himself. She barely spoke English. My mother had to go get this Argentinian neighbor we had to translate. That's how she found out."

"What was the woman's name?"

"Maria. I think she was just kind of a housekeeper or something, and then he probably started sleeping with her and had her move in. He was always doing that with women. He liked housekeepers, maids, young women, anyone who didn't ask too much of him."

"Maybe he loved her," Ian said, and his words seemed to fill up the room. *We've never said those words to each other,* Sweeney thought to herself. *We've never*

150

ever said those words.

"Maybe," she said quickly. "Stranger things have happened."

"The thing is," Ian said, closing the dishwasher and looking at her as though she had disappointed him, "sometimes there isn't any reason for what people do. Sometimes it's just love."

They had left about a thousand things unsaid, but she was tired and — he was right — a good bit drunk, and for now, for tonight, she didn't want to think about any of it. So she kissed him, hard and very seriously. "I just want you to take me to bed," she said. "I don't want to talk anymore."

"We have to talk," he said.

"Later," she whispered. "Just take me to bed."

And he did, though later, in the light from the hallway, she saw that he was still sad, as though he'd been promised something and never gotten it, as though he was still waiting to see if he would.

THIRTEEN

The opening of "Still as Death: The Art of the End of Life" was held the second week of September. The heat wave had hung on kicking and screaming, and at four o'clock it was still ninety-five degrees, the humid air hanging oppressively over the entire eastern seaboard and most specifically over the Hapner Museum.

Sweeney had been at the museum all day and had run home at three to shower and change. She'd barely had time to down a quick iced coffee before heading back to meet Ian and Toby outside the museum. By the time they arrived, Ian from work in his perfectly pressed suit and tie and Toby wearing jeans and a white button-down shirt that looked as though it had been dried out the window of his Jeep, she had worked herself into a frenzy of self-consciousness.

"Do I look all right?" she demanded of them as they walked up, talking seriously.

Seeing their dark heads bent toward each other made her even more nervous. What were they talking about? Toby had suggested that they meet for a late lunch and walk over to the museum together, and Ian had been pleased that Toby had thought of it.

"We don't see Toby enough," he'd said to Sweeney after the phone call. "We should have him over for dinner."

In fact, Toby had been away a lot. He'd sold his finally finished novel — a semiauto-biographical tale about his relationship with his Italian poet father — and had used his advance to travel for most of the past year. He'd been in Europe for three months and then gone hiking in Ecuador and Peru for another four months, and the upshot was that Sweeney felt she hadn't seen much of him lately. He was her best friend. He always would be. But watching his familiar lanky form coming toward her, she realized that she felt a little abandoned.

"Yes, you look lovely," Ian said, kissing her and looking a little perplexed. "Of course you do."

Toby, who had known Sweeney for far longer and therefore knew exactly the right thing to say, kissed her on the cheek, stood back to look at her long black taffeta skirt, sleeveless white linen blouse, and layers of jet beads, and said, "You look perfect. Exactly what you should wear to an exhibit titled 'Still as Death.' "

"Okay. Ready?" Ian said, taking her hand.

She looked up at him. "You don't think the outfit's too . . . strange?"

He hesitated, and the hesitation was all she needed to be racked with another wave of self-doubt. Ian didn't always approve of some of her stranger vintage ensembles. "No. You're fine. You're beautiful." He kissed her forehead and smiled at her.

"Okay, okay, we should probably go in." But she still felt off, as though she'd forgotten something. She looked up at the banners announcing the exhibition and allowed herself a little moment of pure happiness. She had been planning this exhibition for almost three years. In some ways it was what all of her work up to this point had been about. And then, just as suddenly as the pleasure had washed over her, she felt an equally strong wave of emptiness. It was done. What now?

Olga was just inside the door, taking coats and pointing the attendees toward the hors d'oeuvres. She looked more attractive than Sweeney had ever seen her, her short gray hair slightly wavy, as though she'd had it set, and her sturdy body dressed in black pants and a crisp white blouse that was open to show off her elegant neck and pale throat. Sweeney had never seen her in anything other than the dumpy uniform she wore for cleaning, and it struck her for the first time that Olga must have been pretty once.

Sweeney greeted her, and Olga nodded back with a look of disdain, or perhaps preoccupation. There was a line of people backing up behind them, so she just took Ian and Toby's arms and led them toward the long table covered with cheese and crackers and the attractive but pedestrian hors d'oeuvres provided by the university dining services.

The three of them got drinks — Sweeney was too nervous to eat — and found Fred and Lacey Kauffman chatting with Harriet and some of Sweeney's colleagues from the History of Art Department.

Harriet gave Sweeney a tight smile and said, "Very nice, Sweeney. Very interesting," patting her perfect hair as if to reassure herself it was still there.

"Thanks, Harriet." Sweeney had never seen her in a social setting and wasn't surprised to find that she was just as ill at ease as she was at work. Harriet excused herself, and Sweeney could feel everyone breathe a small sigh of relief.

"Why do I always have the feeling that Harriet's mad at me?" Lacey asked them. Sweeney had always liked Lacey, a tall, pretty woman from Quebec who made high-end hand-knitted sweaters that sold in boutiques all over Cambridge and Boston. They were beautiful and Sweeney had thought about buying one once, then changed her mind when she saw that they cost upward of $500.

"Hello, Madame Curator," Fred said with one of his big smiles, though when Sweeney leaned in to kiss him on the cheek, she caught him glance over her shoulder in a preoccupied way. He was wearing a chocolate brown linen blazer and trousers, and the monochromatic brown made him look even more ursine than he usually did, though his height and round belly made him look like a teddy bear rather than a grizzly. His curly gray hair was desperately in need of a cut.

Sweeney introduced him to Toby and hugged Lacey, who immediately engaged Ian in conversation about his work. She had a way of making people feel fascinating that Sweeney appreciated. You always left an encounter with Lacey Kauffman feeling just a little bit better about yourself than you had before it. Sweeney caught Fred watching his wife, his face unguarded and supremely relaxed for a moment before reverting to the tenseness Sweeney had noticed. Still talking to Ian, Lacey reached out and took Fred's hand.

Sweeney looked around. The place wasn't packed, but the turnout was certainly better than she'd hoped for. And it was still early. She saw a number of people from the university, as well as some members of the public she didn't recognize. And she was touched to see that some of her students had come.

"It turned out so well," Fred was saying. "You should be very proud of it, Sweeney. Really."

Tad, looking uncharacteristically dapper in a red shirt, waved from across the room. Sweeney watched him go back to his conversation with an elderly man in a rumpled sports coat and, oddly, since it hadn't rained in weeks, galoshes. There was something about him that said money, though, and she pointed him out to Fred. "Who's that talking to Tad?"

He looked. "Oh, that's Cyrus Hutchinson. Guy who gave the canopic chest?"

Willem had shown her his prize that morning, and she knew how excited he was about displaying it. "Tad's on chaperone duty?"

"I guess so. Willem's trying to keep Hutchinson happy. Obviously. He's so delighted. He's been taking people down to the basement to show it off all night."

Ian and Toby were chatting with Lacey, so Sweeney turned to Fred and said in a low voice, "Lacey's so great. Ian was saying that he hoped she'd be here. I think she could make anyone feel good about himself."

She'd said it lightly, but Fred gazed at Lacey and said, "Yeah. She's amazing that way. I swear to God, the first time I met her it was like . . . like I'd all of a sudden become a rock star. You know? I felt like crap that night, and when I walked out of that dinner party with her phone number in my pocket, I felt like I could take over the world." He watched his wife as she laughed at something Toby said and, seeing the look on his face, Sweeney felt as voyeuristic as if she'd walked in on them in bed.

She waited a beat and then said, "You were here in 1979–1980, right?"

"Yeah. In graduate school," he said in a guarded way. "Why do you ask?"

"Do you remember an intern named Karen Philips?"

He nodded. "She was a nice kid. We all

felt bad about what happened to her."

"You mean that she killed herself?"

A student waitress passed carrying a tray of meatballs skewered with toothpicks. Fred took one, popped it in his mouth, and turned his attention back to Sweeney. "Yeah. She was here during the robbery and she was tied up and left in one of the study rooms. I always figured she was so traumatized about it that it affected her, made her depressed."

"Did she seem depressed?" Fred looked guarded again, and Sweeney caught him scanning the room. *He's looking for someone,* she told herself. "Fred?"

"I didn't really know her, Sweeney. I can't say whether she was depressed or not. She just seemed kind of, I don't know. Off. Not her usually chipper self."

There was something slightly ironic in his tone, and Sweeney knew he didn't want to talk about it anymore. Still, she couldn't stop herself from asking, "Did she strike you as honest?"

"Honest? How should I know? Why are you asking me about her?"

"Sorry. I just heard something about her and . . . Forget it."

He studied her for a minute. "Okay. I have to go. There's someone I need to talk to over

there. But I'll see you later, okay? Con-
grats."

Ian and Lacey went off to look at the
show, leaving Sweeney and Toby alone.

"So how do you feel?" he asked her. "The
show seems to be a great success."

"Honestly? Sick to my stomach. Outside,
I got . . . I don't know, so sad and empty all
of a sudden."

"Well, there's always a letdown after
something like this. You've been working on
this for almost a year now. Besides, now you
have to figure out what you're going to do.
About work, about a place to live. About
Ian." He hesitated, then said, "By the way,
he told me about London while we were
walking over here. What are you going to
do?"

"I have absolutely no idea." She watched
a couple — students, she decided — kissing
and whispering at the other end of the gallery as they looked at a cabinet of canopic
jars. She wondered if they knew that the
jars had been used to hold human viscera.

"You're going to go, aren't you?" He was
watching the couple too.

"What do you mean? You make it sound
like I should."

"Sweeney. I don't want you to go. You
know that. But I don't know, it just seems

like you guys have gotten pretty serious. I just assumed you'd want to . . ."

"I don't want to talk about it," she said as Willem approached them, steering a young guy dressed in black by the arm.

"Sweeney," he said, ignoring Toby completely. "I'd like you to meet David Milken, from *The New York Times.* He was hoping you could show him around a bit." Milken looked more like a painter than a critic, right down to his black turtleneck and black cowboy boots.

"I'd love to," she said, feeling nervousness overtake her for a moment. This was probably the guy who would be writing about the exhibition.

"David, Sweeney is one of our brilliant young things. I've been so excited about 'Still as Death.' " The thing about Willem, Sweeney thought as she nodded good-bye to Toby and led David Milken toward the first section, was that he seemed self-involved sometimes but was actually always looking out for the best interests of the museum. If your own interests coincided with his, you were in luck. He had been so involved in the planning and execution of the exhibition — necessarily since the Egyptian burial items were his specialty and not Sweeney's — but he seemed willing to give Sweeney all the credit.

"These are canopic jars," she explained to Milken, showing him a few examples from the twenty-second dynasty. "The jars were made of alabaster and they held the organs that the deceased would need in the after-life."

"Yuck." But he was smiling. "What do they represent?" He looked through the glass at the little jars, round bottomed and topped by carved heads.

"Funerary deities. The four sons of Horus." She pointed to each one. "The one that looks like a baboon is Hapy. He guarded the lungs. Then there's Imsety, the only human-headed one. He's the liver. The jackal, Duamutef, is the stomach, and the falcon, Qebehsenuef, is the intestines."

"Who's got the brains?"

"Oh, they didn't think we needed our brains in the afterlife."

"Really?"

"Yeah. It's interesting to compare that sentiment with the Christian belief in the ascendancy of the soul."

"That's true. We Judeo-Christians tend to want to leave the guts behind. We only care about the brain, don't we?" He ran a hand over one of the smooth stone sarcophagi. "Did all the Egyptian kings get buried the way King Tut did? Like Russian dolls?"

"The body had to be preserved," Sweeney said. "And the layers and layers of wrapping and protection did a good job. I've always thought there was an interesting dichotomy about that, though. They were really very earthy, preserving the organs and all that. But how was the guy supposed to get out of the twenty coffins they put him in?"

Milken laughed and Sweeney took him into the next room to show him the photographs of gravestones. "See how they evolve," she said. "We move from these very Puritan images of skeletons, very corporeal, really, and then on to the much more spiritual ones." She pointed to photographs of round-faced souls' heads. "The appearance of these sort of coinicides with new theological ideas of heaven and the afterlife."

"It's all about the afterlife, isn't it?" Milken asked, wandering around the crowded gallery, looking at the photographs.

"To a certain extent, though I'm even more interested in looking at those words from a different perspective. 'Afterlife. Life after.' What happens to those who have to carry on with life after someone has died. That's who this art is for. That's why we have gravestones and canopic jars and

163

postmortem photography."

Milken wanted to know how she had gotten interested in memorial photography, and Sweeney talked about how she'd seen Civil War battlefield photos of the dead that fascinated her and how she'd been astonished the first time she'd seen a postmortem photograph of a young child, dressed in finery and propped up in her bed.

She stood back and let him take in the photographs. Sweeney had discovered that people needed to look at them in silence in order to really see them. When he'd finished, Sweeney showed him around the final gallery.

"These are amazing," he said, looking at the collection of memorial decals Sweeney had included. "I didn't even know about these."

"I love them. I think it's really interesting that we kind of decorate our personal space with our ideas about death. Buddhist households have shrines, of course, and the Puritans saw their macabre gravestone carvings every day as they moved about their communities. We Americans live in our cars, so what do we do but make them into rolling memorials."

She told him good-bye and went to find Ian and Toby, who were talking with Lacey and Jeanne. For the occasion, Jeanne had adorned herself in a vaguely Greco-Roman dress that draped extravagantly around her chest in swirls of blue silk. Her hair was coiled on either side of her head, completing the look.

". . . that he doesn't understand how women are discriminated against at this university," she was saying. "It's all just bullshit. I really see it as my role to educate them."

"How did it go?" Ian asked, giving her a peck on the cheek.

"Pretty good. He seemed really interested."

A young guy in a splashy Hawaiian print shirt came up to them and said, "Hi, Jeanne."

"Trevor." She flushed, which Sweeney had never seen her do before. Jeanne wasn't flustered by anything. "Everyone, this is Trevor Ferigni." They did an awkward round of handshaking.

"I loved the show," he said to Sweeney. "It was really cool." He had a California sort of breeziness about him and an absolute confidence that you didn't see often in students. Was he a student? He had to be. But how did he know Jeanne? Jeanne usually didn't give male students the time of day. Sweeney had heard complaints about it, actually, and some male students had done an analysis of her grading patterns that revealed that women were something like ten times more likely than men to receive an A in her classes.

Jeanne, her fingers shredding the cocktail napkin she was holding, said, "Did the *Times* guy want to talk to me too? You told him about my upcoming exhibition, didn't you?"

There was an awkward silence. "Oh, yeah," Sweeney said. "I think I did mention it."

"Oh?" Jeanne looked wildly around the room and then said, in a falsely nonchalant voice, "Maybe I'll just go see if I can find him. I'm sure he'll want to come."

"Good idea," Sweeney said. They all watched her make her way across the gallery toward the stairs, followed by Trevor. At the entrance to the galleries, she said something to him that made him leave her at the stairs and head down the hallway in the opposite direction. When she'd gone, Sweeney leaned in and said, "He left already, but I couldn't bear to tell her."

"Poor Jeanne," Lacey said. "Is she getting along with Willem any better?"

"No. I think it's getting worse. Everyone's

going to be really glad when her show is over and they don't have to deal with each other anymore."

"I still don't understand why he's letting her do it," Lacey said.

"Someone somewhere must have ordered it," Sweeney said. "It's the only thing I can think."

Toby said he had to get going, so she and Ian walked him downstairs, then came back up to chat with some of Sweeney's colleagues for the next hour. As things started to wind down, Lacey said, "I wonder what happened to Fred. He went out to make a phone call, but that was a while ago. I think I'm ready to get going."

"He probably just got stuck doing public relations," Sweeney told her. "Tell you what, I'm going to visit the ladies' room and I'll look for him, tell him you're ready to go."

She didn't see him in any of the exhibition galleries, nor could she find him near the bar. There was a line at the bathroom on the main floor and so she decided to try the restroom in the basement. She'd been down here many times before and she knew Willem had had people in and out of the gallery all night looking at the canopic chest, but as she came down the stairs she felt suddenly and absolutely alone. The cavernous basement galleries had always creeped her out a little; the stone arches provided strange, shadowy nooks and crannies, and the lack of natural light made it feel like a dungeon. The sarcophagi placed around the room didn't help any.

She had just turned the corner when she heard a strangled sob and looked up to find Jeanne standing in front of her, staring straight at Sweeney and holding her hands out in front of her. As Sweeney's eyes adjusted to the light, she could see that the front of Jeanne's dress was stained with something dark. *Something's happened,* she said to herself. *Something awful.*

Jeanne let out another sob and gestured wildly toward the back of the gallery. "Olga," she got out. "Olga."

Sweeney turned in the direction Jeanne was gesturing and saw a black-clad leg protruding from behind a stone pillar near the temporary exhibit where the canopic chest was being housed. "Is she hurt?" Sweeney asked Jeanne, rushing over and bending down to see if Olga was okay.

When she saw the dark blood, bright against the marble floor, she knew that Olga was not okay. It was the amount of blood, she realized, and the brightness of it, that caused her to stand up again and step back from the body. But she couldn't help seeing Olga's face, surprised and pale, the wound on her forehead and temple, the glistening blood, a rude spike of something white that must be bone. She noticed again the lovely cheekbones that she had never seen before, Olga's delicate throat. And as she looked up, thinking to herself, *Jeanne's killed her. Jeanne's killed Olga,* she saw the open lid of the cabinet where the canopic chest was kept, and the splintered wood, and she saw the three alabaster stoppers in the shape of a baboon, a jackal, and a falcon.

Three stoppers, she realized as she turned to Jeanne. Three where there had been four.

FOURTEEN

Afterward, Sweeney realized that it was evidence of how upset she'd been that she didn't even think about the fact that Quinn would eventually show up in response to the 911 call that Denny made from the phone on the main floor.

Once Willem had been located and they had told Denny to secure all the doors downstairs (Lacey displaying a sudden flair for police work and asserting that the thieves might still be in the building, or at the very least there might be a witness who had seen something) and gotten her a glass of whiskey from the bar, Jeanne calmed down enough to explain that she had gone downstairs to see if David Milken was still down there and, seeing something on the floor near the canopic chest, had gone to investigate.

She had found, she choked out, Olga, lying on her back and not moving, and she had dropped to the floor to see what had happened, not seeing the blood until it was all over her. "I kept trying to feel for her pulse," she told them. "But I didn't know what it was supposed to feel like and I just kept getting in the blood."

Sweeney, who had found and been comforted by Ian and then convinced everyone to gather on the main floor to wait for the police, discovered that she kept watching Jeanne's face for any sign that she was lying. She certainly seemed genuinely distraught and shocked, but then wouldn't she be pretty broken up if she had had some kind of altercation with Olga? She just couldn't get over the feeling she'd had when she'd first found Jeanne, the statement that had flashed through her head: *Jeanne's killed Olga.* She remembered Quinn telling her that it had taken him a long time to learn that more often than not, things were as they appeared. "If I arrive at a house and there's a dead girl there and there's a guy standing over her with blood on his hands, that guy better have a pretty damn good reason for being there," he'd told her. "And I can guarantee you that ninety-nine point nine percent of the time, that guy did it. But that's not how the justice system works. The system is set up for the one-tenth of a percent of the time he didn't do it."

But why would Jeanne kill Olga?

Quinn wasn't the first to arrive. He was preceded by a dozen or so uniformed cops who searched the galleries, secured the doors, and made sure no one left the building. Sweeney heard Willem explain the sequence of events to one of the cops and then pointed out Jeanne. "She found the body," he explained. "She's a bit on edge, but I'm sure she'll answer your questions." As always, he was very calm, very in control. It didn't surprise her that a murder in his museum didn't throw him, but Sweeney would have thought he'd be more upset about someone trying to take his new acquisition.

And then Quinn arrived. He was with a young woman Sweeney hadn't met before, and she remembered what he'd said about breaking in a new partner. The new partner — if that's who she was — looked too young to be a homicide detective. She was small but strong, her athlete's body clad in jeans and a simple T-shirt, her dirty blond hair in a ponytail. Sweeney watched her check in with the cops who were already there, then wave Quinn over to talk to them. He shook hands with everybody, friendly but somber, and she wondered if he ever slipped and grinned in these situations, if he ever forgot why he was there.

"You all right?" Ian asked her, encircling her with his arm and searching her face.

"Fine." She realized that she had never actually seen Quinn work a crime scene before. She'd never seen him in his element this way, asking questions, giving orders, taking charge from Willem, who had filled a kind of vacuum for authority that Sweeney now saw must always exist in a situation like this. The rest of them just stood around, whispering, passing what was probably bad information back and forth until it took on an air of veracity. Sweeney hadn't told anyone about the missing stopper, but word had somehow spread that there had been an attempted robbery.

She watched Quinn's tall form bowing gracefully toward one of the security guards, who was explaining something to him. He was wearing a short-sleeved shirt, and the muscles of his arms moved as he gestured with his hands. She could see the long scar that moved down one bicep — she hadn't noticed it at his house — and she couldn't help remembering lying on that cold, concrete floor last fall, Quinn in her arms, his blood flowing onto her hands, and waiting for the police to come and get them. She shook her head, trying to clear the memory, and when she looked up, she realized that he had seen her and she looked away so he wouldn't think she'd been staring at him.

"Do you want to sit down?" Ian asked her. "You look a bit wobbly."

But then Quinn was standing right in front of them. "I should have known you'd be here," he said, grinning just a little, though only Sweeney knew that it was a grin.

She tried not to smile too broadly, and she saw something else in his face — a twist of his eyebrows, the slight incline of his head, an apology for how he'd behaved at his house, she thought.

"Did you really find the body?" There was a thin mist of perspiration on his forehead and she could smell him, his sweat, his spicy deodorant, his laundry detergent. The scent was familiar to her now, and she realized she would have known him by it, or at the very least she would have thought of him if she'd passed someone else on the street who used the same deodorant or soap or whatever it was.

"No. But I guess I was second on the scene." She became aware of Ian standing next to her and turned to him. "This is Ian Ball. Tim Quinn. Detective Tim Quinn."

"Do you work at the museum as well?"

Ian looked at Sweeney and then back at Quinn, and said, "No, I just came to cheer Sweeney on." They shook hands and she saw Quinn search Ian's face.

There was an awkward silence and then Quinn said, "Did you see the victim earlier tonight? We're trying to get our time line down."

"She was doing coat check," Sweeney said. "We saw her when we arrived at four." She checked her watch. It was now eight-thirty. She had found Jeanne standing in the basement around seven. "I saw her at a couple different points in the evening, talking to people, helping out." The last time had been when she'd seen Olga talking to Fred. What time had that been? "I saw her up here in the gallery around six, I'd say. And I didn't see her again until . . . well, until Jeanne found the body." She thought of something. "But when I knelt down, to see if she was still alive, the blood was still running from her wound. Pretty fast. That means it hadn't been long, doesn't it? How long does it take blood to clot?"

"Not long," Quinn said. "Thanks. That's a good reference point for us. All right, I'd better get started. You'll all have to stay here for a while. We'll need to interview everyone." He turned to Sweeney. "Did you know her? The guy over there who's the head of the museum said she was Russian or something."

"Yeah. I think that's right. Though I think she'd been in the country for a while."

"That thing down there . . . the . . ."

"The canopic chest?"

"Yeah. Mr. Keane said it was Egyptian. That they used it for putting bodies in or something."

"Not bodies. Internal organs. The liver, the lungs, the stomach, and the intestines." She enjoyed the look of disgust that came over his face.

"And would something like that be worth a lot of money?"

"A fair bit," Ian said.

"Really? Well, there you go." He winked at them and headed over to where the young woman was taking down information from everyone who'd been left at the museum. There were some who worked at the museum, along with a few colleagues from Sweeney's department, a few stragglers whom she didn't recognize. Suddenly she found herself scrutinizing everyone. There was a tall guy in a dark suit who seemed vaguely sinister to Sweeney, but perhaps he just had one of those unfortunate faces.

Sweeney knew they'd have to ask everyone where they had been during the time leading up to Jeanne's discovery of the body. She and Ian and Lacey had been talking upstairs, of course. Who else had been in the room? She tried to remember. There had been a group of people she didn't know standing over by the entrance to her exhibit. She remembered that one of the women had been wearing a long embroidered coat and now she caught sight of the coat across the room, along with the two men and the blond woman the woman in the coat had been talking to. Then there'd been a group of five other members of the History of Art Department. That made another nine, and they had all been on the third floor when she'd gone downstairs. Then, of course, there had been someone in the bathroom on the main floor. Oh, and she remembered being introduced to three members of the Women's Studies Department who had come too. She saw them standing with Jeanne.

She assumed that whoever had tried to steal the canopic chest was long gone, but Quinn was going to have to find out if anyone had seen anything. As far as she knew, she and Jeanne were the only ones who had gone downstairs to the basement, though of course Willem had been taking people down and showing them the chest. And there was Fred. Where had Fred gone? Lacey had said he'd gone to make a phone call.

She felt like she'd gotten to know Fred well over the past few months, but when she thought about it, she knew almost nothing about him other than the fact that, like her, he'd gotten his graduate degree at the university. She knew he and Lacey had a daughter in college and a grown son who lived in Seattle, and that he took photographs in addition to studying them. But beyond that, she didn't know much at all.

"Now that's what I'd call a Boston accent."

Sweeney turned to Ian. "What?"

"Your cop friend. He's got quite an accent."

Sweeney waited a beat. "And you've got quite an accent yourself."

His face fell a little. "I didn't mean anything by it."

"Okay." They stared at each other for a minute, and she relented. "I'm sensitive about Boston accents, I guess."

"I like *your* accent."

"Well, I don't really have one." Ian just raised an eyebrow.

She was too tired to pursue it. "Let's go over there." She pointed to where their fellow detainees were sitting on folding chairs at the other end of the gallery.

"I wonder how long we'll have to stay here," Fred was saying. "I mean, what can we really do? If anyone had seen them, they would have already told the police, don't you think?"

"They're probably trying to get a time line in place, so they can figure out exactly when it happened," Sweeney said. "They'll want to know where we all were, who we remember being here, that kind of thing. And they're going to have to talk to each of us individually, so you'd better count on being here a while."

"I'm sure there are security cameras," Ian told them. "They'll be able to look at the tapes and at least see who entered and left the building. Whether they'll be able to track down the stopper is another question. It's amazing how quickly artifacts disappear into underground networks. I doubt it will ever be recovered. I've seen it many, many times. Though I suppose it's worth much less separated from the rest of the chest."

"It was incredibly bold," Willem said, "trying to take it when everyone was here." He sounded personally offended, as though the art thieves had done it as an affront to Willem.

"That was probably the point," Ian said. "Think about it. Your security is much more lax during something like this than at any other time, right? It was quite clever, actually."

Willem didn't say anything. Sweeney could see him eyeing Ian, making the judgment that he was a little arrogant, a little too sure of himself.

"But think about all the people who were coming and going." Lacey wrapped her shawl a little more tightly around her shoulders. "Anyone could have come down at any time."

"Jeanne and I did go down," Sweeney pointed out. "And Olga did too."

There was a long silence. Sweeney knew that both she and Jeanne were thinking the same thing. If they'd gone down a little bit earlier, it might have been either one of them surprising the thief or thieves.

"You didn't see anybody, did you, Jeanne?" Fred asked.

Jeanne shook her head. Someone had found a sweatshirt for her to put on over her bloodstained dress. It was sized for a large man and came nearly to her waist, her hands disappearing inside the sleeves.

They watched Tad approaching them. "I'm allowed to go, apparently," he said. "But they want to talk to everybody."

"What did they ask you?" Fred asked in a low voice. Something in his tone made Sweeney turn to look at him. He seemed nervous, his eyes darting back and forth between Quinn and the other people waiting to be questioned.

"Oh, just where I was, did I see anyone going downstairs, did I see anyone leaving or anyone who seemed nervous or anything like that. I couldn't offer a whole lot. I had gone to get more seltzer for the caterers. I was in the supply closet on the main floor, so I didn't see anybody at all." He gave a long sigh, as though he was relieved. "Well, I'm going to get going. I'll see you all tomorrow?" They nodded and he flashed a rare smile — Sweeney realized she'd seen Tad smile only a handful of times — and turned to go.

But he didn't make it very far before he was stopped in his tracks by the voice of one of the uniformed cops who were rushing up the stairs. "Detective Quinn," he called out. "We need you downstairs. Right now. I think we've got something."

They all watched as Quinn and the young woman raced out of the gallery and disappeared down the stairwell. Despite the fact that there was a uniformed cop guarding them, everyone left in the gallery went out onto the open hallway and looked down over the balcony. The voices floated up and reached them where they stood.

"We found the other head," one of the uniformed cops was saying. "Someone dumped it in the trash can by the door. And it's covered in blood."

FIFTEEN

"She was a Soviet Jew. From Moscow, I think," Willem Keane was saying. "I've known her for thirty years now, and I never heard the story of how she ended up here, but you know there were a lot of them who came over in the late seventies. Remember the refuseniks?"

Quinn had no idea what he was talking about, but he nodded and let Keane go on. "She was a very private person, not particularly friendly. She hid behind the language barrier sometimes, I think. Her English was actually pretty good, but she would pretend she didn't understand so she wouldn't have to talk. She was afraid of people, of personal interactions, I think."

"Did you know anything about her family? Was she married? Where did she live?" Quinn asked him.

"Oh, no. I don't think she had anybody. We can check the personnel file, but I believe she rented an apartment somewhere in Jamaica Plain. She'd moved around a good bit while she worked for us. Perhaps she had friends in the Russian or Jewish community, I don't know. She never talked about anything beyond her job here at the museum."

"How did you come to hire her?" Quinn asked.

"It wasn't me, but I was here then. I believe it was through a benefactor. We can find the name for you if you want. He had taken on the cause of Russian Jews who had come over and was helping them find jobs. In those days, I think it was easier for someone just to call up and say he wanted to find a job for a friend. He'd given a lot of money to the museum. Now Olga would have to go through personnel like anyone else. She was very satisfactory, though. She did her job well."

"Who should we notify? About her death?"

"I was thinking about that," Keane said, crossing his legs and leaning back comfortably in the chair. "She never mentioned anyone. I suppose the only thing to do is to go to her apartment and see if any of her neighbors know anything more, see if there are any letters at the apartment, anything like that. I'd be happy to help in any way I can. I liked her very much."

"And of course it looks like she may have saved your chest from being stolen," Ellie said. She had been silent up until now, following Quinn's instructions as they'd come in. Both Quinn and Keane turned to look at her.

"That's right," Keane said. "I'm grateful, though of course if I had my choice, I would prefer she hadn't had to sacrifice her life." He said it just a little too fast, as though he was embarrassed that Ellie had reminded him.

"Right," Quinn said. "Of course." Ellie's comment had thrown him off. "If you could tell me about the security procedures here at the museum . . . ?"

"Yes." Keane settled back in his chair, on firm ground now. "Certainly. You'll want to talk to our director of security and the company that handles it for us. After the theft here twenty-five or so years ago, we improved our security a lot, though there's always more that can be done. Basically we have extensive video surveillance in all of the galleries and at all points of entry or exit. Then there's security at every door leading from the administrative offices and the storerooms into the galleries. All staff have electronic passkeys that they wave in front of the device and then enter a password. I'm sure there are tapes from the cameras."

"Yes," Quinn said. "We arranged with Mr. Moran to contact the security company to get all of those tapes. We'll be viewing them as soon as possible."

"Good. Of course, we have a state-of-the-art alarm system as well. All points of entry. That's for when the museum's not open. But many of our display cabinets are alarmed as well. I attended a conference on security a couple of years ago that led me to insist on the extra protection. College and university art museums are extraordinarily vulnerable, apparently. They have some priceless art and artifacts and are usually woefully unprotected. It's a miracle there haven't been more thefts like this one."

"Attempted thefts," Ellie said.

"Yes. Right." Keane glanced at her. "Attempted thefts."

Quinn paused for a moment, in order to figure out where he wanted to go next. Thanks to Sweeney, he couldn't help wanting to know more about the 1979 theft, but Keane probably wasn't the person to ask. Quinn was sure he'd have his own prejudices and theories. He looked around the office, which was decorated with what looked like castoffs from the museum's collection, a couple of rugs hanging on one wall, a piece of fabric covered in symbols and drawings of women on another. Keane's desk had a few small Egyptian artifacts on it, a golden woman's head and a small buff-colored pyramid. Quinn assumed they were copies. "Have you had any threats or unusual communications of any kind?"

Keane gave him a sardonic look. "You mean has anyone written me a note telling me they're going to rob my museum? No. I can assure you they have not."

"Okay. Now, can you tell me what you did tonight. Just give us a time line of your evening."

Keane looked around the room, as though he couldn't quite believe he was being asked to do this. Quinn gave him what he hoped was a stern look. "Certainly. I was upstairs for most of the evening, talking to guests. At about six o'clock, I took Mr. Hutchinson down to see the chest." He said it as though he'd already explained all of this to them and they were annoying him by asking him to repeat it.

"Mr. Hutchinson?"

Keane came close to rolling his eyes. "I told the other cop. Mr. Hutchinson donated the chest and I took him down to show it to him. When we were done, I escorted him back to the main floor and said good-bye, and then I came back upstairs."

"Did you see Mr. Hutchinson leave the building?" Hutchinson hadn't been on the list of people in the museum at the time the body was found.

"Yes."

"We'll need to get in touch with him."

Now Keane looked angry. "We are talking about a seventy-nine-year-old man, a banker and distinguished alumnus of this university, who has given a priceless gift to the museum. Surely you can't be suggesting that he is also an art thief."

"No, but he may be a witness," Quinn said. "So you said good-bye to him and then you came straight upstairs? Did you see anything unusual?"

"I did visit the restroom on the lower floor," Keane said. "But I did not see anything unusual. In fact, I did not see anything usual, either. There was no one down there." He held his head a little higher, and Quinn decided that he now knew where the phrase "looking down his nose" came from. There was real arrogance in Keane's voice, as though he couldn't understand why this cop was suddenly in a position of authority over him.

He and Quinn stared at each other for a minute, and then Quinn said, "Mr. Keane, I am trying to find out who murdered one of your employees and tried to steal what I understand is a very expensive piece of art. I don't know why you are reluctant to answer my questions, but if you continue to be so, I will find myself wondering about it even more." It was the kind of speech he always wanted to make but could never quite think of at the time.

Keane inclined his head a bit and said, "You're right. I'm sorry. Of course I want to help you."

"Okay. What time was it when you went down to the basement and found it empty?"

"I would say it was about six thirty-five or so."

Quinn looked at Ellie. That was only twenty-five minutes before Jeanne Ortiz had found Olga Levitch's body. They'd pinned the murder down to a twenty-five minute window. Now the security tapes would actually be useful to them. "Go get Jimmy and those guys to start viewing the tapes," he told Ellie. She nodded and left the room.

"And after you showed Mr. Hutchinson the chest, you locked the cabinet back up again, right?" In their initial investigation of the cabinet, it had appeared as though it

189

had been broken open. The wood near the lock was splintered and gouged, and the crime-scene services was taking castings of the marks to try to figure out what kind of a tool had made them. It was one of them who had called Quinn over and said, "The lock was open, Tim. Look, you can see that it's disengaged. Whoever made these marks was trying to make us think that he'd broken in, but it was as simple as lifting the top."

Tad Moran had been adamant that Keane would never have done something as careless as to leave the cabinet unlocked, but Quinn was betting that he had.

Now, faced with the question, Keane looked offended. "Of course I did."

"The cabinet was damaged, but the lock appears not to have been broken."

Keane didn't seem to get what he was saying. He just sat there.

Quinn prompted him. "Mr. Keane, the lock on the cabinet was open when the cabinet was damaged."

"Well, I know I locked it when I took Mr. Hutchinson back upstairs." But he sounded less sure this time.

"Is there any possibility that you left it open? I'm sure you can appreciate how important this is. If you are absolutely certain that you locked that cabinet, then we're looking for someone with a key. How many other people in this museum have keys to that cabinet?"

He seemed to grasp the point. "I don't know how I could have . . ." He blanched, as though he'd just realized that if the chest had been stolen, it would have been his fault. "I suppose that . . . I was very excited about it and it was just a temporary exhibit, so I'm not accustomed to locking them. The newer ones lock automatically. Oh, God." He put a hand to his heart. "If it had been successfully stolen . . ."

Quinn decided to go for it and ask Keane if he had any ideas about the 1979 theft. "Did you have any suspicions about who it might have been?"

"Well, I guess it isn't any secret that the FBI suspected it was the same people who later broke into the Gardner. Some kind of organized crime."

"And that made sense to you?"

"I suppose. It certainly seemed like a professional job."

"Okay, that's all I have for now. I'm sure we'll be in touch in the next couple of days. And we will need your help in locating family members for Olga Levitch."

"Yes. Okay." But Keane didn't get up.

Instead he sat there, his hands worrying in his lap. Quinn had the feeling that if he just waited, he would find out what it was that was making Willem Keane so hostile. "Detective Quinn," he said finally. "You must understand that we depend upon donors and benefactors to grow our collection here at the university. If they . . . well, if they feel that our security is somehow lacking, they will be less likely to do so. Particularly if I did in fact leave the chest unsecured. I was hoping that we could keep the fact that there's been a breach of security, well, quiet."

Quinn stood up and went over to open the door. "Mr. Keane, there's been a murder. I'm sorry if the museum gets bad publicity, but our first order of business has to be figuring out who killed Olga Levitch. Do you understand?"

Just as Ellie came back into the room, Keane rose and smiled hello to her as though nothing but light conversation had been exchanged for the past half hour. "Of course, Detective," he said. "Of course."

Sixteen

"Who's next?" Ellie asked, sitting down in the chair where Keane had been sitting. She stretched her legs out, getting comfortable, and looked up at him, her blue eyes shining with excitement. She looked like a kid who'd been brought to the circus.

He snapped at her, "Don't sit behind his desk. That's his desk. We're using his office, but it doesn't mean we get to sit at his desk."

She jumped up and sat awkwardly in the chair she'd been sitting in before, embarrassed now.

He asked, "You got the security tapes?"

"Yeah, yeah. I have Johnny on it. They have to get someone from the security company to come over and figure out how to access them. It may take a little while. They're going to get it all set up and give us a call when it's ready."

"What do you think about that thing with the chest being left unlocked?"

She seemed surprised that he wanted her opinion. "I guess you can kind of understand how it happened. The rest of the cabinets in the museum lock automatically. And he said too that he didn't usually open cabinets to show things off. It was just that this one wasn't specifically designed for the chest, so it was hard to see it unless you opened it up. That's what he said, anyway."

"Did you buy that? I'm not sure I do."

She thought for a moment. "I know what you mean. That part seemed a little insincere to me. You know what I did buy, though? When he said that he was so excited about showing it off that he opened the cabinet even though he knew he shouldn't. I really believed him when he said that."

Quinn grudgingly admitted to himself that irritating habits and all, Havrilek was right about Ellie. She had a good feeling for people, for when they were lying and when they were telling the truth.

"But how did the thief know it would be open? Was Keane in on it? Did he leave it open on purpose?" That didn't make any sense. Why would Keane help someone steal a piece he'd just gotten?

"The thief didn't have to know. Remember he tried to break it."

She was right. "But that's just . . . What

are the chances the thief got that lucky? I mean, come on. We don't see that kind of luck very often in our profession. You know that."

She shrugged, and he watched her for a minute. There was something about the way she sat that bugged the shit out of him. Her knees were pressed together and her hands rested awkwardly on them. As though she could read his mind, she leaned back in the chair, trying to look more casual.

"Can you do me a favor and listen this time?" He hadn't meant it quite as harsh as it sounded. "I mean, just let me lead the questioning. I have a rhythm and . . ."

Her lower lip did something funny and she looked down at her lap.

Jesus Christ. "I'm sorry. Just listen and let's try to get through this." She nodded, still looking down at her thin hands.

He checked his list of witnesses and the notes he'd jotted down about each one from the initial conversations with the guys who had first arrived on the scene. Fred Kauffman, who was in charge of photography at the museum, had said he'd gone downstairs to get something out of the office, then gone outside to use his cell phone and come back in just as the police were being called. Quinn was wondering whether he'd seen anyone leaving the museum.

But when he asked that question, the answer he got made him suspicious. Kauffman was a nice, friendly-looking guy, on the short and round side, with curly gray hair and a face that reminded Quinn of one of Megan's teddy bears.

"No, no. I didn't . . . I mean, I saw a lot of people leaving, but just, you know, people who had been at the opening."

"Were you watching the main entrance to the museum the entire time you were on the phone?"

"Not exactly. No. I mean, I was talking so I was paying attention to that . . ." His answer kind of stuttered out, as though he was making it up as he went along.

"And who were you talking to on the phone?"

Kauffman nearly jumped in his seat. "Just a friend. Why do you need to know?"

Quinn, following a hunch, said, "Well, we'll need to check with this friend, of course, in order to pin down exactly where everyone was and when."

There was a long silence, and then Kauffman said, "Look, I told my wife and everyone that I was going out to make a phone call, but actually, I just needed a breath of fresh air. I wasn't talking to anyone. It sounds silly now, but I had told my wife that's what I was doing and she was there when the policeman asked us."

"Why couldn't you tell them that you needed to get outside for a minute?" Quinn tried to pretend that he was merely curious, but he was actually very suspicious. Kauffman was about the jumpiest guy he'd seen in a long time.

"It was stupid. I just . . . my wife would have wanted to come with me, and I really just needed to be alone. I can't explain very well. I was so tired of talking to people, of playing host, and I just wanted to get out. I walked around the yard and came back about fifteen minutes later. When I walked through the front entrance, I knew something had happened. Sweeney was standing there yelling at Denny and he was on the phone and she said something about Olga and then they told me."

Quinn asked a few more questions, then let him go. He noted that Kauffman seemed relieved but tried not to make too much of it. After all, most people were relieved when they finished being questioned by the police.

Next was the uptight-looking woman who had accosted Quinn when he first arrived to tell him that it was very important to keep "his men" from touching the works of art.

She'd pissed him off by looking down her nose at him and saying, "You may not realize how fragile they are." He had to admit, though, she looked like the kind of person who might be able to give him a minute-by-minute account of everyone's movements over the course of the evening.

"Ms. Tyler, is there anything you can tell us. Anything you noticed that might help us?"

"Oh, I don't think so. I don't think you're looking for someone who would have been noticed."

"Excuse me?"

"You're not looking for someone stupid enough to do something to bring attention to himself or herself. Himself, I'd think. Organized criminals are usually men, aren't they?" She smiled at the look on his face. "This wasn't just some person who walked in off the street, Detective. This has to be the same people who robbed the museum before, don't you think?"

Quinn, who had decided that she was probably right, asked her a few more questions and moved on. They made their way through the guests and the few students who had been upstairs when Olga Levitch's body was found. Nobody had seen anything out of the ordinary, but then none of them had gone down to the basement.

Quinn rubbed his eyes. It was ten now and he'd been up with Megan a couple of times in the night. Megan. He felt a wave of guilt. He'd asked Patience to sleep on the couch and she hadn't minded — she never did when he had to work late — but he still wondered what Megan thought when he wasn't there to put her to bed. Sometimes, he saw the way Megan looked at Patience, with absolute and total love and trust, and he felt a little jealous. Of course she looked at him the same way, but when it came right down to it, hour for hour, Patience took care of her more than he did. It made him nervous, thinking about how his daughter had invested so much love in someone who could be taken away from her, the way her mother had. He was the only one who couldn't be taken away. He had to be.

Quinn rubbed his eyes, told himself to stop wallowing in parental guilt, and told Ellie to go get Ian Ball. Quinn studied him as he came in, walking as though he'd practiced the exact way he wanted to walk into a room to be questioned by the police. Quinn had had a roommate in college, a guy who had been a really, really good soccer player, and he moved the way this guy did, gracefully, full of his right to be moving in the world. It struck Quinn that he was just the kind of guy he'd expect to see with Sweeney. His black hair reminded Quinn of the Kennedys, and his glasses and the neat blue shirt and green tie under his dark suit made him look like an ad for men's clothes. Quinn sat up a little straighter, suddenly aware that he'd come rushing out wearing a polo shirt he'd taken out of the laundry. A few hours out, it was beginning to smell a little funky.

"So you were upstairs in the gallery the whole evening?"

"That's right. We arrived around four, and while Sweeney was showing the reporter around and talking to people, I stood with Lacey — I'm sorry I don't know her last name, but she's Fred's wife — and we spoke with some of Sweeney's colleagues. So I'm afraid I can't help you much. We saw the woman who was killed as we came in because she was running the coat check — not that there were many coats to check in this wretched heat." He smiled at Ellie, and Quinn watched Ellie smile back, then blush a little under her porcelain doll skin.

"You're visiting Boston, is that right? But you live in London?"

"Well, in a way. I've been here for eight months now. I've been opening a Boston office of my company. We're an auction house. We're still quite small, but we hope to open some other satellite offices. Perhaps New York or Washington next."

"And your place of residence while you're here?" He gave them an address on Russell Street in Cambridge. Quinn looked up. It was Sweeney's address. They were living together. "And how long do you intend to be at that address?" He felt Ellie glance at him. It was a strange question.

"Don't know, really. I'm trying to convince Sweeney to move to London with me." He smiled. "We'll see if I can wear her down."

Quinn felt hot suddenly, and he couldn't think of what he wanted to ask next. When the silence grew uncomfortable, Ellie said, "So you didn't see anything strange during the evening, anyone who looked out of place?"

Ian Ball laughed. "No. I wish I could help you there. Everyone looked perfectly respectable to me, but I suppose that's how they pulled it off. By looking respectable, I mean."

"Thank you," Quinn said. "I think that's it." He wanted the guy out of the room.

Ian Ball stood up. "I've dealt with a few of these thefts before," he said. "I'd be pleased to help you identify some contacts. If you'd like."

"Thanks. We'll let you know." Quinn stood up and waited until he'd gone before looking at Ellie. She was watching the door as though she could still see the handsome ghost of Ian Ball lingering there.

"Let's do the rest of the people who were upstairs," he said, making some notes in his notebook.

"It might be helpful to . . ."

"I said, let's do the rest of the people who were upstairs."

Silently, she went out and came back in with one of the History of Art Department faculty members.

They finished with the rest of the witnesses, including Fred Kauffman's wife, who told them that she'd been upstairs all evening and that her husband had too except for when he'd gone outside to make a phone call. Quinn decided there wasn't any reason to tell her the truth. Not yet, anyway. He let her go.

Denny Keefe was next. They'd already talked to the other guard who had been on duty, but he'd reported just what Quinn had expected him to report, that he'd done his rounds, hitting each gallery every thirty minutes, and hadn't seen anything out of the ordinary. He warned a couple of guests about getting too close to paintings. Other than that, nothing.

Keefe was an older guy, with gray hair slicked back against his head in the old-style way that Quinn's dad and his friends had worn their hair. Keefe even smelled the way they'd smelled, kind of musky and herby, like some ancient, mysterious potion.

"You were at your post near the main entrance throughout the evening?" Quinn asked him.

"Yeah, that's right. That's the protocol. One officer at the front, one doing rounds."

"Anything out of the ordinary last night?"

"Not really. A lot of people coming through all at the same time. That's kind of stressful for us, 'cause we got to check all of them and the line kind of builds up. Other than that, it was pretty easy. People stayed upstairs for the most part. There was the thing with the kid, though."

"The kid?"

"Yeah, a student. He had a bag with him, like the kind you would put a computer in, you know? And he wanted to bring it in. I told him he couldn't. No bags bigger than a purse. But he was kind of mad about it. He made an issue of it, you know, said it wouldn't be safe in the coat check. Finally, he left it there, but he was mad. You could tell."

"What did he look like? Did you know who he was?"

"No, I hadn't seen him before. But he had on this Hawaiian kind of shirt. It was just like one I used to have, back in the fifties probably. Red and orange, with those palm leaves on it."

Quinn wrote that down.

"So you were by the front entrance all night. You didn't step away, even for a second?" One of the other guards had told him he'd walked by the front desk at six-thirty and hadn't seen Denny Keefe.

Keefe looked down. "Well, once things quieted down, I had to use the restroom. I was going to try to get Patrick to come up and take over, but he was up on the fourth floor, so I just ducked in for a quick whiz. Oh, sorry." He'd forgotten Ellie was there. "I'm telling you, though, I was gone maybe two minutes, three tops. I shouldn't have, I know, but boy, I had to go, and at my age, you can't leave it too long." He smiled at them, trying to make a joke, then said, "You don't think that's when this person got out the front door, do you?"

Quinn felt sorry for him and said, "I doubt it. We'll check the tapes again. What time did you say that was?"

"I'd say six-forty, something like that."

They told him he could go and Quinn looked down at the list. He felt his stomach pitch a little.

"We just have to do Sweeney St. George and then we'll be done with everyone," Ellie said. "And by that time, they should have the tapes ready to look at."

"Okay," Quinn said, opening the door. "You can go get her. But let's talk to her down there."

"Down where?"

"In the basement by the cabinet. She was the second person on the scene. I want to know if anything struck her about it. She's had some experience with this kind of thing, and I think her impressions may be valuable. Bring her down in the elevator, though, so we don't walk anywhere we don't have to down there."

It was highly irregular and he knew it. Ellie looked as though she was going to say something, then nodded and went out. He stepped out of Keane's office and went down in the elevator, trying to get hold of himself. In the reflection of the steel doors, he could just barely make out the outline of his face. He used the hem of his shirt to wipe the sweat off his face. Christ, it was hot. There didn't seem to be any air-conditioning in the elevator.

It had thrown him, seeing Sweeney. He'd been feeling bad about the way he'd treated her when she'd come to his house a few weeks ago, though he wasn't sure what to do about it. Why had he been so mean to her? He'd been trying to figure that out, and the closest he could get was that he was mad at her for never calling him back. Last fall, after they'd gotten back from Concord, they'd gotten together for coffee a few times and he'd thought . . . What had he thought? He looked at his blurry image in the elevator door. *Be honest, Quinny.* He'd thought about asking her out, just for dinner, maybe. He'd wanted to talk to her, he'd wanted to tell her about his English class. He'd wanted to tell her about Megan, about all the words she could say. One day, walking around Cambridge, he'd seen exactly the place he wanted to take her, a little restaurant with candles on the tables and a bouquet of roses on a little table by the door. It seemed like the kind of place you could talk and nobody would mind if you closed the place down.

He'd called her to ask her about it, but she'd never called back. Then she'd shown up at his house, asking him to go and open up a cold case just to satisfy some kind of personal curiosity. It had been stupid, that thing about going out to dinner. He didn't know what he'd been thinking.

The elevator opened in a little alcove off of the basement gallery. They were right next to the cabinet, and Quinn reminded himself to check and see if there were tapes from the elevator. The killer could have escaped that way, though he still would have had to go out the main entrance and dump the stopper.

Quinn stood by the cabinet, looking down at where the body had been. They had finished with Olga Levitch and taken her away to be carved up in a postmortem that would tell them for sure what had killed her. Quinn didn't need to be told. She'd been killed with the stopper. Head trauma, followed by death. He could see it all clearly, the faceless figure, bent over the cabinet, the cleaning woman coming upon him, crying out, the figure turning and raising the stopper, hitting her over the head, then turning and running, dumping the stopper in the garbage can before disappearing into the night. Something occurred to him. There must have been an accomplice with a vehicle. The chest wasn't huge — you could put it in a bag or wrap it in a coat, but you wouldn't want to go too far carrying it like that. He made a mental note to check with traffic enforcement, see if any vehicles had been idling outside during the evening.

"Hey," Sweeney said, coming out of the elevator, Ellie behind her. Her long, dark skirt swished against the floor as she walked. Her arms were lightly freckled, like her face, and in the low light of the basement, her blouse was blindingly white.

He almost smiled, then remembered Ellie was there and said in a businesslike way, "I was hoping you could tell me if everything looks just the way it did when you first saw the body."

"Sure." She studied him for a moment, then asked, "Are you okay?"

Quinn turned around so Ellie wouldn't see his face, and ignoring Sweeney's question, asked her, "What struck you when you came over? Just tell me what you remember."

She stepped toward the cabinet and said, "I remember that the blood was the first thing I saw. It would be, wouldn't it? I mean, Jeanne had already told me something had happened to her, so I suppose I was looking for it, but as I told you, I remember that the blood was kind of running out. I guess I saw the wound and so I could see that that was where the blood was coming from."

"You realized the stopper had been stolen immediately, right?"

"Yeah, well, there had been four of them — there are always four — and when I looked there were only three."

"And you're sure there wasn't anyone here?" It had just occurred to him that the thief might have been hiding in the basement, then slipped out in the commotion after the discovery of the body.

"Pretty sure. I think I would have felt him there, if you know what I mean. But on the other hand, I was so upset that I may not have been paying attention."

"After you saw the body, you and Ms. Ortiz both went upstairs, is that right?"

"Yes."

"What I'm trying to figure out is if the crime scene could have been altered in any way. Does everything look the same to you?"

She stood there, and he could tell she was checking all the details off. Cabinet, splintered wood, the three stoppers in the chest. "It looks the same," she said.

"Thanks. Now, you came downstairs to use the restroom?"

"Yeah. There was someone in the one on the main floor. I came around the corner." She pointed to the stairs. "And Jeanne was just standing there."

"And in your opinion, was her shock real?" He could feel Ellie behind him, disapproving. She's a witness, he knew she was thinking. Why is he asking her to speculate about what another witness was thinking or feeling?

Sweeney met his eyes, and he could tell she knew what he was thinking. "You mean . . . ? I think she was upset. There's no doubt about that. Although . . ." She trailed off and he felt his heart speed a little.

"Yeah?"

"She was so upset, almost too upset. Do you know what I mean?" She told him about the thought that had gone through her head when she first saw Jeanne. "Maybe I've just become an old hand at this murder thing, but it wasn't like she knew Olga. And it wasn't like she really cared about Willem's canopic chest. So why was she so upset?" She shrugged her shoulders. "I don't know. It just seemed weird to me is all."

He knew there were other things he should ask her, but he was too tired to think what they were. "Why don't you get going. We'll be in touch."

"Okay," she said, still studying his face. "I'll talk to you soon?"

He nodded, trying to seem indifferent,

and turned away as she and Ellie stepped into the elevator, listening to the doors open, then shut again, and the elevator hum up through the walls.

The basement seemed huge suddenly, cavernous and silent, and he stared at the chest. What had Keane said it was made of? Alabaster. The alabaster almost glowed in the low light. Sweeney had said they put organs in it and it occurred to him that they might still be in there. The elevator hummed again and he heard the doors open and then Ellie's footsteps behind him.

"It's great that you already knew her." Something in her voice made Quinn think of icy lemonade.

Quinn turned to look at her and found himself meeting her wide blue eyes, the clear suspicion on her face. He deserved it, deserved anything she'd want to say to him right now, he knew, and he wanted to apologize to her, to confess the riot of jealousy and uncertainty that had gripped him as Ian Ball told him about Sweeney moving to London. He wanted to tell her about Maura, about Megan, about every-thing. But of course he wouldn't.

"Let's go," he said. "I want to see what's on that tape."

SEVENTEEN

The next morning, Sweeney left Ian in bed with the slumbering General and walked up to Davis Square for pastry and the papers. They hadn't gotten home until nearly midnight, and she should have used the opportunity that a Saturday morning offered and caught up on her sleep, but she'd had strange dreams all night, dreams in which she'd been running from someone or something through a series of dark rooms.

And, she remembered as she walked along in the soft heat of the early morning, she had dreamt of her father. He'd been standing in front of a house, a low, compact house made of gray wood set against a dry, orange-brown landscape. She had spoken to him, and he'd nodded at her, then disappeared inside. Suddenly they were at the Hapner, in the basement galleries, and her father was leaning over the stone sarcophagus, looking into it, rapt. When Sweeney leaned over his shoulder to look down into it, she saw a little diorama of her father and a dark-haired woman standing in a living room assembled like a stage set, fighting with each other, her father's voice high and shrill, not the way she remembered it at all. When she turned to her father to ask him what was going on, he had smiled and nodded again and disappeared. Then she was alone in the basement of the museum, and she knew, suddenly, terrifyingly, that she was being pursued. The galleries were dark and the artifacts in their dim glass cases mocked her as she ran, uncertain where her pursuer was.

She stopped for a second and stood watching a squirrel run across the tiny front lawn of a newly renovated triple-decker at the end of her street. It stopped every ten feet or so to look around, listening for danger.

The dream wasn't as odd as it seemed. First of all, she and Ian had been talking about her father just a few weeks ago, so it made sense that he would show up in her dreams. And they had also talked about her father's girlfriend, or whatever she had been, in Mexico. So that was why she'd shown up. And of course after what had happened last night, she was just working through her fear about being in the basement, about finding Jeanne and then seeing Olga's body. Still, the dream bothered her and she wasn't sure why.

She got a dozen crullers at her favorite bakery, along with some orange juice, and bought a *New York Times,* checking the arts section as she walked back home. There was David Milken's review of the exhibition on an inside page, a glowing review, she was happy to note, but it was overshadowed by the larger article detailing Olga's murder and the attempted theft of the canopic chest, and it struck her that however much a success the exhibition had been, people would always remember that Olga had been murdered at the opening. That was what murder did. It overshadowed, blanked out, erased everything normal.

Back at the apartment, she made coffee and poured herself a large glass of orange juice, splashing in some leftover champagne from the fridge to make a mimosa. Her dream had rattled her, and she decided that she needed something to steady her nerves. A mimosa was festive. She'd make Ian one too. Then she finished reading the papers while the General had his breakfast and spent a good half hour cleaning his sleek black fur before disappearing out the window for his daily rounds.

She made up a tray with the coffee and crullers and the mimosas and brought it into the bedroom, where Ian was still sleeping. She took off her jeans and got back in bed, poking Ian's back and propping the tray up on her lap.

Then she opened the *Globe* to read its coverage of the attempted theft.

The story quoted Willem as saying that Olga had apparently prevented the theft of the invaluable object and that he was only sorry she'd had to pay with her life. Quinn was quoted too, saying that the police were interviewing witnesses and that any help the public could offer would be much appreciated. It was a classic nonanswer answer.

Sweeney knew there were security cameras in many locations around the museum, and if the cameras hadn't caught the actual murder, they probably had caught every person who'd come through the main entrance. Sweeney was betting that Quinn already had a complete guest list. But he'd prefer to make the thief/murderer think that he didn't have any idea who he or she was.

Ian picked up the *Globe* and read the story.

"Does it strike you as strange that someone would try to steal the chest during a show?" Sweeney asked him. "I mean, how would he or she know that a guard or someone wasn't going to walk in at that moment?"

"Well, he solved one of the major problems that any art thief has, which is access. He didn't have to break into the building because the building was already open." She knew that Ian was actually quite knowledgeable about security, having had to come up with a system for securing valuables at the auction house.

"Your cop was different from how I thought he would be," Ian said after a minute. "The way you described him, I had this image of . . . I don't know. More of a *cop,* if you know what I mean." Sweeney did know, but still she considered being offended on behalf of all cops.

Instead she said, "He's got this nanny, this beautiful girl. From Rwanda, I think. She was speaking French, anyway. She has this long scar down the side of her face."

Ian put down the paper. "They used machetes."

"Yes."

They were silent for a moment and then Ian pulled her over to him. She breathed deeply against his chest. He smelled of bodies, of salt and coffee.

"Have you thought at all about London?"

She felt herself stiffen against him. She considered making a joke, telling him she often thought of London, but she knew it wasn't the thing to do. Instead she said nothing, hugging him tighter as if she could squeeze away the question, as if she could take away the very air that had carried it.

He let her, squeezing her back, and her hand dropped to his hip, rubbing circles on it, and then lower, and his desire replaced his need to know.

Sweeney felt out of sorts and aimless all that weekend. Her work on the exhibition was finished and she didn't have anything to do until January, when she'd be teaching again. She had planned it this way so that she'd have some time for research on a new book about funerary items around the world, but now she was regretting the empty months ahead of her.

She and Ian spent much of Saturday and Sunday fielding phone calls from friends who had heard about the murder and wanted to make sure Sweeney was okay. Toby, who seemed almost disappointed he'd left before the fireworks, stopped by on Saturday afternoon and ended up staying for dinner. Watching him and Ian chattering happily away over the pasta carbonara

Sweeney had made, she felt oddly jealous. It wasn't that she didn't want them to be friends. In fact, it made her life a whole hell of a lot easier that they liked each other, but their chumminess made her feel . . . trapped somehow.

"You seem really upset," Toby said when she walked him down to his car. His curly dark hair was even curlier than usual in the humid air, and his glasses kept slipping down his nose. She watched him push them up for the twentieth time that night and smiled. Toby pushing his glasses back up was a visual snapshot she carried with her when he wasn't around. "Was it finding her? Or did you know her?"

"I didn't really know her," Sweeney said. "And I didn't really find her. Jeanne did."

"But you were there."

"Yeah. But that's not it. I'm just kind of at loose ends. The show's done. I should start the research for the book, but this has kind of thrown me."

"And you still haven't decided if you're going to London."

"I still haven't decided if I'm going to London." She leaned on the passenger side door of his Honda. "What do you think I should do?"

"I think you shouldn't ask someone who

loves you as much as I do for objective advice about a relationship that's going to put an ocean between us."

"Really. Come on. I want your opinion."

"My opinion is that Ian is a great guy and that he's sickeningly in love with you. But neither of those things really matters. What do *you* think?" He went around to the driver's side and opened the door, blowing her a kiss over the top of the car. "Sorry. Thanks for dinner. And be good. I worry about you when you're at loose ends."

She waved and watched him go. She wasn't sure what he meant by it, but she realized he was right. It was when she didn't have anything to do that she usually got into trouble.

After brunch on Sunday, Ian announced that he had to go to the office for a couple of hours and Sweeney decided to go for a walk. She needed some time to think, and walking was the way she did it best. It was still hot, so she put on a tank top and shorts and flip-flops and started out, crisscrossing her way through the neighborhoods around Davis Square.

It wasn't as though she'd been friends with Olga, she told herself, so she ought not to fool herself into thinking that that was why she was so . . . disquieted. She had known Olga for a lot of years, she supposed, but she hadn't really *known* her. Sweeney had always tried to smile and be pleasant, but Olga hadn't seemed particularly interested in even a nodding acquaintance. But then she must have been fairly terrified of getting to know anyone, having gotten out of the Soviet Union at a time when Jews were persecuted and had to live in fear. Sweeney forgot now who'd told her that Olga had been a refusenik, one of the Soviet Jews who had applied for a visa to emigrate, been refused, and then been subject to suspicion by the government. No wonder she'd been so unpleasant sometimes.

There was a kind of monumental injustice to the fact that someone who had probably never owned much of anything in her life had been killed in the course of an art robbery.

It was the robbery, Sweeney decided, that was giving her pause. It seemed too much of a coincidence that she had only just discovered that Karen Philips had been in the museum at the time of the robbery and that there should then be another one. But as Quinn had reminded her, sometimes coincidences were just coincidences.

She walked on, thinking about Ian. Toby

was right. It didn't really matter what he thought about Ian. It only mattered what she thought. She knew she cared about Ian, was attracted to him, though less so in the last few weeks, she reflected, then wondered why that was. He had been so good to her, and he made her feel . . . prized. She wasn't sure why that was the word that came to her mind, but it was. And he wanted her to go to London with him. So what was she going to do?

What would Quinn say if she were to ask him what she should do? Suddenly, his opinion on the matter seemed very important. But she couldn't very well call him up and ask him, could she? Perhaps if it just came up in conversation. She shook her head, trying to clear it. What was she thinking, asking Quinn for advice on her love life? He would think she was crazy.

She found herself wondering where he was. Probably at the museum, going over the crime scene. She assumed that if the security cameras had picked up anything, they would already be making arrests. Remembering what she'd read about the 1979 robbery, Sweeney decided it had to be connected. In order to kill Olga, the thiefs had to be pretty cold-blooded. This wasn't some amateur who'd decided to take the chest and see what he could get for it. This was someone who was willing to kill for it. That was interesting. She wondered if Quinn had thought of that, though she supposed the thief might have been surprised by Olga and killed her even though he hadn't meant to. Certainly the fact that the theft had been aborted backed up that theory.

The problem, Sweeney told herself, was that she needed something to focus her mind on. What about the collar? She'd never been able to find it for the exhibit. Tad had said that there wasn't time to launch a search for it, and Sweeney knew that now there was even less incentive. But if the collar was really missing from the museum, then someone had to have taken it, and it had to have something to do with Karen Philips. It had to have something to do with the robberies. The latest one proved Quinn wrong. Sometimes coincidences were more than just coincidences.

Eighteen

"What I don't understand," Quinn said, "is how they managed to get the stopper out of the building without it being recorded on any of the surveillance cameras. How is that possible?"

He tried to keep the anger out of his voice, but he knew he hadn't been very successful. As a cop, he believed in security. He believed that you put security procedures in place to discourage crime and that when discouraging it didn't work, your procedures ought to help you catch your thief.

Rick Torrance, the head of the security company that had designed all of the university museums' security systems, glanced at George Fellows, the Hapner director of security, and gave a little shrug.

"I'm right there with you, Detective Quinn," he said. "You won't find any argument from me. What happened in this case is what happens in a lot of cases. The museum chose public access over security."

George Fellows stepped in, eager not to let Torrance's statement about "the museum" include him.

"I should tell you that the decision to display the canopic chest in a temporary cabinet without the proper surveillance or alarming was made in direct opposition to my recommendations. The only reason I signed off was that they assured me it would be for one night only."

Quinn said, "I guess it's kind of like what my old man told me about getting a girl pregnant. It only takes one night."

Torrance laughed out loud and Fellows allowed himself a small smile.

"I just don't understand how this happened," Quinn said. "We've looked through hours and hours of tape and there's nothing I can use."

It was true. He and Ellie had gone through all of the tapes and hadn't seen anything out of the ordinary. People entered and left the museum, but there was no way of knowing if one of them had killed Olga Levitch. And more important, no one dropped anything into the garbage can where they'd found the stopper. It had already been gone over for forensic evidence and hadn't yielded anything, even fingerprints. One of the technicians told Quinn that the thief had probably worn gloves.

"If you wanted to steal something from this museum, how would you do it?" Torrance asked Quinn.

"I don't know. I suppose I'd break in through a window or something and hope I could get out before the police arrived."

Rick Torrance smiled and sat back in his chair, obviously pleased with Quinn's answer. "That's actually the last thing you'd want to do," he said. "By the time you were two inches inside that window, I'd know you were there. I'd even be able to take my time coming to get you." He reached for the plan of the museum sitting on the table at headquarters and spread it out in front of them.

"I'm famous for what we in the museum security world call overdesigning," he said. "There isn't a work of art or an entrance or an exit that isn't covered in some way. All of the windows in the museum have contact alarms as well as glass-breaking detection devices. If they're opened or the glass is broken, a silent alarm alerts the security guard on duty and calls the police. If the intruder somehow makes it beyond the window, his movement will be picked up by the motion sensors on the floor in the gallery. Again a silent alarm is sent to the security guard on duty and the police. If he should somehow make it beyond the motion sensors, he would certainly trip the alarms connected to the actual works themselves. All hung paintings are wired, all artifacts displayed behind glazing are in alarmed cabinets. In short, unless there was a monumental breakdown of the entire security system — an almost impossible eventuality — you'd never do it.

"No, what you'd want to do, what I'd want to do, is try to take the thing when the museum was open and occupied."

Quinn was about to jump in and ask a question when Fellows said, "Mr. Quinn, the work of creating a museum security system is all about balance. How do we balance the protection of the museum's assets with the desire of museum staff to keep the collections accessible to the public? There's an added goal with academic institutions, of course, which is to make the collections available for educational purposes. Our students need to be able to get close enough to the works to study them but not close enough to endanger them. Do you understand?" Quinn nodded.

"During an event like the one last night, we are perhaps the most vulnerable," Fellows said. "During the daytime, the amount of activity in the museum provides a level of security that cannot be underestimated. Almost our best line of defense is the average museumgoer who might notice something strange. It's like having one hundred guards out there patrolling the floors. And we need them, because during opening hours, we lose many of our protections — motion sensors, for example, and many of the alarms. Last night, we had people in the museum, so most of those alarms were off, but all of the people were clustered on the top floors. The cabinet containing the canopic chest was in a temporary location and the exhibit did not have the appropriate level of security."

"It was just about the perfect time to steal it," Torrance said.

"A perfect storm, if you will." Fellows gave a wry little smile.

"You make it sound like someone knew what he was doing," Quinn said.

"Oh, yeah. It had to be someone who knows this museum," Torrance said. "Someone who knew that this event was going on."

"Could it be an inside job?" Quinn asked.

"Sure, of course it could. Though I'll tell you, if I had clearance, if I worked at the museum, I would take advantage of that and do it some other time. If you're already in the museum, if you have security clearance to move around, then everything we've said no longer applies. At that point, you want to do it when the museum is empty."

That made sense to Quinn. "Okay," he said. "Tell me about the system you've got here."

Torrance handed him a diagram of the museum covered with little x's and circles. "The museum is equipped with a standard closed-circuit television system. There are twenty cameras throughout the museum, one at every main entrance and one in each gallery. You can see the location of each on the map. The cameras aren't fixed. Instead they sweep the room at sixty-second intervals. The system here still uses tapes.

"The spot where Olga Levitch was killed is outside the sweep of the camera," Torrance continued. "There normally isn't an exhibit there."

Quinn nodded. They'd heard all of this from Moran and Keane. "What about the passkeys?"

"The passkey system requires staff to wave an electronic card in front of a sensor at the four doors between the galleries and the staff offices in the annex. But those wouldn't have been used during the opening."

"You deal with this stuff a lot. If you had to guess," he asked Torrance, "do you think this is related to the 1979 robbery?"

Torrance laughed out loud, as though Quinn had made a very funny joke. "You're asking me a big question, Detective Quinn, but I'll tell you. I'd say it is. There's something similar about the MO, the feel of the MO. I've looked at the files on that investigation pretty completely, and I'm convinced that was a professional job carried out by someone who had done extensive research or possibly with the benefit of inside information. I think we've got the same thing going on here."

"Thanks," Quinn said. "That's what I'm thinking too."

He thought about Sweeney coming to his house, telling him about the missing jewelry. He doubted there was anything in that, but it was interesting that she'd been thinking about the 1979 theft. What had he told her, that the FBI was probably on top of it? Well, they'd be involved now and he'd make sure they were on top of it.

When they had gone, Quinn turned to Ellie. "So what do you think?"

She seemed nervous, checking his face to make sure he really wanted her opinion, and Quinn felt guilty for a moment. "I agree with the idea that it's connected to the other theft," she said. "Or at least the same kind of deal. Professional job with research or inside information. The way I look at it, someone who worked at the museum probably wouldn't have the skills or the connections to pull off something that big, but if he hooked up with someone who did, well there you go, they're all set. The professionals can carry it out, sell the stuff. The person providing the information gets paid for that." She tucked a piece of stray hair behind her ear and hesitated, then said, "There was something like this in Cleveland, except it was a supermarket. One of the employees was selling information about the shift changes, how the cash from the registers got transferred into the vault when the managers took their breaks. We figured out that whoever did it had to have had someone on the inside. I got a job at the supermarket." She gave him a small grin, meeting his eyes for a second, then looking away. "That sucked, let me tell you. Bagging groceries? Anyway, there was this one guy who came in with all this new stuff and he wanted to take everyone out for drinks. That was him." He could see the pleasure on her face, thinking of it, and it made him uncomfortable somehow, as though he'd seen her naked by mistake.

"Sounds like good work. Havrilek told me you did a lot of that back in Ohio. Good work, I mean." He was going to ask her why she'd moved east, but her face suddenly shut down, all her features collapsing into worry, and she stood up.

Quinn filled the awkward silence. "I talked to an FBI field agent this morning. They're going to help us out any way they can. And I think one angle that may be good is to look at who would have bought the chest if it had been successfully stolen."

"That guy, the English guy who was at the opening. He said he'd be happy to help if we needed him. He knows about the art world, that kind of thing, right?"

Quinn grudgingly admitted to himself that she had a point.

"Listen," he said. "I want you to come with me to look at Olga Levitch's apartment, and then I need you to do some legwork on this girl, okay? Luz Ramirez." They'd almost forgotten about her in the excitement over the attempted theft at the museum. They needed to get back to her before the trail went cold. And he felt like he wanted to work this museum thing alone for a little while, just put his head down and work on it, without having to deal with

Ellie, with the two hundred ways she had of irritating him.

He could see her push down her disappointment. The museum case was the big time, the one that would get her noticed. But she was a good soldier and she said, "Okay. Yeah."

"Let me know what you need, okay?"

"Sure." She nodded and then looked away, and he was afraid she was going to start crying. He almost relented, but then he thought of all the crappy cases he'd worked as a junior detective. This was the way it worked. You had to put in your time.

"Good," he said. "Let's go see what we can find in her apartment."

NINETEEN

They'd gotten Olga Levitch's address through the university's payroll department after the address Keane gave them turned out to be outdated. As they pulled up in front of the ugly brick building on a run-down street, Ellie looked up at the building and said, "I wonder if this is what she thought she was coming to when she came to America."

"Hey," Quinn said. "It's better than what a lot of people have."

But it was pretty awful, a hostile-looking group of teenage boys hanging around out front and hypodermic needles littering the sidewalk. The front door was locked, and when they asked the boys where they could find the manager, they shrugged and pointed around the side of the building.

The malnourished-looking woman sitting in front of a small portable TV in the building manager's office told them she was not the manager, but when Quinn identified himself and informed her that he needed access to Olga Levitch's apartment, she stood up, took a key off the Peg-Board on the wall, and handed it to him, all without taking her eyes from the soap opera on the television. "Bring it back when you're done," she said, a hand picking obsessively at her overly permed hair. Apparently the police often needed access to apartments in the building.

"Hey," Quinn said, shouting over the voices of the glamorous people on the screen. "Did you know her?"

The woman looked up blankly. "She didn't talk to anyone. She was afraid of the police. One time there was a fire alarm and we had to get everyone out of the building, and she wouldn't come out. She was afraid they were going to torture her or something." Someone started sobbing on the TV and she snapped her head back, afraid she'd missed something. Quinn rolled his eyes at Ellie.

Number 7 was a tiny studio apartment on the second floor. When Quinn opened the door, they were assaulted by the overly sweet scent of apples and cinnamon. The source of the fragrance was a pink basket of potpourri sitting on the only table in the room, a round kitchen table with a blue linoleum top. "Jeez," Ellie said. "That's pretty strong. I think you're supposed to put it inside something."

"I bet the cooking smells in a building like this are pretty bad," Quinn said, picking up a handful of the potpourri and letting it fall between his fingers. He looked around the room, taking in the single bed, neatly made, with its white bedspread and a single pillow in a pink pillowcase at the head. There was a small bathroom through a door at the end of the room and a small closet next to the bathroom. The kitchen consisted of a half-sized refrigerator and an electric hot plate on top of a rolling butcher block that was pushed against the wall. Underneath the butcher block were what appeared to be all of Olga Levitch's kitchen things: three nice china plates with a rose pattern on them, two matching teacups and saucers, an old Folger's coffee can containing three forks, four knives, a large silver serving spoon, and a spatula.

"Not much here," Quinn said. "Look around and see if you see anything like an address book or a phone list." Ellie went to the table where the potpourri was and leafed through a stack of papers.

"These are just receipts, for groceries it

looks like." She looked around the room. "There's no telephone, is there?"

Quinn looked too. "You're right. So much for a phone list. There's nothing here. How could someone have gone through so much of her life without buying any more stuff than this?" He took a quick look in the closet. Olga Levitch had owned four dark green uniforms, which she must have worn to clean, two identical olive cardigan sweaters, a pair of jeans that looked as though they had never been worn, and a couple of skirts and dresses that were old enough to have been brought over from Russia. There was a pink bathrobe that seemed to be the only comfortable thing she owned, and a matching pair of slippers.

On the top shelf of the closet was a shoe box. Quinn got excited for a moment, thinking it might hold some secret journals or old family photographs, but it held a pair of shoes, green silk pumps that wouldn't match anything else in the closet. That was it. Quinn closed the closet door and looked around the room again.

But there was one more thing. On the windowsill was a blue box, made of fancy cardboard and stamped with some kind of logo on the outside. There was a little card taped to the back. He opened it and read,

"Happy Holidays from Cyrus and Susanna Hutchinson."

"What's inside?" Ellie asked, reading the card over his shoulder.

Quinn opened the box and took out a still-sealed bottle of scotch whisky. He didn't recognize the brand, but he knew it was expensive from the writing and the little picture of mountains and a lake drawn on the label.

"This bottle probably cost two hundred dollars," he said.

Ellie whistled. "Did you know that American and Irish whiskey is spelled with an 'e' but Scotch whisky isn't?" she asked him. "Just whisky with a 'y.' "

"If it didn't have that card on it, I'd be thinking she had a thing for very expensive booze," he said. "Because the thing I'm wondering is, where did all her money go? She wasn't rich, but she would have made more money than this." He gestured around at the apartment.

"Maybe she gave it to charity," Ellie said. "You sometimes read about these people who live like recluses and then when they die it turns out they were millionaires and they gave everything to a cat hospital or something."

"That's a good idea," he said. "Check on

it. Call around to some of the charities. She was a Soviet Jew, I guess. Russian, whatever. Keane said something about refuseniks. Figure out what he was talking about and see if they have any charities for them."

"Okay." Ellie, looking pleased, wrote it down in her book.

"I think that's it," Quinn said. "Let's go downstairs and break it to the soap opera addict that whoever the manager is has to find another sucker to rent this rat hole."

TWENTY

Sweeney found Willem in his office, tapping away on his computer keyboard and looking generally cheerful, as though a murder hadn't occurred in his museum only a few nights before.

Aida was playing on the CD player on his bookshelf, and he was humming, mouthing a few bars of Italian here and there.

"Sweeney, just the person I wanted to see," he said. "I've decided to extend the dates of the exhibition. It looks like we're going to be closed for a while, and I don't want this to preclude people from seeing it, especially after that wonderful write-up."

"Thanks, Willem." Sweeney felt kind of funny about his evident good cheer. It was nice of him to have made the decision, but couldn't he have waited a few days? "Hey, I guess we never found that eighteenth-dynasty collar I got interested in, did we?"

His face clouded over. "I'm furious about

that. I don't know what could have happened to it. What kind of a museum are we? Where pieces just disappear from storage. I went and had a look around myself and I couldn't find it. It must have been taken or misplaced. I'm very sorry." He looked up at her. "But you wanted it for the exhibition, right? You're not still interested in it?"

"It was beautiful. I'd love to see it, even if we're not going to display it."

"Yes, although it's fairly unremarkable. If we had to lose something, it's not a bad thing to lose. Was that all?" He glanced back at his computer screen as though he considered the conversation finished.

"Willem, there was a student intern here named Karen Philips. She committed suicide her senior year. Her name was in the file on the falcon collar. It looks like she was maybe doing some research on it. Did she ever talk to you?"

Willem cocked his head and fixed his eyes sadly on a point over Sweeney's shoulder. "That was the most awful . . ." His voice trailed off. "I remember she was interested in funeral jewelry. She was pretty excited when the piece was donated."

Sweeney took a deep breath. "I was thinking. The date on her note in the file is the same as the date of the robbery. Doesn't it make sense that maybe it was taken during the robbery?"

Willem looked up at her, a smile spreading across his face. "You know, you just may be right. She was in one of the study rooms when I found her. She could have been examining the collar, and in the chaos after the robbery, we wouldn't have looked to make sure that something from storage was there. We were too concerned with the big items taken from the gallery. I think you may have it."

But Sweeney saw the flaw in her theory. "But wouldn't Karen have said something? Surely she would have known if it had been taken."

Willem thought for a moment. "She was in shock, really shaken up. I found her and I remember the way she looked. It's possible that she just didn't think of it. Or . . ." He didn't finish the sentence, but Sweeney followed his line of thought. *Or maybe Karen had taken it herself.* She left Willem and went down to make copies of the file on the collar.

Her cell phone rang just as she was finishing up, and she looked down to see Quinn's number on the screen.

"Are you doing okay?" he asked when she answered. "And are you some kind of witch or something? You show up at my house talking about a robbery at the museum, and bang! A couple of weeks later, someone tries to rob the museum."

"Now do you believe me that there's something strange about all of this?"

He laughed. "I still think that you're drawing connections between things that aren't necessarily connected, but I have to admit the attempted robbery is pretty suspicious."

"So you think the two robberies are connected? They have to be, don't they?"

There must have been someone else in the room because he said, in a slightly stiff voice, "Certainly seems that way. Listen, I was hoping we could talk." He hesitated. "I was also hoping I could talk to Ian. I need someone who knows about art dealing, how someone might try to sell an artifact. Hypothetically."

"Oh." She felt her face flush. "Of course. Yeah, maybe we could . . . Do you want to go out for a drink tonight and we can talk? Can you get a babysitter?"

"Yeah, Patience is pretty good that way. How about six-thirty at Flannery's?" It was a pub in Central Square.

"Good," Sweeney said. "I'll see you there." She corrected herself. "*We'll* see you there."

In her office, she sat at her desk and

looked out the window, watching late commuters drive by. The idea of going out for a drink with Quinn and Ian made her suddenly jittery. Why was that? If Ian was going to be in her life, she was going to have to get comfortable introducing him to her friends. But Quinn wasn't exactly a friend.

What was he? In Concord, she had come to think of him as a friend. They had been engaged in a mutual pursuit, had spent a lot of time with each other under fairly intense circumstances. What had Toby said, that he thought she was attracted to Quinn? Well, she probably was. After all, he was a good-looking guy. She did like him. She thought he was a good father and he had shown himself to be a good policeman. Who wouldn't be attracted to him?

But, she told herself, it's more than that, isn't it? A couple of times over the past year, she'd awakened from a dream and known that she had dreamt of him again, dreamt that they were kissing, dreamt that she was running her hands through the short hair at the back of his neck. It was what she remembered, the bristly feel of his hair beneath her fingers.

But that was perfectly normal. People had sexual dreams about all kinds of odd people, didn't they? Their bosses, their relatives. It didn't mean anything.

She shook her head. It was perfectly normal. There wasn't anything wrong with her at all.

TWENTY-ONE

She spent the rest of the day responding to e-mail and generally cleaning up details left over from the exhibition. When she was done, she went online and Googled Arthur Maloof to see if anything interesting came up. The first thing she discovered was that he had died a year previously. His obituary in *The New York Times* gave her the basics: humble beginnings, educated at the university, a successful career as an international financier, and an interest in collecting antiquities from ancient Egypt. Toward the end of his life, he had become an enthusiastic philanthropist and had donated pieces from his collections to many of the great American museums. Along with references to his collections of Egyptian statuary and reliefs, she found an inordinate number of photographs of him in a tuxedo at fancy charity events. But there wasn't anything suggesting that he wasn't on the up-and-up.

When she took a break around three to go get some extra catalogs she'd left up in the museum offices, she found Fred by the mailboxes, leafing through a stack of manila envelopes. He was trying to stay cool in tan Bermuda shorts and a T-shirt.

"Hey, Fred."

He'd been opening one of the envelopes and he turned when he heard her voice. "Sweeney. Hi. What are you doing up here?"

"Just getting these." She found the catalogs sitting on a chair outside Tad's office, where he'd told her they'd be. "Hot, huh?"

"I know. Lacey said I looked like a schlub, but I couldn't stand wearing anything more than this. How are you holding up?"

"Okay. It's weird having it so quiet around here, though, isn't it?"

He nodded. "Willem doesn't know what to do with himself, and Tad finally went home after lunch."

"Fred, did you once tell me that Tad has a wife who's really sick?"

"Mother. He takes care of her. I always figured it was why he didn't go for an academic career. Chances are he would have had to move for a job."

"What does she have?" Sweeney found herself curious about Tad's life.

"I don't know. I remember something

about her heart. I think she may just be one of those people who always have something wrong."

"An invalid. That's what they used to call them."

"That's right. An invalid." Fred said it in a kind of funny, faux-British accent.

She walked with him back toward his office and the elevator. "Olga didn't have any family, did she? I wonder if there'll be a service."

"I doubt it. If there wasn't any family. Maybe the museum will do something."

"We could mention it to Willem," Sweeney said. "I know he really liked Olga." Fred did something with his eyes when she said Willem's name that made her ask, "What?"

"Nothing."

It had to be about the Potter Jennings show. "Is he going to host something for your book?" she asked innocently.

"We'll see." The hallway was fairly dim, but as they reached his office, Fred's face was suddenly illuminated by the thick sunlight coming in the window at the end of the hall. As he turned to Sweeney, she saw that his eyes were rimmed with red and that he hadn't shaved in a few days.

"Are you okay, Fred?"

"What? Oh, yeah, fine. It's just been so

crazy around here. We've been having all kinds of security meetings about upgrading the systems. Willem's going to turn this place into Fort Knox. And I'm trying to get the book off to a good start."

"Is Lacey throwing you a book party?"

"I don't know. Maybe." Something on his face told her not to ask any more questions. Could he and Lacey be having problems? They seemed like a pretty tight couple to her, but she didn't know them very well when it came right down to it. She knew that Fred had been putting in a lot of long hours at the museum lately, but she'd assumed it was because of his book.

By the time Sweeney left at quarter to six to meet Quinn and Ian at Flannery's, she had worked herself into a state of nervous abandon. When she'd called Ian, he had sounded pleased.

Central Square seemed full of people. It was still over ninety-five degrees and Sweeney could feel droplets of sweat running down her back beneath her tank top. There was a strange smell in the air, as though the city itself was sweating, oozing out the odors of the rainwater and sewage and earth that lay just beneath the surface. Flannery's was a slightly seedy, dimly lit pub, with old green-shaded lamps that hung too low in the aisles between the old leather booths and that people were always banging their heads on. At one time, Sweeney had gone there a lot for the Irish music sessions, but she realized it had been months since she'd been — since Ian had arrived, probably.

She got there early and ordered a scotch, paying for it with cash and finishing it quickly, then opened a tab and ordered another to have on the table when they got there. She'd drink that one slowly so Ian wouldn't make an issue of it. She felt much better having had the drink, and by the time Quinn walked in at six on the dot, she was starting to think that this might turn out to be a good thing. She liked Quinn, she wanted to continue to be friends with him, and if he and Ian got along, then that would make it all so much easier. Ian was her boyfriend. She cared about Ian. And he should get to know Quinn. There. It would be fine. She would figure out a way to convince Ian to stay in Boston and they would be great friends with Quinn and everything would be fine.

Dressed in khaki shorts and a gray T-shirt, his forehead shimmering with a fine mist of perspiration, he looked like he'd jogged over. Sweeney was suddenly glad she hadn't gone home to change. She'd thought about it, but since Ian would probably arrive wearing one of his impeccable suits, she didn't want to make Quinn feel uncomfortable. "Sorry about this," he said, pointing to his clothes. "I was playing with Megan outside and I lost track of time. I'm going to just . . ." he headed in the direction of the restrooms and Sweeney watched him walk across the bar, the muscles on the backs of his calves articulating as he moved.

When he came back, his face pink and clean looking, he looked once around the bar. "Where's . . . ?"

"Ian's on his way. He couldn't get out of work until six," she said.

"Oh." He sat down as the waitress approached their table. Quinn ordered a Sam Adams.

"I'll have one too," Sweeney said, draining her whiskey glass and pushing it toward the waitress. "It's so hot."

"I know. Poor Megan. I gave her a bath, and a few seconds later she was all hot and sweaty again."

"How's she doing? She looked so grown up the other day."

"She's great. She says 'juice' and 'elephant' and 'snuggle.' That's her new word: 'snuggle.' "

"That's pretty cute." Sweeney smiled at him. There was a look that he got when he talked about Megan. His whole face relaxed and his eyes did something at the corners.

"So, I was hoping you could tell me a little bit about the museum," Quinn said once they had their beers. "How long have you been working there?"

"Well, all of the history of art faculty have their offices at the museum," she said. "Or rather in the building behind the museum. So I've technically been working in a building attached to the museum for three years or so. But it was only this summer that I started working *in* the museum. I've been planning this exhibition for three years, but I really started spending time there around April or May, I guess."

He took a long sip of his beer. "Who are the staff who work there all the time? On a typical day, who would be in and out of the place? Who would know about, say, the fact that the chest was only in a temporary exhibit?"

"Well, let's see. It's a lot of people. There are all the curators. Willem. His official title is director of the museum and curator of Egyptian antiquities, or something like that. Then there's Lucinda Hack, who's the curator of European paintings. She's been on a kind of sabbatical in Italy, though, so she's not around this fall. And then there's Fred, who's the curator of photography, and Gerry Peterson, who's in charge of American collections. He's teaching a course this fall and hasn't been around a lot. Then there's Tad, who's the assistant to the director. He helps Willem with all kinds of stuff, mostly administrative but some curatorial. There's Harriet, the collections manager." She stopped to think. "Then there are student interns and volunteers and the conservators and the students who are studying conservation. Then of course there's me. And Jeanne Ortiz. Did she explain to you? She has a show starting in January so she's been working on that. We were around this summer, so we heard a lot about the chest. Willem had been badgering the guy for years, hoping to get him to donate some items from his collection."

"Anyone else? What about all of the other faculty members who are in the building? The offices of the art history department are over in the annex behind the building, right?"

"Well, yeah, but they don't come over to the museum a lot. The buildings really are kind of separate. A lot of them work in the museum from time to time, but they're not a part of the regular scene, if you know what I mean."

"But they're around enough to know about something like the chest?"

"Mmmm. Some of them. I think anybody might have known about the chest. I mentioned it to my aunt, who I happened to talk to the night it arrived and who I know is interested in Egyptian stuff. People talk about things, you know. Do you think someone inside the museum tried to take it?"

"It's possible. It's also possible that someone from the outside heard about it and tried to take it. Maybe it was your aunt."

Sweeney smiled, thinking of her aunt Anna, who was small and gray haired and illustrated children's books and always seemed to be in a bad mood, even though she wasn't. "Maybe. So there wasn't anything on the security cameras, huh?"

She watched his face as she said it, but he saw through her and smiled. "You know I can't tell you that. Here's a question, though: How aware were you of the security system in the museum?"

"You knew it was there. I've spent a lot of time in museums so I know what the cameras look like. I figured there were probably silent alarms on most of the pieces, motion detectors, that kind of thing. I got into it a little bit because we had to figure out where to situate some of the sarcophagi — those big stone coffins — and other pieces so we could alarm them. Though you usually don't have to worry about anyone stealing a sarcophagus. It's hard to carry out."

He laughed. "I guess so. How about the security? Getting in and out of the building? How do they work that?"

"Well, there's a guard on duty all the time. Denny or someone else. When the museum's open, you can go up to the museum and History of Art Department offices from the elevator or stairs on the main floor, or through doors on each floor. You have to have a passkey and a password, though, and only the essential staff have them. Willem gave me one, but only because he's known me for so long. Normally guest curators would have to be with a staff member. We're supposed to wear these ID badges, but once everyone knows you, you really don't have to. I stopped after a month or so, and none of the people who work there regularly ever wear them anymore. You just wave at the guard as you go in."

"How did they work it the night of the opening?"

"It was as if the museum was open, I

guess. Denny and another guard were on duty, and he was walking around checking on the galleries."

"What do you think of the people who work with you there?" he asked after a minute. "Is there anyone who strikes you as dishonest?"

"Nothing like that," she said. "Fred was pretty eaten up about the whole thing this morning. He seemed very . . . distraught."

"What about Jeanne Ortiz? What's she like?"

"I like Jeanne, but I'm about the only one. She and Willem don't get along at all, and I think she kind of drives Tad and Fred and Harriet crazy, though they don't make it as obvious as Willem does." She took a long sip of her beer.

"Harriet seems like a piece of work."

"Oh, God. She is. But she's so honest it's annoying. So, you really think it's related to the 1979 theft?"

He grinned, hesitated for a minute, then said, "You know I shouldn't discuss this with you, but yes. It certainly looks that way to me."

She told Quinn about her conversation with Willem. "So even if you think I'm completely crazy to be suspicious about the disappearance of the collar, you have to look

255

into Karen Philips, because she was working at the museum then. Just look to see if they interviewed her after the theft, okay? And see if you can find out anything more about her death."

"All right, all right." He grinned again. "But I would have done it anyway."

"Sure you would have. You just don't want to admit that you need me to do your job."

"I need you to do my job? Is that right?" He reached out and picked up her empty beer bottle, rolling the neck back and forth between his fingers. "Should I just make you my partner? Is that it?" He was flirting with her. It gave her a strange little thrill.

"I don't know. Your new partner is pretty cute," Sweeney said, flirting back.

"I don't think cute is the word." And as he said it, he seemed to remember himself, and he sat back in his chair and finished his beer, not looking at her.

There was a moderately awkward silence and then they spoke at the same time.

"I'm sorry I . . ."

"I should have . . ."

They laughed. "What I was going to say was that I'm sorry we kind of lost touch," Sweeney said.

"Me too." He blushed and then he said, "Megan takes up a lot of my time, and I'm taking an English class. Remember you told me I should?"

"You're doing that? That's great. How's that going?"

"Good, I guess. I have my first paper due next week. On *The Rime of the Ancient Mariner.* It's been so long since I had to write a paper. And now with this, I don't know when I'm going to do it . . ."

"Sorry I'm late." They looked up to find Ian standing over the table. "The phone rang just as I was leaving." He smiled and kissed Sweeney on the cheek.

"You remember Tim Quinn, right?"

He nodded, shaking Quinn's hand. "Of course. Good to see you again."

Sweeney had been right. He'd come in his suit from work, and next to Quinn in his shorts and T-shirt and Sweeney in her jeans and tank top, he looked like their older, more respectable father.

Ian ordered a glass of white wine and they made small talk about the weather until it came, along with another beer each for Sweeney and Quinn.

"So what is it you were hoping I could help you with?"

Sweeney glanced over at Ian, taking in his fine-boned face, his blue eyes, intelligent beneath his glasses. She could see his dark beard just starting to come up on his cheeks and chin.

Quinn looked relieved. "Say the chest had been successfully stolen. How would you get rid of it afterward?"

Ian took Sweeney's hand under the table, rubbing her knuckles with his thumb. "The thing is," he said, "most thefts of priceless art, they would have been set up beforehand. In other words, the real top-level art thieves don't just take something because they think it might be worth a lot of money and someone might want it. They steal it because they know exactly how much it's worth and because they *know* that someone wants it."

"You're saying someone specifically wanted that chest?"

"That's right. It wouldn't be very efficient otherwise, would it? I mean, you might risk your neck taking it and then not be able to find a buyer."

"Who are we talking? International?"

"I'd say so," Ian said. "If I remember correctly, the Gardner museum theft was supposed to be the Boston mob, right? On behalf of the IRA."

"We don't know for sure. That was one of the theories. There was a guy who came forward a couple of years ago and claimed to know where the paintings were and said he could get them back in exchange for the release of an IRA prisoner. The IRA haven't been afraid to use art theft as a method of financing their operations. There are other international crime syndicates we could talk about too, but the key thing is that these crimes are always very well planned.

"I was wondering about the significance of the chest being Egyptian," Quinn said. "Do you know about any Middle Eastern groups that might be involved?"

"Not off the top of my head," Ian said. "My understanding is that thefts of antiquities in that part of the world tend to be carried out by criminal figures on the ground but masterminded by international bigwigs."

Quinn nodded, impressed. "So how would something like the chest be sold?"

Sweeney watched Ian sip his wine, then take off his suit jacket and hang it over the back of his chair. *Elegant,* she thought. He was the most elegant man she'd ever known. "The person who would buy something like the chest — or who would buy any piece of stolen art — is obviously very wealthy, someone for whom money is no object. This person has no compunction about owning stolen goods, and must not care that he or she can never display the object. It has to be someone who loves art so much, someone who is so gratified by the . . . the nearness of a thing of beauty, that he or she is satisfied with mere ownership. This is important. There are very, very few people in the world like that. Most of us would hardly find it worth owning something extraordinary if we couldn't show it off."

"So there are unscrupulous art dealers who would broker this kind of deal?"

"That's right. I'm sorry to say I have many colleagues who can be bought for the right price. The art dealer might act as the go-between. He might have contacts with these wealthy clients who are looking for specific works of art. He might put the word out that a certain piece is desired. You see what I mean?"

Quinn nodded. "How do I get in touch with these people?"

"Tell you what. There's a guy I know in London. He's a good enough chap, but I've always suspected him of having questionable connections. I could kind of drop a hint to him. Ask him if I knew someone who was looking for something like the chest, who would I talk to. You get the idea."

"Sure, okay," Quinn said. "Are you going to be going back there soon?" He glanced at Sweeney as he said it.

"That," Ian said, "depends on Sweeney."

She felt herself flush. "Well, we're still figuring that out," she said, her voice a little too high to her ears. "We have a lot to figure out about all this . . ." She reached for her beer and tipped it up, forgetting she'd already finished. They both watched her, and she tried to cover up by waving the waitress over. "Where is that waitress? Doesn't she know I need another drink?"

Ian studied her for a minute, then turned back to Quinn. "I'll ring him up. I can do it tomorrow and let you know. I won't use his name, obviously, but he may give me a direction you can go in."

Quinn looked uncomfortable and said, "Thanks. Well, I should be getting home." He stood up, then seemed to remember something. "Sweeney, I wonder if you could keep me updated on what's happening at the museum. You know the routine."

"He wants you to spy on your colleagues," Ian said, smiling, but with a little bit of an edge to his voice.

"Sure," Sweeney said. "I'll let you know if anything comes up."

He smiled at her in an unfinished way. "Great. Then I'll talk to you soon."

"Why did you tell him about London?" Sweeney asked once they were out in the balmy night, walking back toward her apartment. Her pleasantly buzzed feeling had turned to dull sadness. She'd had one drink too many. Or too few. She'd tried to get Ian to go somewhere else for another after she'd finished her last beer, but he'd said he was tired and wanted to go home, and she hadn't pressed the issue because she knew she'd get a lecture about her drinking.

Ian took her hand. "Well, he asked me how long I was going to be in Boston. I didn't know what to tell him. Besides, he's your friend. I thought maybe he could convince you."

She pulled her hand back. "I don't like being forced into things. You had no right to go around talking about it before we've decided anything."

"Well, why don't we decide it, then, so I can *go around* talking about it."

"I'm not ready to decide. I'm trying to get ready for class, and this whole thing with Olga . . ."

"Well, when will you be ready to decide? Because it doesn't seem like you're getting any closer, and I need to start making plans." He turned to look at her and she could see that he wasn't angry, but rather hurt, and for some reason, seeing it on his face made her angry.

"Why can't you understand that I just need a little time?"

"Because it isn't as though I'm asking you whether you want to buy a carpet from me. I'm asking you if you love me, if you want to move to London with me. But I'm starting to get a feeling of what the answer is."

"What's that supposed to mean?"

He raised his eyebrows.

She stopped and looked at him. "Are you saying that you don't think I love you?"

"I'm saying that you don't act like someone who does. I don't know what to think. I keep telling myself that you're not over Colm, that you need more time to get over him, and that if I wait around patiently, eventually you'll be ready, but I'm getting tired of waiting." He walked ahead, leaving her standing there beneath the maple tree at the end of her street.

She hurried and caught up with him outside her building. In the dusky light, it suddenly looked old, sad. Perhaps it *was* in need of a renovation. She hadn't noticed how bad it had gotten. She stared up at the building, feeling the scotches and beers doing their work. She was a little nauseous now and she closed her eyes for a minute. When she opened them again, he was standing in front of her.

"I don't like it when you yell at me," she said. "It makes me feel like the worst person in the world." He blurred in front of her then, and she stepped back to steady herself, stumbling a little on the sidewalk. Everything spun and she closed her eyes again, but that only made it worse.

"I don't like it when you drink so much," he said. "It seems to be a bit of a regular thing lately."

There wasn't any use telling him she'd had only a beer or two because she now felt like she was going to throw up. She pushed past him, running up the stairs and fumbling for her keys in her pockets. The apartment was dark and she stumbled over something on the floor in the hallway, then banged into the bathroom and sank down on the floor. She had been sure she was going to be sick, but the feel of the cold tile against her cheek calmed her stomach, and she closed her eyes, drifting off for a moment before Ian's voice came out of the darkness.

"Are you going to be sick?"

"No," she managed. "I don't think so."

She felt him lift her to her feet. "Well, you don't want to fall asleep in here."

She let herself be led into the bedroom, felt him ease her tank top over her head, help her step out of her jeans. She got under the top sheet in her bra and underwear, her head throbbing now. There was pressure against her back and she reached down and felt the General's fur. He had curled up against her back, and his purring sounded too loud, the vibration like a jackhammer in the quiet room.

"If you want me to move out, I'll move out," Ian was saying. He sat down on the bed next to her and stroked the hair away from her forehead.

She turned and tried to focus on him, but in the darkness he was only a shape. "Oh, no. That's not what I want." She heard herself say the words and felt him begin to stroke her hair again, but she could feel herself slipping into dark, kind sleep. She tried to fight it, forcing her eyes open and trying to sit up. "I've made such a mess of things," she said, and just before everything went dark she remembered that it was something her mother had said. *I've made such a mess of things. Oh, Sweeney, I've made such a mess of things, haven't I?*

■ ■ ■ ■

When she woke up, it was still dark, and through her blinding headache, she made out the numbers on the clock next to the bed: 3:30. She rolled over toward Ian but found the bed empty. She sat straight up, trying to ignore the pain in her head, and listened to the silent apartment. Where was he? She felt a moment of panic. What had he said last night? That he'd leave if she wanted him to?

But he hadn't gone. He was sitting at the kitchen table, working on his laptop, the General curled up on the table next to him.

When he saw Sweeney, he got up and took the bottle of Advil from the shelf over the sink and got her a glass of water. She took two tablets and finished the water, then leaned against the sink. "I feel like shit," she said. "But I can't sleep."

"Neither can I." He watched her, and it struck her that he was scared.

"I'm sorry. I'm not going to do that again. You're right that I've been drinking too much."

He got up and came over to her, and she reached out for him. They stood like that, her face pressed against his cheek. "I do

266

love you," she whispered into his ear. "I do."

His mouth was pressed hard against her ear and he said, so quietly she wouldn't have heard it otherwise, "I love you too."

After a few minutes, he pulled away and went through to the living room, then came back holding his briefcase. "I got these yesterday," he said, taking out a thin white envelope. "They're tickets to Mexico. Five nights at what's supposed to be the best resort outside Oaxaca City, which apparently is a great place for Day of the Dead, and then three nights at the youth hostel of your choice. I don't quite understand why that's an important part of the equation, but . . ."

She reached for him again and held him tight.

"So you'll go with me?" he whispered.

And though she wasn't sure what he was really asking her, she whispered back, "Yeah," and pulled back to look at him. "I'll go."

TWENTY-TWO

Lacey was still up. Fred pulled into the driveway and sat in the car for a few minutes, watching the lit kitchen window. It was nearly midnight and all the other houses on the street were dark, but that one rectangle of yellow light both beckoned him and kept him in the car. What was he going to tell her? He'd hoped she'd be asleep and he could slide into bed, press himself against her back, and answer any murmured question about where he'd been with a whispered, "Work. It's okay, go back to sleep."

But Lacey knew him too well for that. Over the last few days, he'd caught her watching him, and he knew she knew something was wrong. It was evidence of just how well she knew him that she hadn't asked. She knew it was bad and he was afraid. For all of Lacey's warmth and openness, she was terrified of conflict, bad news. When they'd gotten the call that her mother had died, Fred had almost had to pin her down on the living room couch to give her the details. She had run from him and put her hands over her ears like a child, as though it hadn't happened if she didn't hear it.

He felt tears come to his eyes. *Oh, Lacey.* What was he going to do?

"Hey," he said, coming in the back door. "I thought you'd be asleep."

Her hair was unbraided and fell in kinky waves over her shoulders. She faced him but didn't look him right in the eyes as she said, "You thought I'd be asleep? Why would you think that? You didn't tell me you were going to be late, you didn't answer your cell phone. I thought you were dead!"

She had been crying. And from her face, he could see she really had thought something had happened to him. Her face did something to him, and he embraced her, nearly crying himself. "Oh, Lace, I'm so sorry. I should have called. I'm okay, everything's okay." It wasn't true, of course.

She pushed him away and went to the sink, where she turned on the water, then turned it off again and turned to look at him. "Well, where were you? Are you going to tell me?"

He sat down at the table and put his head in his hands. "No, because I don't want to lie to you."

"So don't lie to me!" The loudness of her voice surprised him. "Tell me. Freddy, what is going on? Are you having an affair?"

"No, it's nothing like . . ." He didn't even know what to say. "Do you love me, Lacey?"

"Of course I love you." As angry as she was, she didn't hesitate and it gave him hope. Maybe there was a way to make it all come out right.

"Well, I need you to love me. I need you to just love me as much as you can, without knowing what's going on, without knowing anything." Suddenly he was more sure of this, that this was what he needed, than of anything he'd ever said to her.

"How can you ask me that? How can you ask me to say that without telling me?"

"Do you love me? Would you love me if I had done the worst thing you can think of. Whatever that worst thing is? Would you still love me? Would you help me?"

"Freddy? What have you done?"

"Lacey, don't you see? It doesn't matter. If you would love me anyway, then you don't need to know." He was sure of his logic and he smiled at her. He stood up and lifted her hair and buried his face in it, smelling the fresh green scent of her shampoo. "Do you remember the night we met?

I've been thinking about that lately, all the time. You were so beautiful and you were so kind to me. I loved you from the minute you opened your mouth." He nuzzled her neck, just smelling her, taking her in. "Would you?" he whispered.

She thought for a moment. "I would still love you. I would help you."

He took her in his arms, kissing her face, her throat, her shoulders. "Okay, then," he said. "Okay."

TWENTY-THREE

Agatha Williams was much prettier than Sweeney had thought she'd be. When Sweeney had asked Ian if he knew anyone who specialized in antiquities, he had said that, as it happened, the woman who handled antiquities for him was over from London for an auction and he was sure she'd be happy to have lunch with Sweeney to tell her a little bit more about Egyptian funeral jewelry.

"Are you sure?" she'd teased him. "I'll be able to get all kinds of dirt on you."

"It's a chance I'll have to take. Besides, everyone from the London office has been dying to meet you. Aggie can report back. It'll have to do until they can meet you in person." He'd given her a little grin and disappeared into the bathroom for his shower.

Sweeney wasn't sure what she'd been expecting, but "Aggie," when she arrived at the restaurant near the university Sweeney had chosen for their lunch, wasn't it. She was Sweeney's age, if not a little younger, and instead of the severe bun Sweeney assumed someone named Agatha would have her hair tied up in, Aggie Williams had long, straight dark hair that fell around her perfect face and shone under the lights above their table like polished stone. It was exactly the kind of hair that Sweeney had wished she had when she was ten and her own, impossibly curly, hair never seemed to do what she wanted it to do. It had certainly never fallen around her shoulders and the shoulders of her expensive linen suit the way Aggie Williams's did.

"It's so nice to finally meet you," she said in her crisp Oxbridge accent when Sweeney sat down. "We've all been so curious about the woman who could get Ian out of London." Her lips were painted a perfect red, not too bright, and Sweeney found herself wishing she'd put on lipstick.

"Oh. Really?" Sweeney wasn't sure what else she was supposed to say to that.

"He's such a Londoner," Agatha went on. "When he said he was going to live in Boston for a few months, we couldn't quite believe it." There was a little bit of an edge to her words, but then, as if regretting it, she smiled and said, "You must be very special."

Now Sweeney really wasn't sure what to say, so when she looked up to find the waitress standing over them, Sweeney asked for water and ordered a Caesar salad.

"So Ian tells me you've gotten interested in antiquities," Aggie said after she'd ordered too. "How can I help?"

"I'm not sure exactly. I'm doing some research into this collar and I just don't know enough about the field to know what I'm looking at." She handed over a copy of the file photograph of the collar and let Aggie take it in.

"Very nice. What do you know about it?"

"Just that it's supposed to be eighteenth dynasty. It was given to the museum by a collector named Arthur Maloof and . . ."

"Maloof?" Aggie looked up.

"That's right. Why? Did you know him?"

"No. I've heard of him, though." She held the copy up to the light and peered at it. "Any information on where this came from?"

"The file said it had been in the collection of a British explorer who dug it up in the 1890s or something." Aggie was looking skeptically at the photo. "It's identified as eighteenth dynasty, from Giza."

"It's not," Aggie said. "But here comes our food. Let's talk about something else while we eat, and then I'll tell you what it really is." Sweeney didn't dare argue with her.

Their salads came and they ate for a few minutes while Aggie told Sweeney about her trip. "I'll be in Washington for a few days and then finish up in New York. There are a couple of auctions. It's been lovely doing all this travel. Usually Ian does it. I've got to enjoy it while I can." Her accent was perfectly crisp. Her eyebrows dipped and rose, and she said nonchalantly, "Of course, I don't have much time left. We're all looking forward to having Ian back next month and of course you as well. I'd love to show you around London a bit, introduce you to some of my friends."

Sweeney felt her stomach drop a little. "Next month?"

"That's what I was led to believe. I'm sorry, is that not the case?"

"Oh, no, we're just still working out the details." She felt a hot flash of anger at Ian. How dare he go ahead and tell them they were coming back together without consulting her?

Sweeney almost had to grit her teeth as she asked, "So, what did you mean when you said you'd tell me what the collar really is?"

"Well, it's not eighteenth dynasty." She pronounced it "din-isty." "Not at all. It's older, Middle Kingdom, and I'm pretty sure it didn't come from Giza. Look, I don't know what you're going to do with this information, but it looks to me like a piece that was taken out of one of the tombs at Dahshur. There were a number of princesses entombed there, and the caches found at Dahshur represent probably the best examples of dynastic jewelry ever found. The pieces aren't as showy as the better-known New Kingdom pieces found in Tutankhamen's tomb, but they are so much more delicately constructed. A number of pieces from the princesses tombs are at the Cairo Museum and they're stunning. I think your museum has one of them here. But I think it may have been stolen."

"From the Cairo Museum?"

"Possibly, but it's more likely that it was taken from one of the tombs around 1914. It's also possible that it was found in an undiscovered tomb more recently and sold on the black market. It's hard to see in this copy, but it's really beautiful. See the detail on the falcons, and the beading. I bet it's exquisite in real life."

"That's what I liked about it," Sweeney said. "I think that's why it caught my eye. It's so much more feminine than the other pieces you always see."

"You've got a good one. Eye that is." Aggie checked her watch. "I'd be careful about anything having to do with Arthur Maloof's collections."

"Why?"

"I don't want to go telling tales out of school. I may have to deal with his estate at some point. But if that piece is stolen, it could be embarrassing for the museum. I should be on my way. It was lovely to meet you." Aggie left Sweeney with money for her portion of the check and gave her a smile that was, Sweeney decided, more than a little bit wicked. "I think a lot of him. Ian." The way she said his name, lovingly, as though the very taste of it in her mouth was delicious, made Sweeney's stomach feel funny. "So do a lot of people. I hope we'll see you in London soon."

Twenty-Four

Quinn's day had started at six A.M., when Megan had woken him up and demanded to be dressed in the same pink dress she'd worn the day before. When Quinn had patiently tried to explain to her that the dress was dirty and that she'd have to wear something else, she'd screamed and insisted on it until he'd finally relented and taken the musty-smelling dress out of the hamper. He felt like he'd been doing that a lot lately, and he'd tried to explain to Patience that Megan wasn't very flexible when it came to fashion, but for some reason, Megan let Patience dress her in anything.

When he got to headquarters, he found a message from special agent Steve Kirschner, one of the FBI agents who had worked on the 1979 Hapner robbery, along with the original case files from Cambridge PD's investigation and the files from the investigation into Karen Philips's death. He called

Kirschner back and arranged to meet with him at headquarters at five, then headed across Central Square to get a coffee before delving into the files.

He was just starting on the files when Ellie came into the conference room and sat down across from him. "Hey," he said. "I got the FBI files on the theft. I want you to help me go over them."

"Okay," she said. "But I got something on Luz Ramirez. Thought you might like to go with me."

"What'd you get?" So far, they'd hit a dead end on the case. No one in the neighborhood had been able to tell them anything, though having to use a translator always made him realize how much he depended on being able to read people's expressions and weigh them against the words being said.

Ellie took out her notebook and beamed at him in a self-satisfied way. "I found a friend of hers in the neighborhood who was willing to talk. She'd been working at a salon." She pronounced it with the accent on the first syllable.

"A what?"

"A hair salon."

"Oh. Did you get a name?"

"Yeah, it's called My Blue Heaven, down

on Mass. Ave. She didn't know the exact address, but I'm sure I can find it in the phone book."

"Great. Why don't you go down and talk to them, see if you can find anything. That's good work, Ellie. Really."

She allowed herself a small smile. "Don't you want to come with?"

"No. I've got some things to do here before the FBI guy arrives."

"Shouldn't I stay so I can talk to him too?"

Quinn turned to look at her. "No." Her face fell a little, then resolved into anger. He'd never seen her angry before. Her small, feminine features seemed to curl up, her eyes cast down, her mouth twisting.

"Are you mad at me or something?" She stood very straight, her head held rigidly, her chest thrust out a little. Her whole body was tensed, like a cat's, and he had the sense that she might spring on him if he pissed her off.

"What?" He turned to look at her again. "No. Why do you say that?"

"Because it seems like you are."

"Well, I'm not mad at you. Why would I be mad at you?"

"It just seems like you are."

"Look, if you're going to be a cop, you need to have a thicker skin. I'm not mad at you, okay. Maybe I'm a little distracted because I've got two big investigations going right now."

"I *am* a cop."

"What?"

"I said I am a cop. And *you* don't have two investigations going. *We* do." They glared at each other for a minute, then Ellie said, "By the way, I talked to Cyrus Hutchinson. He said he gives a lot of people, including Willem Keane, bottles of that scotch for Christmas. He said that maybe she stole it from Keane's office." Then she made some kind of face at him, a child's scowl, and left the room.

Quinn didn't know if he should laugh or swear.

He decided on the latter. "Goddamn!" He'd have to go talk to Havrilek, tell him that it wasn't working out with Ellie, that he needed a new partner. Frankly, he didn't think she was detective material, but that was up to Havrilek.

For now, though, he needed to call Keane to see about the scotch, and then he had to go through the files and prepare for his meeting with Agent Kirschner. He put Ellie out of his mind for the moment.

Tad Moran answered the phone, and when Quinn asked to speak to Keane, there was a short hesitation before Moran said, "Can I tell him what it's about?"

"No. I'd just like to talk to him." His encounter with Ellie had put him in a bad mood. "Is he there?"

"Yes. Hold, please." Quinn listened to the endless silence of the telephone system and then there was a click and Keane came on.

"Hello? Detective Quinn?"

"Yes, Mr. Keane. I had a quick question for you. We found a very expensive bottle of scotch in Olga Levitch's apartment. There was a card on it from Cyrus Hutchinson. He claims that he didn't give her a bottle, but rather gave one to you. I'm —"

Keane cut in, "You didn't tell him you'd found it, did you?"

"Yes, we needed to —"

"Oh, Christ! Do you see what you've done? He'll know I gave it to her. Detective Quinn, you've created a real problem for me. Mr. Hutchinson is an important bene-factor of our museum. I'm not a scotch man, so I gave it to Olga, as a kind of holiday treat. But now he knows, and I'm guessing he's pretty offended. Damn!"

Quinn was so taken aback by Keane's indignation that he didn't know what to say.

"Well, what do you have to say for your-self?" Keane demanded. Quinn felt as though he were being scolded by an angry schoolteacher.

"Mr. Keane. As I told you at the museum, we are investigating a murder here. If you've been inconvenienced, I'm sorry, but I'm sure that if you think about this for a couple of seconds, you'll see why we had to ask." He hung up the phone, because he'd said all he wanted to say and because he didn't want to give Keane a chance to admonish him again.

The mystery of the scotch solved, he turned to the file on Karen Philips's death.

She had been found by a friend whom she was supposed to meet for lunch and campus security had been the first ones on the scene. If there was ever a straightforward kind of a suicide, Quinn thought, it was a hanging, and everyone who had investigated this one had treated it as such. Everything seemed to be in order, from what he could tell. At no point had anyone expressed any doubts about whether she had done it herself. Death had been due to asphyxiation, there were marks around her neck consistent with a strangling, etc., etc. She had used a piece of hardware-store baling twine.

But one thing caught his eye. On one of the pathology reports, someone had scribbled at the bottom, "No rope burns on hands." Quinn knew what the pathologist or whoever was getting at. He'd seen the hands of a couple of suicides who had tied the noose themselves. If you weren't used to handling rope, and you tried to make a noose out of a brand-new length, it was going to show on your hands.

But there wasn't anything else, and he put the little detail aside as a very remote "maybe" before turning to the file on the robbery. The call to 911 had been made at three twenty-three P.M. on November 4, 1979, by Tad Moran, who had told the 911 dispatcher that he and other staff of the museum had returned from a staff meeting to find the security guard on duty, Denny Keefe, tied up and in need of medical attention. In fact, police were already on their way to the museum, since a silent alarm had been activated behind the ticket booth. Quinn assumed that Keefe had seen something suspicious, activated the alarm, and gone outside to confront the thieves, which was when he'd been attacked.

While officers were en route to the scene, Tad Moran had called again, this time to say that museum staff had discovered that a number of antiquities had been removed from the museum. There were the reports of the officers who had responded to the call, which described what they had found when they arrived. The museum staff had returned from a meeting in the adjacent building to find Mr. Keefe tied up near the entrance door. He had been badly beaten but was alive and was immediately transported to the hospital.

According to the report, police had found no signs of forced entry and so the assumption was that the thieves had simply walked in, pretending to be members of the public, then subdued Keefe and taken their time opening the Plexiglas display cabinets with hacksaws and other tools. The individual works hadn't been alarmed, so the first cry for help had been Keefe's activating of the silent alarm.

After the police had been called, Willem Keane had remembered that a student intern was working in a basement storage room and had gone to check on her. Quinn knew it must be Karen Philips to whom the officer writing the report was referring. He skipped ahead. Sure enough, it was noted that Keane had found Karen Philips in the storage room, her mouth covered with duct tape and her arms and legs taped too. Keane determined that nothing had been taken from the storage room.

Quinn skipped ahead to the witness interviews. There was a list of everyone who had been at the staff meeting, and he felt himself perk up a bit when he read the names. Among them were Willem Keane, Harriet Tyler, Tad Moran, and Frederick Kauffman. It was like old home day. If someone had given the robbers inside information, he or she was probably still around.

The first interview with Denny Keefe had been in the hospital, once he'd regained consciousness. He said that two men dressed in business suits had entered the museum around two-thirty. He had nodded hello to them and then continued his conversation with a volunteer who had been on duty but was going home. He said good-bye to her and returned to his post behind the ticket desk. He said that he had checked the closed-circuit television monitors every once in a while but hadn't seen anything out of the ordinary. The next thing he remembered was being attacked from behind. He described the men as being of medium height and build, one with gray hair and one with brown hair. They had not been carrying any luggage or large bags, as far as he remembered.

The next interview was with Willem Keane, who was described as the "curater of Egypt antiquities." What was it about cops? They had to be about the worst spellers in the world. Keane — and the other staff members — didn't have much to say. They had gone over to the Jansen Museum next door for the meeting and come back around three-twenty to find Keefe bound on the floor behind the ticket desk.

The only thing that was of interest to Quinn was that Keane had gone alone to check the museum and then again to look for Karen Philips. He'd have to check, but he was pretty sure that it was against the museum's security procedures for any member of the staff other than the director of security to respond to a possible breach of security by himself or herself. But things must have been pretty chaotic. Quinn doubted that anyone had been thinking about security procedures.

Quinn glanced up at the clock. Agent Kirschner would be arriving soon, so he skimmed over the rest of the papers in the top file.

Finally, he came to the Cambridge PD's interview with Karen Philips. He assumed the FBI had conducted a much more extensive one when they'd been assigned the case, but she had given the basics in the initial interview. She had been working alone in one of the study rooms in the storage area and had opened the door to let some air in. The interviewing officer had noted that she seemed nervous about this detail, since it was apparently against security protocol. She had heard men's voices in the basement gallery and, in her surprise at hearing a loud noise, had knocked over a stool when they had broken into the first cabinet. They were alerted to her presence and had come in and taped her mouth as well as her arms and legs. She had given a description of the men but seemed unable to remember much about them.

All in all, it was pretty straightforward. But somewhere, Quinn suspected, someone had lied.

"The body was found right next to the chest," Quinn told Special Agent Steve Kirschner. "Ms. Ortiz said she didn't notice that the cabinet had been breached. It was the second person on the scene who noticed that one of the stoppers was missing."

Kirschner, Quinn decided, had to be nearing retirement. He still looked fairly young, his gray hair cut in a short crew, his trim body lean and rangy. But he had the bored energy of someone who wasn't going to have to live with the consequences of anything he did anymore. He was professional enough, but Quinn knew the signs. He reminded him of Marino, his old partner, who had checked out even before he'd hurt his back.

Kirschner looked through the crime scene photos Quinn had given him. "It seems pretty clear that he — or they, I guess — were in the process of taking the chest and were surprised by the cleaning woman. What was her name again?"

"Olga Levitch," Quinn said.

"Yeah." He looked around. "It's a pretty similar MO to the 1979 theft, isn't it? Coming in while the place is open to the public but at a time when it won't be full of people. Pretty smart."

"I guess," Quinn said. "Isn't that sort of Museum Theft 101, though?"

"Nah," Kirschner said. "This is a little more nuanced. Think about it. They would have had to have inside info about the staff meeting. And I'm thinking the same thing about the opening. You know? You might see in the paper or whatever that there was going to be an opening, but you wouldn't know what the situation was going to be — that the basement gallery was probably mostly empty, that this is where the chest would be — unless you knew a lot about this place."

"You're right." Quinn thought for a moment. "You had any guesses about who the inside person was way back when?"

"Not really. Everyone checked out okay, though . . ."

"What?"

"I don't know if it's even worth mentioning, but the director, Hector Ribling. He struck me as kind of a cold fish. I always wondered about him."

"Really?" Quinn knew that Ribling, who had retired ten years ago, hadn't been at the opening. But perhaps he was still in contact with the museum staff and could have passed on the necessary information.

"Don't get your hopes up. He died a couple years ago. I'd been keeping tabs on him."

"Damn. So how does this work? I've never had something that overlapped with you guys before. And this one's complicated because the art theft didn't actually occur."

"Well, we'll work our intelligence, see if we can find out anything there. If I were you, I'd look closely at everyone who was in the museum during that opening. I'm betting there's someone there who knows more than they're saying."

"That's my plan." They both looked at the

photos of Olga Levitch's body, outlined in blood on the marble.

"The dead woman," Kirschner said. "Any chance she had anything to do with it?"

"Doubt it. She'd worked here a long time, but if she made any money from selling out the museum, she sure didn't spend it on herself. I saw her apartment. I'm telling you. She came over from Moscow or somewhere and it had to be worse than anything she'd have gotten over there."

"Maybe she was sending it home. That's what a lot of these immigrants do."

"I guess. We're looking into charities, but we haven't found anything." Quinn was pretty convinced that Olga Levitch didn't have anyone to send money to, but it gave him an idea. Had any of the other people with intimate knowledge of the museum spent large amounts of money in 1980?

"You know, there's something else I should tell you," Kirschner said. "I don't know if there's anything to it, but it's an open investigation, so . . ."

"Yeah?" Something in his voice made Quinn pay attention.

"I don't know how much you know about art collecting and museums." He waited for Quinn to give some indication of how much he did know, but when it didn't come, he went on. "We've been in touch with the Egyptian authorities." He lowered his voice as though the walls themselves could hear. "There's some question about the provenance of some of the pieces they've got. It's complicated, but some of the things were donated by a man named Arthur Maloof. He apparently had a family collection that had been in place since before 1970, which is when the UNESCO convention prohibiting things being taken out of Egypt went through. I can get you more information if you want, but basically, if you can prove legitimate ownership of antiquities before then, you're in the clear. Some people, though, have figured out ways of making things look legitimate. They create fake documentation for these family collections, old labels, handwritten documents, some of it's amazingly real looking. You should see it. Anyway, we're looking at all the places Maloof placed items from his collection. We don't have anything specific yet, but the museum is certainly on the list."

"Is Keane implicated?"

"Oh, no. He seems to be a victim at this point, if it turns out Maloof faked the provenances of any pieces at the museum, but obviously it's embarrassing for him. It's difficult because Maloof is dead, so we're dealing with his estate."

"So you think it might be related to the murder?"

"I doubt it, but someone did try to steal an Egyptian piece. By the way, I looked into Hutchinson, today, because of this latest theft, and there doesn't seem to be anything wrong with the piece he donated. Anyway, I thought you should have all the facts. I'll get you the relevant information. As I say, nothing's been proved. The investigation is still open." He stood up. "And I need to go."

"Right. Hey, do you remember interviewing a Karen Philips? At the time of the 1979 theft?"

"That was about twenty-five years ago," Kirschner said. "I'm retiring at the end of the year. To be honest with you, my memory's gotten worse and worse the closer I get."

"She was a student intern at the museum. According to the files, she was working in one of the storage areas in the basement, I think it was. She had propped the door open and the thieves discovered her, tied her up."

"Oh, yeah," Kirschner said. "I'd forgotten there was another witness. It's funny you asking about her. It seemed pretty clear that she was tied up the whole time, but I remember I wondered about whether she was the one who'd passed on the inside scoop. We kept asking her about what had happened, and she didn't want to talk about it. Just said they'd tied her up and that was all. She sort of gave us a description, but she seemed scared to me. Or . . ." He thought for a moment. "It was more like she was in shock. You know when someone's seen something really awful. I remember thinking that somebody had scared the crap out of that little girl."

TWENTY-FIVE

It wasn't hard to find the names of the women who had been members of the WA-WAs at the same time as Karen Philips. Sweeney went back to the yearbooks in the library and found, in the extracurricular activities section of the yearbook for the year before Karen died, a picture of a group of serious-looking young women — Karen at one end — sitting on a couch, with the two in the front holding a banner reading, WOMEN ANGRY, WOMEN ACTIVE. Below the picture, the caption read, "L–R, Mary Haster, Angie Bellini, Rose Moreham, Davida Singleton, Felicia Hu, Susan Esterhaus, and Karen Philips." Sweeney wrote down the names of the other women and headed over to the alumni office. She identified herself to the secretary and said she was working on a project related to the history of women in higher education and needed to contact some alumnae. The secretary easily found the women's current contact information in the database and wrote the numbers on a scrap of paper.

When Sweeney and Ian had woken up that morning, it had looked a little like rain, the sky gray and congested, the air humid and full of heat. Nothing had come of the rain clouds, but the air was still so heavy Sweeney felt she was wading through a swimming pool as she made her way back to her car.

At home, she changed out of her sweat-soaked clothes. She found the General curled up on the cool tiles in the kitchen and bent to scratch his ears. "The heat's too much for you, huh?" He blinked his eyes open for a moment, then closed them again.

She got herself a cold beer from the fridge, telling herself it was the only thing that was going to cool her down, and started calling the WAWA women, as she'd come to think of them.

It took a while to find someone at home, but when she got to the fifth woman on the list, Felicia Hu, she was at her home in Manhattan. When Sweeney explained what she was doing and that she wanted to know more about Karen Philips, Hu hesitated for a minute before saying, "I haven't thought about her in years. God, it's so strange that something that affected me so deeply at the time could just kind of . . . leave me. I'm sorry, what did you want to know about her?"

Sweeney explained that she taught at the university and had gotten interested in women's organizations throughout the university's history. "I learned about Karen Philips's suicide and I thought it might be interesting to examine the reasons behind it."

"I never really heard that there was a reason behind it."

"So you were surprised?"

"No, I didn't say that. I should explain that Karen and I weren't particularly close. If you want someone who knew her well, you should call Susan Esterhaus. I can give you her work number if you want. Anyway, I was saying that I wasn't really surprised. She had been depressed for a while before she did it. We all knew it, all the WAWAs, but no one could get her to talk about why. She obviously wasn't sleeping, and she seemed angry. It was during that time leading up to her suicide that she got really involved in the group."

"She hadn't been involved before? Her picture was in the yearbook photo."

"Yeah, they must have taken it around the

holidays because I remember she didn't really start coming to meetings and helping us with events until that fall."

"We're talking about the fall and winter of 1979?"

"That's right. I graduated that next year and Karen was class of eighty-one. She had gone to a rally we put on, something about sexual violence against women, and she came to the next meeting and said she wanted to get involved. She was really passionate about the organization. We were happy to have her."

"When did she start seeming depressed to you?"

"It's hard to say. It was gradual, but I do remember seeing her after the Thanksgiving break and she looked terrible. She said she hadn't been sleeping well, but again, she wouldn't talk about why."

Sweeney wrote that down. "Did you know about the robbery at the museum?"

"Oh, yeah, everyone knew. Karen was a bit of a celebrity on campus after that. I mean, to a bunch of college students from the suburbs, getting tied up during the commission of a major art heist was pretty wild stuff. Karen hated talking about it, though. When people asked her about it, what it had been like, she just said she didn't remember much about it. It was a kind of thing with her. It was almost like it embarrassed her in some way."

"You say you didn't think there was a reason for her suicide, that she was just depressed. You're sure she never said anything to any of you? She hadn't been dumped by a boyfriend, anything like that?"

"Karen didn't have any boyfriends as far as I know. And she had gotten pretty militant toward the end of that year, going on about how all heterosexual relationships were a kind of slavery. She wasn't a lesbian. She had had some relationships with men. But something had happened to turn her off of dating. Oh, and she had gotten upset about some of the things going on at the museum too. I remember that."

"What do you mean?"

"Well, she had gone to Egypt, on a study trip, the summer before our senior year, and I guess she saw some things that really bothered her. My family's Chinese, and she told me that all of our great treasures were in American museums instead of Chinese ones and wasn't that a crime? She said that visiting the museum in Cairo had made her so depressed because they couldn't even afford to properly display their own history because so many of their most valuable items had been stolen by Westerners. White men, she said, white men in sun hats. I remember her saying that so vividly."

"Was there a specific piece that she was angry about?" Sweeney was thinking about the collar. If Karen had discovered that the collar had been illegally taken out of Egypt, maybe that's what she'd been so angry about.

"I don't think so. I think it was the idea of it. Something happened to her when she was in Egypt. She got radicalized." Felicia hesitated, then asked, "I have to get going in a couple of minutes. Was there anything else?"

"Just one more question. What did the WAWAs do?"

Felicia laughed. "The name sounds kind of silly now, doesn't it? At the time, it was very important to us, you know, we weren't just angry like all the feminists who had come before us, we were going to actually *do* something about it. We had rallies for ERA and we did a lot of yelling about the number of women faculty on campus. I don't know how old you are, but the late seventies and early eighties were a strange time to be a young woman. We'd won in so many respects. We were on campus. In theory, we could be anything we wanted to be, we could sleep with anyone we wanted to sleep with, but the place where things hadn't changed a lot was in the way that men thought of you. It's hard to explain. I knew so many women who had been forced into things they didn't want to do, date rape we'd say now, but they literally didn't know how to say no. We weren't prepared, you see. We'd been given all this freedom and we weren't ready for it. Anyway, you should call Susan. She knew Karen better than anyone." Felicia Hu gave Sweeney a Chicago number and asked her to pass on her best. "We had a reunion a few years ago. All the WAWAs. It was interesting to see what everyone had done with her life. Susan became an academic. I'm a lawyer. There are a good few of us lawyers. Angie Bellini became a Unitarian minister. Do you know Jeanne Olsen? Ortiz I guess she is now? I think she's teaching at the university too."

"Yeah, I know Jeanne well."

"She was around a lot too in those days. She went to Smith, but we always kidded her that with no men around, there wasn't enough for her to be mad about so she had to come and create trouble here. She was a sort of unofficial member of the WAWAs. I've got to go, but call Susan."

Sweeney thanked her for her time and

hung up the phone.

She turned on one of the six fans she and Ian had placed throughout the apartment and drained her beer, pressing the empty bottle against the back of her neck, then dialed Susan Esterhaus's number in her office at the University of Chicago. When she answered, Sweeney identified herself and told her what she wanted to know.

"That's a coincidence," Susan Esterhaus said. "I can't talk now. I have about a thousand things to do because I'm flying to Boston tomorrow. I'll be at the university on Saturday, speaking at a rally Jeanne Ortiz is helping to organize. Why don't you come and we can talk there?" Sweeney told her that sounded good. "Karen wasn't the real thing," Susan Esterhaus added, as an afterthought. "Not a real radical, I mean. But I liked her just the same."

TWENTY-SIX

Her inquiries at a standstill until the rally, Sweeney decided to go back to the museum to finish cleaning up the copious paperwork connected with the exhibition. She boxed up her files and was heading down the stairs to the main floor of the museum when she saw Quinn coming up in the opposite direction.

He was so out of context here that it took her a moment to recognize him. "Hey. What are you doing here?"

"Talking to some people. Going over the crime scene." He grinned, happy to see her.

"Oh, yeah? Where are you going now?"

"Actually," he said, "you caught me. I was going to look at your exhibit. I was kinda curious about what funerary art looks like. I know all about your gravestones, but . . ."

"You want me to go with you?" She'd been looking forward to getting home and back in front of the fans, but it would be fun to show him around.

"Sure. You can give me the official tour. Unless you have to get home or anything."

"No, I'd love to show you."

They went back up to the third-floor galleries. "It's really strange having the place so empty," she said.

"How long will the show be up? You got kind of a raw deal out of this whole thing, didn't you?"

"They'll keep it up until January probably. Willem's being good about that. Do you think you'll let us reopen by then?"

"Oh, yeah, we should be finishing up pretty soon. We need to make sure we haven't missed anything, and the university wants to be sure the security system is adequate."

"I bet Willem won't have any trouble getting the money he wanted for a security upgrade now."

"Had he been turned down for the money?" Quinn had guessed it from his conversation with Rick Torrance and George Fellows about museum security.

"Oh, yeah. I'd heard that much through the grapevine. But I think you'd be hard-pressed to find a director of a college or university art museum who didn't get his dream budget turned down every year. It's always a balance between what could be and what's possible. My department chairman said that to me once when I asked for money for a research project."

"I asked my FBI contact about Karen Philips," he said suddenly. "He said he did interview her. She was working near the storage area when the theft occurred, and he said she seemed scared."

"Really?" Sweeney turned to look at him. He was grinning.

"Are you going to say you told me so?"

"I never say that. Although . . ." They laughed.

"Can I ask you something? You have to keep it confidential." She nodded. "Have you ever heard anything around the museum about someone named Arthur Maloof?"

Sweeney stared at him. "Yeah. He donated the collar to the museum — along with some of Willem's best pieces — and a friend of Ian's said she thinks there was something fishy about him." She told him about her conversation with Aggie Williams.

"His donations are being investigated. I guess the Egyptian government and the FBI think some of the pieces in his collection were taken out illegally."

"I don't understand it," Sweeney told him,

thinking out loud. "The falcon collar was incorrectly identified. Was it a mistake, or did someone do it on purpose in order to make it easier to steal? But why would Maloof have done that? Was he trying to hide the fact that it had a suspicious provenance?"

They'd reached the top of the stairs. " 'Still as Death,' " Quinn said, reading the black letters over the entrance. "So this is it."

"Yeah. This is what I've been doing for the last three years of my life." It had been so busy the night of the opening that she hadn't really had a chance to see the whole effect of the installations. Now, looking around at the walls, she realized it was perfect. The black and cream color scheme she'd chosen for the galleries was a nice complement to the dark cabinets and framed photographs, and the square labels with their scrolled titles fit the feel of the exhibit perfectly.

He looked carefully at the sarcophagi and unguent jars, the small canopic jars she'd included in the exhibit, reading the explanations about how the Egyptians had prepared their dead for entombment. She watched as he took it all in, wandering from room to room.

"Are all these people really dead?" They'd come to the postmortem photographs, and he wandered silently, stopping to read the little cards below each one.

"Yeah. It was very common. People kept them as a memento of the person who had died."

"It's awful," he said. "All these children."

She stood next to him, their shoulders almost touching. "I know. I had a hard time working on that part of it."

"Megan," he said. He didn't need to explain. "I couldn't stand it."

Sweeney looked up at the photograph in front of them. The girl in it couldn't be more than four or five. "I thought about Megan when I was . . . As I said, I had a hard time choosing the ones of children."

"Yeah?" He glanced at her and stepped closer, so that their shoulders were touching again, and they stood in silence for a few minutes staring at the photographs. In the glare from the glass, she caught their reflection, the two tall forms, her long curly hair forming an indeterminate halo around her head, his short hair making his skull seem blocky and strange. She had a sudden sense of their oppositeness, the male and female qualities of them, the way they seemed polar bookends in the reflecting glass. She wanted to tell him this, wanted to express something to him that she had suddenly realized, but she was struck dumb.

The space between them was charged with energy. She could feel the warmth of his body passing through his shoulder and into her skin. Then he moved ever so slightly, shifting from one foot to the other, and the energy changed, dissipated.

He walked across the room, leaving her standing in front of a cast of a 1720s gravestone. "So, Ian seems like a nice guy," he called back over his shoulder.

"He is." She bent down to pick up a blank piece of notepaper from the floor, crumpling it and putting it in her pocket. "Better than I deserve."

"Oh, come on," he said lightly. "You deserve the best." She felt as though she'd set him up to say it and she jumped in so he wouldn't think she had.

"No, I mean, I think it's just that . . . in a way, I don't feel like I'm ready to be in a really serious relationship, you know? But that's ridiculous. It's been almost three years now since Colm died, and I should be moving on. I guess I am moving on."

"You are living with someone."

She laughed. "I guess I am. I just don't know about this whole London thing."

"Can't he stay here?"

"No. He has a daughter in Paris, and he hasn't been seeing enough of her since he's been over here. He's got the office here up and going, so his job is over there. And I should really be thinking about what I'm going to do next. My building is going to be sold and I haven't even told him yet. I don't know why. It's like I want things to just stay the same, you know what I mean?"

He was looking at her with an expression on his face that she couldn't quite read.

"I don't know," he said. "I don't know if I do. I haven't wanted things to stay the same a lot lately. I want to move on, I want to get over Maura's death. I just can't seem to do it."

"Have you ever thought about . . . you know. Dating. Marrying again? I don't know, sleeping with someone?" She had meant it to sound jokey, but suddenly the air between them was charged again.

In the gallery lights, his face was all angles and his hair blended into the color of his face so that he looked like a stone statue. He turned and said quickly, "Yes," and then he was gone, into the next room, leaving Sweeney standing there, listening to his voice come back toward her saying, "I have to get going. I left a notebook in the basement."

"Yeah. Okay. I'll come down with you." She joined him in the hallway, but they didn't look at each other as they went down the stairs.

The basement was in shadow, the Egyptian exhibits spookily illuminated along the walls, the stone pillars creating strange little pools of darkness. The potted trees in the center of the courtyard almost looked like a real forest, the leaves casting odd animal shapes onto the pale marble.

"Careful," Quinn said, catching her arm as she stumbled at the bottom of the stairs.

"Thanks." She felt the hot skin of his forearm against her hand. He stopped suddenly. And in the instant she turned to look up at him to see why, she knew two things. One was that she wanted to kiss him, the other was that something was wrong. It was pure déjà vu, the room, the look on Quinn's face mirroring the shock she'd seen on Jeanne's face, and she followed the direction of his gaze.

There was someone on the floor, in almost the exact center of the room. They stood there for a moment, just staring at the body, as though they didn't know what it was, and then Quinn whispered, "It's Willem Keane," and he was moving across the room. Sweeney turned to see him crouching by the body, and she crossed the room too and knelt down next to him, taking in the details. It was as though she was seeing the whole thing again, Olga's body and the blood, except that this time it was Willem and the blood was on his mouth, on his cheeks, on the floor, and she thought of Macbeth. Who would have known? So much blood. And she thought, *All of us, all of us have this much blood.* And then, *We are all this close to death.*

TWENTY-SEVEN

Quinn and Ellie stood in front of one of the stone pillars in the basement and watched as Willem Keane's body, now zipped into its plastic shroud, was lifted onto a gurney and wheeled toward the elevator. Ellie had arrived within ten minutes of his call, and she had been pretty helpful, he had to admit, helping to secure the building and getting an initial list of everyone who had been there that afternoon. She'd gotten the security tapes ready for viewing already, and he'd watched her in action with Sweeney, making sure she was okay, getting her a glass of water, asking if she needed a ride home, and waiting with her until Ian Ball came to pick her up.

"I talked to the family," Ellie said suddenly, confusing him. "They let me look around in her room. I found a textbook."

"What?"

"Luz Ramirez. A textbook. College chemistry."

"Oh." For a second he thought she'd been talking about Willem Keane's family. Willem Keane didn't have any family. Tad Moran had already told them that. There was a brother in L.A. whom he offered to notify, but apparently they'd been estranged for years.

Watching Tad Moran's face when he heard the news, though, Quinn had decided that maybe this guy was as close to family as Keane had gotten. Moran said he'd worked for him for more than twenty years, and he had the look that Quinn knew so well from years of being the one to knock on the next of kin's door, pure, disbelieving grief, the kind that made you fall down, the kind that made you lose control of your bodily functions, the kind that would eventually, mercifully, wipe all memory of those first few minutes of knowing from your brain.

Ellie went on in the way she had of stringing a new sentence on the end of the old one. "Which is strange, because she wasn't in college. She worked at this salon and she hung around with her friends, but the family told me she definitely wasn't in college. So I couldn't figure out why she would have something like this. I talked to the girls at the salon where she worked. Most of them didn't have much to offer, but one of the hair stylists, who's also from El Salvador, she told me that Luz told her she was in love. She told her his name was Jason and he was a 'college boy.' She met him when he came in to get his hair cut."

Quinn just listened, sensing she didn't want him to talk.

"Remember that outfit she was wearing? We both thought it looked like something you'd wear to a job interview? Well, I was thinking that maybe it was the kind of thing someone like Luz might wear on a date with a guy who she saw as different from the boys in her neighborhood. A guy she really liked."

Quinn was impressed. "Okay," he said. "So what do we do next?"

"I was thinking I could call all the colleges in town, ask to speak to someone in the Chemistry Department, find out if they have any students named Jason. What do you think?"

"I think that's pretty good," he said. "I think you've got it."

She watched as the gurney was wheeled into the elevator and the doors closed. They were silent for a few minutes. "If you don't want to work with me anymore," she said finally, "you could tell Havrilek that we don't get along. I bet he'd transfer me."

"Do you not want to work with me anymore?"

She brushed a piece of slightly greasy hair out of her eyes and tucked it behind an ear, looking down at the ground as though she was afraid of him. "No, but it just seems like . . ."

"Like I have a problem with you?"

She nodded.

He thought for a minute, trying to figure out how to get out of telling her the truth. "I don't. It's me, so you shouldn't worry. No, I want to work with you, and I'm sorry if I've been short with you. I have a lot on my mind right now." He reached for the easy, the uncomplicated explanation. "You may have heard about my wife." Her quick glance up at him told him that she had.

"I'm sorry," she whispered.

"Thanks." He looked across the gallery. "I'm going to need your help on this now," he said. "This is getting messy. The museum wasn't open to the public today. Unless he let his murderer in or someone was really freaking smart about breaking in, it was someone who had access to the building."

"Murderer?"

"He didn't jump. There were contusions on his face. Someone hit him before he went over, and there are marks on the banister upstairs that indicate there was a struggle. He was on the fourth floor, outside the gallery where Jeanne Ortiz's show will be."

"Was she here?"

He nodded. "All day. She said she didn't hear anything. She'd been working in the gallery and went for a walk around the museum at some point, to clear her head, she said. She seemed pretty nervous to me." In fact, she'd seemed more than nervous. She'd seemed so edgy that Quinn was afraid she might jump over the balcony herself.

"Who else was here?"

"Everyone. Tad Moran, Fred Kauffman, Denny Keefe."

"Sweeney St. George? Was she here earlier?"

"Yeah." He didn't look at Ellie. She knew he and Sweeney had been together when they found the body. Had she added a little something, a little emphasis, to Sweeney's name, or was he just being paranoid?

"But he could have let someone in, couldn't he?"

He was tired, but there was so much to be done now. He'd have to call Patience and see if she could stay. Luckily, she didn't seem to mind. He forced his mind back to the matter at hand. "It'll be on the tapes anyway," he said. "Let's see what we've got."

They took them back to headquarters and viewed them in one of the conference rooms. Ellie went to get sandwiches for dinner, and he ate his BLT while they watched the static shots of the front entrance to the museum. The tapes confirmed the times that all of the museum employees claimed to have arrived that morning. Because the museum was closed, there was a long stretch of inactivity between ten — when Keane himself had been the last to arrive — and one-thirty, when Fred Kauffman had gone out for a sandwich and then come back an hour later. Keane himself had gone out around two and returned holding a paper cup of coffee.

He and Sweeney had found Keane's body at six, so it was the late afternoon they were interested in. Ellie fast-forwarded the tapes, both of them watching for any action.

"Wait. Stop," Quinn said. "Look at that. Who's that?"

She rewound back to the point where a figure appeared at the main entrance to the museum. It was a man, dressed in a shirt, tie, and sports coat, and carrying a newspaper in one hand and a tote bag in the other.

"I think it's Cyrus Hutchinson," Ellie said.

"I Googled him before I called him about the whiskey, and there were some pictures of him online. From charity events, that kind of thing." They watched as he slowly climbed the steps to the museum and tried the front door, then appeared to wave at someone on the other side of the glass.

"He must be calling one of the security guards to open the door," Ellie said. Sure enough, the door opened, and Quinn saw Denny Keefe in the corner of the television screen before they both stepped out of frame.

"Keane must have been expecting him. I don't think they would have let him in otherwise," Quinn said. "Let's see when he leaves."

They watched for another few seconds. But instead of seeing Hutchinson leave through the main entrance, they saw what looked like a teenage boy wearing a backpack approach the camera, try the door as Hutchinson had, then cup his hands around his face and peer through the window. This time, though, they saw Keefe come to the door, speak to the boy for a few minutes, then close it again.

"He's not letting him in," Quinn said. "Do you know who that is?"

"Uh-uh," Ellie said, watching as the boy

stood in front of the door, waiting for something. After a couple of minutes, the door opened again and the boy spoke to Keefe, gesturing with his hands as though he was trying to explain something. Finally the door was pushed open and the boy stepped in. "They let him in," she said.

Nothing happened for the next hour. "Okay," Quinn said, checking the time stamp. "It's now five-thirty. We found him at six and neither one of them has left yet. When did they leave?"

His question was answered when they saw Hutchinson walk out through the front door at five forty-five and the boy come out a few minutes later. After that, no one arrived or left until six-ten, when a group of uniformed police arrived in response to Quinn's call. A few minutes later, Ellie herself came running up the steps and was let in by the uniformed cop at the door.

Quinn stopped the tape. "Ellie, tell Johnny to locate Cyrus Hutchinson. I want to talk to him as soon as we've got him. And I want to talk to whoever we can get from the museum. I want to know who that kid is. Get him going on that, and then we can see what else is on the tapes."

She ducked out for a minute and came back as he was getting the first of the tapes from the inside of the museum loaded in. "He's on it," she said.

There wasn't much of interest on the gallery tapes. They watched Jeanne Ortiz come into the fourth-floor gallery where her show was going up and spend a few minutes measuring walls, then go out again.

"There's not going to be anything," Quinn said. "They were all over in their offices. But we should watch just to make sure." The cameras swept the rooms at sixty-second intervals, switching back and forth between the galleries.

Ellie fast-forwarded and stopped the tape as two figures came into view in the third-floor galleries.

Quinn sat up. "Oh," he said. "That's me and Sweeney. We . . . I mean, she showed me her exhibition. That was before . . ." He was silenced by the sight of the two of them, standing in the gallery and talking. He watched himself turn to look at her, his head slightly inclined toward hers. They were standing much closer than he remembered.

It was strange, watching himself on camera. He saw that he stooped slightly. Had he always done that? He wasn't sure. Next to Sweeney, he didn't seem as tall as he'd always thought he was, but perhaps it was just that she was taller than most women. The camera seemed to follow them as it swept across the room, and he watched as they stood together, their shoulders nearly touching, his body leaning toward her. Their bodies were like letters, two inverted V's, forming an M. He wanted to lean forward and stop the tape, but he couldn't, and he and Ellie watched for an agonizing thirty seconds before the camera swept away and switched to one of the other galleries. They were silent as they watched the empty rooms. Quinn felt as though she must be able to hear his heart beating out of his chest.

When it finally ended, Quinn leaned forward and ejected the tape.

He felt like he should say something, but he didn't know what it would be and so he just silently turned off the television.

"I'll go check on Johnny," Ellie said and left him alone.

TWENTY-EIGHT

"That friend of mine, the one in London? He said he might have something for your cop," Ian said, covering his wheat toast with the marmalade he bought at a special shop on Beacon Hill. "He said he heard a rumor about the chest."

Sweeney looked up from her own breakfast, toast fingers that she was enthusiastically dipping into a soft-boiled egg. She registered that he'd said, "your cop," and looked up. "What'd he say? Do you want to tell Quinn?"

It had become their little Sunday ritual, the papers and their own particular favorite breakfasts at the dining room table. Ian liked listening to what he called "Sunday morning music": Bach, very loud, making Sweeney's apartment feel a little like a church. This Sunday, she had turned to the ritual to try to enforce a sense of normalcy.

But things were far from normal. Willem was dead.

"You can tell him," Ian said a little too casually. "This fellow said that he heard of a very rich Japanese collector who's obsessed with Egyptian antiquities and made it known that he would pay top dollar for any items that became available."

"In other words, items stolen from other people's collections."

"Right."

"So who might have carried out the theft?"

"Well, he was saying that he'd heard, through the grapevine, that it was the Irish mob in Boston that carried out the 1979 job. They did it on behalf of the IRA, which needed money for guns, and it was planned and executed by guys connected with a gang in Northern Ireland who had carried out some other big art thefts. He mentioned the name Naki Haruhito. I don't know if that'll mean anything to him, but that's all I was able to get."

Sweeney got up to get a piece of paper from the pad next to the phone. "Haruhito with a 'u'?" she asked, writing it down.

"Yes, that's right." He popped the last piece of toast into his mouth. "What are you up to today?"

"I said I'd go to this rally," she said. "I

have to talk to this woman who's visiting, and Jeanne really wants me to go too. She's trying to get me to be the faculty adviser to the women's group. They're called the WA-WAs and she thinks it would be a good thing to have someone younger. I don't know. How about you?"

"I guess I'll go to the office." He seemed annoyed suddenly, and Sweeney watched as he stood up and took his dishes into the kitchen.

When he came back, she reached out to touch his hand. "Was there something you wanted to do? Because I don't have to go to this thing." He looked up to meet her eyes, then looked down at her hand as though he wasn't sure he wanted it there.

Ever since her lunch with Aggie Williams, there had been a layer of chill between her and Ian. She'd been furious about him telling his partners they were coming back to London, and instead of apologizing, he'd asked her what she wanted him to do. "I have to go back, Sweeney. I'm going back. And if you're not going with me, I need you to tell me." He'd seemed tired lately, and she'd felt tired staring at him. She'd finally told him she just needed more time.

And then Willem had been murdered. She'd tried to explain how it had happened that she and Quinn had found the body, but he didn't seem to want to talk about it, and he acted as though he didn't want anything to do with any of it, with the investigation into Willem and Olga's murders, with Quinn, with the museum. "No, you go. I have things to do at the office, anyway. You remember about the dinner Tuesday night, right?"

"With Peter and Lillie?" Ian's partner and his wife were in town, and they were having dinner at some hot new restaurant that Ian had been excited about getting a reservation at for weeks. "It's on my calendar."

"Good. Well, I'm going to have a wash and get going. I'll see you tonight." He didn't kiss her good-bye.

"The thing with the guy in London," Sweeney said as he left the room. "You think this guy really knows what he's talking about?"

"Who knows? There's not much honor among thieves."

"Okay," she said, trying to read his stony face. "I'll tell him."

On the way over to the rally, she watched the hordes of students walking around the yard wearing almost nothing against the heat. Maybe it was Willem's death, but they seemed disgustingly carefree to Sweeney, as though they were on vacation. They weren't really here to learn. They were here to say they had learned something, so they could get high-paying jobs and so they could say their own children were going to an Ivy League school and so forth and so on. If she really thought about it, only about two percent of the students she'd had over the past few years really cared about what she had to teach them.

Jeez, Sweeney, she admonished herself. *What's got into you?*

Was she getting cynical about teaching? She wasn't sure. On the good days, she loved her work, loved the moment when a student saw something in a work of art that he or she hadn't known was there, and she loved the moment where she herself had one of those moments of illumination, where the act of teaching showed her something new. There hadn't been many of those moments over the last year. She wasn't sure why. Perhaps she was feeling that her career had hit a dead end at the university. It was becoming clearer and clearer that she wasn't going to get any of the tenure-track jobs opening up over the next few years. With her lease up, she knew it was a good time to start looking for a new job. She'd had some offers from small colleges in Vermont and

Maine. There was something appealing about the idea of moving to a town where no one knew her, starting over. She had a vision of herself sitting by a roaring fire in a small log cabin somewhere on the side of a mountain, the General sprawled out on the floor. At the moment that she reminded herself that Ian would never consent to move to rural New England, she realized that the fantasy hadn't included Ian. No, if she and Ian were going to be together, she was going to have to move to London.

So what about London? It wouldn't be a bad thing to start over again at a new college or university, a fresh start, a fresh slate of students. British universities operated somewhat differently and she might be given more latitude to pursue her own interests. She sat on a bench for a few minutes, daydreaming. For a while now, she'd had another fantasy, about opening her own museum, a small private museum focused on funerary art. Oddly, it hadn't occurred to her until now that she could probably do it, now that she'd sold some of her father's paintings. And she could sell more if she wanted. It was hard to get used to the idea that a lack of funds was no longer an impediment to the things she wanted to do. It was almost paralyzing, having infinite opportunities. Of course, it was better than not having any opportunities at all.

She daydreamed for a few more minutes as she approached the rally. It was being held at the far end of the yard, and as she got closer she could hear an amplified voice and more voices cheering, and she saw the crowd of people — mostly women students — holding signs and listening to the older woman who was speaking from a makeshift podium. "But you all haven't forgotten," she called out, "because you're here. And with your help we'll make sure that women of your generation never forget." Sweeney saw Jeanne and a few other faculty members standing next to the stage. The woman who was speaking finished up and the crowd cheered. Jeanne was worried about something. Even as she smiled and clapped her hands over her head, her lovely face was twisted in concern.

After the speech was over, Sweeney made her way up to the podium and waved at Jeanne, who smiled when she saw her and beckoned her over. "Hi, Sweeney, there are some people I want you to meet." She introduced Sweeney to a couple of young women who she said were members of the WAWAs. They were both exceptionally pretty, with long limbs and blond hair pulled back in messy ponytails. As she talked to them about their goals for the organization, Sweeney couldn't help thinking about what it had been like to arrive at the university as a sixteen-year-old, younger than everyone she knew, confused about what she was expected to do or be. She'd learned how to study, how to manage her time, how to write a perfect paper, but she'd had no idea how to negotiate the strange gender politics of a college campus. When Sweeney had arrived, the big controversy had been over the definition of date rape. Women on campus were speaking out about men who they said had pushed them to go further than they'd wanted, and a lot of Sweeney's male friends — Toby included — had told her that they were terrified of kissing someone for fear they'd be called a rapist. Some colleges had even started asking students to sign contracts before any physical contact occurred.

One night, Sweeney had gotten drunk at a party in someone's off-campus apartment, passed out on a couch, and awakened in a strange bedroom to find a guy she knew a little from an English class undoing her clothes. She had sat up and pushed him away, and luckily he'd slunk off, embarrassed, but she remembered she yelled after him, "What were you going to do?" and that when she'd seen him around campus, she'd felt humiliated and guilty, as though she'd tried to assault him.

She hoped things had changed for these women, with their summer sun–bleached hair and their hopeful faces.

She had asked Jeanne to introduce her to Susan Esterhaus, and when Jeanne called her over, Sweeney realized that Susan was the one who'd been speaking when she'd arrived. She had long curly gray hair, hippie style, but she was wearing an Armani pant-suit and diamond stud earrings as big as Sweeney's thumbnail.

The diamonds glinted in the sun. "It's great to meet you. Jeanne tells me you're going to be the new faculty adviser."

"Well, I don't know. I want to make sure I have the time to really devote to it."

"Well, it's a terrific group of young women. Really inspiring."

"Yeah, they seem great." Sweeney didn't want to commit to anything. "Is now a good time to talk about Karen?"

"Sure." Susan Esterhaus motioned for Sweeney to step away from the crowd a bit. "What was it you wanted to know?"

"What was she like?" It seemed as good a

place to start as any.

Susan thought for a moment. "I remember she always seemed like kind of an improbable feminist to me. I think she was from Greenfield or somewhere pretty rural, and I had the sense that all of these things we were talking about, equality, empowerment, they were all fairly new concepts for her. But she came alive in the WAWAs and working on this little arts magazine we put together. I was the editor and Karen and I got to know each other working on it. *WAC,* it was called, for Women's Arts Collective. I don't know why we came up with all of these sort of military acronyms, but we thought it was cool." Susan smiled.

"Anyway. Karen. She was a talented artist and a talented art historian, and she was a real asset to our little group. I blamed myself for a long time after her death. I knew she was depressed. I tried to talk to her about it, but nothing doing. I didn't know enough to know that I should have pushed her, should have called her family, whatever it took. But then, I suppose lots of college students get depressed and they don't all kill themselves."

"When did you notice that she was depressed?"

"God, it's so long ago. I can't quite

pinpoint it, but sometime that fall, I guess. Now that I think about it, I'm not sure depressed is the right word. Withdrawn, maybe."

"Scared?"

"Yeah, she seemed scared of something. That's right. I wondered if it had to do with the robbery at the museum. You know about that, right?" Sweeney nodded. "That would be enough to scare anyone. Why are you interested in Karen, anyway?"

"I'm working on a project," Sweeney lied. "Women in the arts at the university."

"Sounds good. I'd love to read it when you're done. I studied sociology, so I wouldn't really know, but I guess Karen was pretty hot shit at the museum. She had gone to Egypt on an archaeological dig the summer before she died, and she was some kind of an expert on jewelry or something. That was what she'd studied over in Egypt."

"Really? That was her area of specialty? I didn't know that. Did she ever talk to you about her work?"

"A bit. She said she'd gotten interested in the jewelry made for women. She said everyone thought of King Tut when they thought about Egypt but that there were all these other lives still to be revealed and discovered. She wrote some poetry for *WAC* about it."

"Really? I'd love to see it."

"I'll see if I can find some old copies. You'll have to endure my second-rate erotic stories, though." She called to Jeanne. "Jeanne, you were around a lot in those days," Susan said. "You were coming down from Smith nearly every weekend for a while there, weren't you? I think that was right around the time Karen Philips died."

Jeanne was watching some young women who had been part of the rally talking to a group of good-looking young men. She looked almost wistful, and Sweeney wondered if she missed the days when male students might have been yelling at the women. "Was I? I don't remember."

"Yeah, we were having all those intercampus planning meetings on ERA that fall and winter, and you were here a lot."

"That's right," Jeanne said vaguely, hardly looking at them.

"So you must have known Karen Philips too?" Sweeney asked.

"I guess so. Not well, though." She waved to someone across the way. "I've got to talk to Catherine. Sweeney, feel free to stick around and talk to some more of the students." She glanced at them quickly and hurried away.

"Is Jeanne okay?" Susan asked once they were alone again. "She seems a little on edge today."

Sweeney told her about the murders at the museum. "I know I'm a little on edge," she said. But she realized that there seemed to be something else wrong with Jeanne. She had seen Jeanne Ortiz angry, excited, annoyed, and unreasonable. But she'd never seen her scared.

TWENTY-NINE

Waiting for Sweeney at one of the outside tables at a café on Brattle Street, Quinn found he was nervous in a way he hadn't been since he'd been about fourteen, meeting a girl for the first time at a pizza place around the corner from his house. He'd imagined sitting at a place like this with Sweeney, imagined the hot late-summer day, the way the air smelled and the way his glass of white wine would taste. But he hadn't imagined that she'd be meeting him to tell him what her boyfriend had to say about international art thieves.

It was stupid. He had to put the whole thing out of his mind. She wasn't the right woman for him. He knew that. He wasn't smart enough, he wasn't educated enough, he wasn't a good enough dresser. Hell, he probably didn't make enough money. They would be friends, or whatever it was that they were, and that would have to be it.

But still, when he spotted her crossing the street and coming toward him, wearing a pair of khaki pants that came to the middle of her calves and a bright aqua T-shirt that matched the blue flip-flops she was wearing, he felt everything stop for a minute and it was all he could do to stop watching her, stop watching her long limbs swinging as she walked like a coltish kid, stop staring at her lightly tanned arms, her throat, her neck . . .

"Hey," she said, sitting down and touching him lightly on the arm. "Sorry I'm late."

"No problem. You want something?" He'd ordered a slice of pizza, though it had come out fancier than he'd expected, with goat cheese and little pieces of herbs on it, and now he wasn't even hungry.

"Maybe an iced coffee?" Quinn gestured to the waitress, and Sweeney ordered the coffee. Then she turned to him and said, "So Ian says to tell you that his friend in London, the one he mentioned? Well, he said something about a Japanese collector who was looking for something like the canopic chest. And he said he'd heard about a connection with organized crime in Boston. Same guys who were talked about for the 1979 theft. Naki Haruhito was the name he got. Does that mean anything to you?"

"No, but I'll have to ask my contact at the FBI. Hey, tell him thanks. This may turn out to be important."

"Sure." There was an awkward silence. That had been the reason for their meeting and now they were finished and her coffee hadn't even come.

"How's everything at the museum?" The building had opened to the public again today, though they had decided to close the basement gallery, mostly to discourage gawkers, since they'd already gotten everything from the crime scene that they could.

"Pretty weird. I've only been over a few times since . . . since Willem's death." The waitress came with a tall glass mug of dark reddish coffee and ice. Sweeney tipped some cream in and stirred, her loose hair falling across her face. "They haven't said who's going to be in charge, not even in the interim, so we don't know what to do with ourselves. How close are you to solving this?"

"I don't know," he said truthfully. "It seems as though it had to be someone from the museum. Or . . ." He didn't want to tip his hand about what they'd found on the tapes, but on the other hand, maybe she knew something about the kid who had been at the museum. They'd gotten something on him from Denny Keefe, who had also identified him as the student who had given him trouble about bringing a bag in the night of the opening. Keefe had said the kid wanted to see Jeanne Ortiz. She came down and got him and they went up to her office. The dean of students had checked out the tape and identified him as Trevor Ferigni, a sophomore from California.

"You know someone named Trevor Ferigni?" Quinn asked.

"Sounds familiar. Who is he?"

"He was at the museum the night of your opening, apparently. And he was at the museum the day Willem Keane was killed."

"Oh, right. The kid who was following Jeanne around. What was he doing?"

"He says he's a former student of Ms. Ortiz's and he had to talk to her about something. He was up in the gallery where she was working for a half hour or so, didn't see anything strange, left and went to the library."

"What did she say?"

"She backed him up. Said he was with her the whole time."

"So what was he doing at the museum?"

"He says he had to talk to Ortiz. But there was something weird about the whole thing. I don't know. She seemed nervous, he seemed nervous. I was just wondering if you knew anything."

She grinned at him. "Have I heard any gossip? No. Can't say I have." She'd finished her coffee. "There's something strange, though. She was around the university a lot during the time leading up to Karen's suicide. I found out from someone who also knew Karen. Jeanne seemed really nervous when I asked her about it."

"You think she had something to do with Karen Philips's death." He told Sweeney that he'd looked at the file and was pretty certain they'd investigated thoroughly.

"I don't know. I'm still trying to figure out how Karen's death and the collar are connected. Maybe she was involved in hiding the fact that there was something wrong with the collar, that it had been stolen. Or, I was thinking, maybe she figured out how valuable it was and she stole it herself." She looked up triumphantly at him, the expression on her face identical to the one Megan got when she'd pulled off the feat of removing her shoes or knocking a bowl of cereal onto the floor.

"And was so guilty that she killed herself."

"Yeah." She grinned at him. "See."

"I don't know. It seems like it must have something to do with the museum, but I'm not there with you yet."

She shrugged. "Speaking of the museum, I should get over there. I have an appointment."

She took a five out of her pocket, but he waved her off. "You're providing me with information after all," he told her. "The least I can do is buy you a cup of cold coffee."

"Thanks." They both stood up and she hesitated for a minute, then said, "Walk me over?"

He nodded and they started walking, not saying anything at first. Finally, he couldn't stand the not knowing anymore. "So, have you decided what you're going to do, about going to London, I mean?"

She didn't turn to look at him, but he felt her tense up. "No. I mean I haven't decided yet." There was a long silence. They'd reached the steps of the museum and only then did she turn to look at him. "What do you think I should do?"

There was something challenging in the way she said it, as though she was daring him to tell her what he really thought, but then she looked away and he wasn't sure what she'd meant and he just said, "I just hope you'll do what makes you happy." Then he said good-bye and left her there, standing on the steps.

Oh, shit, he said to himself as he walked away. *Timmy boy, you're done for. You're really done for.*

He walked around for almost an hour, trying to shake his feeling of melancholy, and he had just gotten into his car when the radio squawked. It wasn't for him, so he turned on the FM and listened to Bruce Springsteen singing about love. But as he pulled out of his parking spot, he heard "Hapner Museum" and he turned the music down and paid attention. They were calling up a lot of units and his first thought was that there had been another murder, but then he realized that they hadn't called him up, so it couldn't be that. He dialed headquarters on his cell phone and asked for Havrilek.

It was a couple minutes before he came on and Quinn pulled over and executed a U-turn so he could get back to the museum quickly if he needed to. "Good, Quinny," Havrilek said when he came on. "Get over to the museum. They're not sure what's going on, but a call came in about a man threatening people with a gun. There are some staff members who are being held hostage inside and the guy's pretty distraught. You know everyone down there, so see if you can help. We don't know yet if it has anything to do with the murders, but I think it's a distinct possibility."

Quinn started for the museum, feeling his stomach fall. Sweeney was at the museum. Unless she'd changed her mind and gone home, she was one of the hostages. He'd been in enough hostage situations to know that these things were often resolved without violence, but when they went wrong, boy did they really go wrong.

There were swarms of cops out front and enough reporters to hold a presidential press conference. He flashed his ID and they let him into the lobby. It was packed full of uniform guys, which told him that the situation was under control for the moment. If the man, whoever he was, was about to go off, they would have cleared the area.

"What's going on?" he whispered to one of the guys he knew from his days as a patrol officer. "Who's the guy?"

"Kid. Student, we think. He's up on the fourth floor with a woman named Ortiz and some of the other staff. The initial call said he had a gun, but we haven't been able to verify that."

"It's not Trevor Ferigni is it?"

"Yeah, I think that's the name. The security guard called it in."

"Who else is up there with him?"

"They don't know. He yelled down that he was going to hurt someone if we didn't back off, so we backed off." There was a kind of low hum in the room and Quinn scanned the uniforms, trying to figure out who was in charge.

"I gotta get up there," he said. "I'll see you."

He didn't know the officer running things from behind the guards' desk, but he introduced himself and told the guy that he'd been investigating the murders and knew everyone. It wasn't strictly true, of course; he didn't know the kid. But if Sweeney was up there he was going to get up there any way he could.

"We've got officers on the fourth floor, talking to him. You go up, let him see you, see if he responds," the officer said. "But don't do anything unless I give the okay."

Quinn made his way up the stairs, and before coming out on the fourth-floor landing, he stopped and took a deep breath. He needed to be calm. If this kid with a gun who may or may not have had something to do with the murders at the museum looked into his soul, Quinn wanted him to see nothing but calm. He forced himself to relax his shoulders, closed his eyes for a minute, and stepped out into the hallway.

It was very, very quiet and there were only three cops there, standing close to the staircase, just standing there, not doing anything. They must have been told he was coming up because they nodded to him and pointed to the opposite end of the hallway where a skinny boy with a shock of blond hair was standing against the balcony holding a gun. Jeanne Ortiz was sitting on the floor, and even from thirty feet away, Quinn could see that she was crying. Behind them, in the doorway of one of the galleries, Sweeney and Tad Moran and Harriet Tyler were standing very still. The look on Sweeney's face — scared and watchful — nearly broke his heart.

Get out of there, he thought, as if Sweeney could read his mind. *You've got cover, you can just duck behind the doorway and you'll be safe.* But there was Jeanne Ortiz. He must have told them he'd hurt Jeanne if they moved.

They all looked up and saw him at the same moment. The boy gripped the gun more tightly and called out, "Stay back." He had on a T-shirt and cutoff shorts and he was wearing hiking boots. Sweeney met

Quinn's eyes, and he saw something like relief there, just for a few seconds, until fear crept back in.

"Who are you?" The words were shouted, breathless.

"My name's Tim. I've been spending a lot of time at the museum," Quinn called out. "It's okay, Trevor. Let's just talk about whatever it is that's making you so mad." He tried to keep his voice even, not condescending, but nonconfrontational.

"Are you a cop?"

"I'm a detective. What's going on here?"

There was a long silence, as though Trevor was deciding what to say. Finally he turned to Quinn and said, "It's her," pointing the gun at Jeanne.

Quinn wasn't sure what he meant. Was he saying that Jeanne Ortiz had killed Olga and Willem Keane? He waited, watching the boy's face in profile.

"She's fucking with me," Trevor said, more quietly this time. "She can't just, just shut me out like that. I didn't even want to do it."

"Trevor," Jeanne said, her hands together in front of her chest in a little prayer. "Can't we just talk about this?"

But he wanted to talk to Quinn. "She got me to sleep with her and then she says we

can't see each other anymore and she can't
. . ." He was crying now. Quinn took a
couple of steps toward him. "She can't *do*
that." He turned to Jeanne Ortiz and said,
"You can't *do* that."

Okay, Quinn thought. *That's what we're
dealing with here.* It was what he'd suspected, and he looked up to meet Sweeney's
eyes again.

"Trevor, just put that down and we'll go
talk about it," Jeanne Ortiz said. "Please.
Trevor." In addition to the fear on her face,
Quinn saw shame there too.

"What are you going to do, Jeanne?" he
asked her, his voice louder, a little more
agitated, in a way that made Quinn ease a
hand onto his holster. "Are you going to tell
everyone that you got me drunk, that you
got a student drunk and, and . . ." He was
crying very hard now, the words barely
intelligible beneath his sobs. "And *seduced*
him and then wanted to kick him to the
curb. Like he was, like he was nothing?" He
was almost shouting now, and Quinn had
the sense that this was where it was going
to go one way or the other. He took a couple
more steps forward, close enough now to
see the dark circles under the arms of the
kid's T-shirt.

"Trevor, if you could just put that down,

then we could talk about this. It sounds like you have good reason to be upset."

"Yeah, I do. I really do." He brandished the gun, and that was the instant that Quinn saw it, really saw it, saw the little piece of plastic along the seam on the barrel, and without really thinking about, he charged forward.

The kid was skinny, lighter than he'd looked, and Quinn had overestimated the amount of force he'd need. The kid hit the ground hard and Quinn heard the "ooof," as the wind was knocked out of him.

"It's a fake, it's a fake," he yelled out, so no one would shoot.

He checked to make sure Trevor Ferigni was breathing and then he called out for handcuffs. He turned and saw Jeanne Ortiz still sitting on the floor. She was really crying now and saying, "I'm sorry, I'm so sorry," over and over again.

It was Sweeney who came forward to make sure she was okay, leaning down and putting an arm around her and helping her up as she said it again and again. "I'm sorry, I'm sorry, I'm sorry."

"So she was boinking the kid?" Havrilek asked him back at headquarters.

"Yup. And she'd decided that she

shouldn't do it anymore. But the kid wasn't willing to be dumped."

Havrilek raised his eyebrows, his pale, Siberian husky eyes studying Quinn. "He in love with her?"

"I don't think he knows what he is." Quinn looked at the pictures on Havrilek's desk. Havrilek had five beautiful daughters. "If he was a nineteen-year-old woman who had been sleeping with her professor and this happened, I think we'd be saying she was forced into it. Not physically, but psychologically. I don't quite understand it. When she wanted to end it, he freaked out. I don't know what he thought he was going to do with that toy gun."

Quinn rubbed his eyes and sat down across from Havrilek's desk. "I'll tell you, for a minute there, I was sure we'd solved this thing. It was perfect. The kid was at the opening when Olga Levitch was killed and he was at the museum when Keane was killed too. But that kid didn't know anything about the murders. He was there to make Jeanne Ortiz own up to their relationship. That seemed to have been his motivation to me, anyway. So we're back at square one with the museum murders. Well, not square one exactly." Quinn told Havrilek about Cyrus Hutchinson being at the museum at the time Keane was killed too.

"What does he say about it?"

"We haven't found him yet. He and his wife aren't at home, his office doesn't have any idea where he is. I'm starting to think maybe we should get someone in New York to look for him."

"But didn't you tell me he's an old man? He didn't push Keane over that balcony." Havrilek looked dubious.

"Maybe it was an accident. Maybe he didn't have anything to do with it. But at the very least, he knows what Keane was doing in the last hours of his life. I want to talk to him."

"Okay. I'll make the call. We'll see what we can do." He narrowed his eyes at Quinn. "Anything else?"

Quinn hesitated. "Yeah, well, maybe." He told Havrilek about Sweeney's tip about the Japanese collector. "I told our contact at the FBI about it. I think he recognized the name, though he didn't give anything away." In fact, Kirschner had muttered something under his breath that sounded a lot like "fuck me." "I'm waiting for him to get back to me."

Havrilek picked up the phone. It was his way of getting you out of the office. But then he put it down again and looked up at Quinn.

"Hey, how about the Ramirez murder? I got reporters breathing down my neck about it."

"We'd hit kind of a dead end, but Ellie's got a good lead. She's working on it now."

"Good." Havrilek watched him for a minute, his eyes narrowed. "How's it going with her, anyway? You doing okay?"

Quinn shrugged, wondering if she'd said something. "Fine. She's smart, if a bit green."

Havrilek watched him some more. "She seem okay to you?"

"What do you mean?"

"I mean, does she seem okay to you?" He sounded mad.

"Yeah, she seems fine."

"Okay," Havrilek said. "If you say so."

Back in the homicide division offices, she was standing in front of his desk, clutching the phone book, a little embarrassed grin on her face. "I think I found something," she said, the words coming very fast. "It took a while 'cause there are so many colleges in Boston and no one was answering their phone. But I just kept calling and anyway . . ." She looked down at the paper she was holding in her hands. "There's a guy named Jason Fowler. He's a chemistry major at the university. I got his address and number right here." She looked up at him, and when he didn't answer, she went on. "There's another Jason at BU, but apparently he's studying in France this semester, so I figure it's gotta be this guy, right?"

For some reason, Quinn couldn't give her the satisfaction of a smile. "Maybe, maybe not. We gotta go talk to him, though. We'll take it nice and easy, just ask him where he was, check on his alibi. If he doesn't have one, though, we're taking him in." This is what it was about, he reminded himself. This is why they did their job. So they could bring the bad guys in. "Good job, Ellie."

They found the apartment and Quinn parked illegally in front of the six-story building. They climbed up to the third floor and Ellie knocked on the green wooden door. She was excited, Quinn could tell, a little smile hovering below her nose, and he remembered the first time that one of his leads had led somewhere.

"He could be at class," Quinn said when no one answered.

"It's nine A.M.," she said. "Aren't college kids supposed to sleep until noon at least?"

"How should I know? I worked my way through college. I had to be at work slinging hash in the dining room at six A.M. most days."

"Me too," she said and grinned.

"Yeah? Where did you go?"

"University of Illinois." That's where that accent came from.

"Criminal justice?" She nodded. "Try that door again."

After another couple knocks, the door opened and a bleary-eyed kid wearing boxers and a white undershirt blinked at them. "Hi," he said. "Sorry about that. I was still asleep."

"Are you Jason Fowler?"

Now he looked wary. "Yeah?" Quinn took in his skinny young body, the too-long dark hair, and unfashionable glasses. It seemed hard to believe that this sweet-faced, nerdy kid could have brutally sodomized someone and then beaten her to death.

"Cambridge police. My name is Detective Quinn. This is Detective Lindquist. We want to talk to you," Quinn said. "Can we come in?"

"Okay." He looked from Quinn to Ellie. "I guess."

They all sat down in the living room, which smelled of fried onions and musty laundry. There were a couple of dinner plates, still crusted with the remains of what looked like fish and chips, sitting on the coffee table, and they made Quinn feel sick to his stomach.

"Do you know someone named Luz Ramirez?" Ellie asked him.

"Yeah?" It was a question. He looked from one to the other.

"When was the last time you saw her?"

"Um. A couple weeks ago."

"Where was that?"

"At the place where I get my hair cut. She cut my hair."

"And?"

"And what?"

"And?" Quinn knew there was an "and."

He looked down at the ground, and it struck Quinn that he was embarrassed about something. "And . . . I don't know why I have to tell you about it. Why do you want to know?"

His confusion seemed genuine to Quinn, but then you never knew. "She's dead," Ellie said bluntly. "Someone killed her."

"Oh, shit!" The kid stood up and Quinn jumped to his own feet, a hand on his holster, thinking he was going to run. But instead he put a hand to his head and sat down again. "Are you serious? Oh shit, oh shit, oh shit. No, really?" His eyes, when he looked up at them, were full of tears.

"Listen, we were supposed to go out. A couple weeks ago, I guess. But she stood me up. We were supposed to meet at that Momma's Pizza place on Mass. Ave. I waited for an hour and she never showed." Quinn took out his calendar and made Fowler show him what night it was. He glanced at Ellie. It was the night before Luz Ramirez's body had been found.

"Had you gone out with her before?"

"No. This was going to be the first time. I . . . I thought she was cute, okay? And we used to talk and stuff when I got my hair cut. And some of my friends, they dared me to ask her out, so I did."

"They dared you, huh?" Ellie asked, an edge in her voice that Quinn had never heard before.

"Yeah," he said. "It was stupid. I didn't think she'd say yes. But she did."

Quinn was about to ask him what time they were supposed to meet when Ellie jumped in again, "What else did they dare you to do?" Her voice was cold, and her face, when Quinn looked over to see what was going on, belonged to someone else. He had seen her play good cop and clueless cop, but he'd never seen her play mean cop. He hadn't thought she had it in her.

"What do you mean?" Jason Fowler

looked at Quinn. "What does she mean?"

"Did they dare you to bag her too? Is that what happened? Were you afraid you were going to lose your bet?"

"No. I . . . I don't know what you're talking about." He seemed confused.

"She didn't want to go along with it?" Ellie started again. Quinn had been impressed with her aggressive questioning, but now he wasn't sure that's what it was. Trancelike, she watched Fowler, then said, "What did she do to deserve it? Did she fight you, is that it?"

Quinn put a hand up. "That's enough," he said, glaring at her.

Jason Fowler turned to him. "No, I didn't even see her. I thought she just stood me up. I swear."

Quinn glanced over at Ellie. Her cheeks were pink and she was sitting forward in her seat as though she was going to strangle the kid. She started to talk and he held his hand up again. "Detective Lindquist," he warned. He didn't like to dress down a fellow detective in front of a witness, but he had the feeling she might completely lose control.

He turned back to the kid. "Is there anyone who can corroborate that?"

"My roommate. My roommate came into

355

the pizza place like an hour after I was supposed to meet her, and I walked home with him. He made fun of me the whole time, like I couldn't even get the shampoo girl, you know. I guess I couldn't. But that wasn't how I felt about her. She was really smart and she was different from most of the girls I know. She liked me because I'm a hard worker and serious and, I don't know, I don't know why I'm telling you this." He seemed so sincere and so scared that Quinn decided he could feel the case slipping away again. He'd be awfully surprised if it turned out that Jason Fowler had anything to do with the girl's death. But he had to check anyway. He got the roommate's name and cell phone number.

"What was that about?" he asked Ellie when they were in the car.

She sat miserably in the front seat, hunched over and staring out the window like a little kid. He wanted to grab her by the collar of her blouse and pull her up, tell her to sit up straight. "I thought he was lying," she said coldly.

"Then you're not as good at this as I thought you might be. But even if he was lying, where does freaking out on him get us? It just puts his back up, makes him more likely to keep lying."

She stared out the window. "Guys like that, they won't just come out and admit it. You have to make them."

He gaped at her. "Ellie, have you gone completely crazy? You know that's not how you get a confession. A guy who really had done something like that, you think he's going to admit it because *you* got in his face?"

"Because *I* got in his face? Or because *someone* got in his face?"

He hesitated. "Look, we all know that people respond differently to different personalities. In our line of work, we can't be sensitive about that kind of thing. There are qualities women cops have that men don't, and vice versa. Right?"

"If you say so." She had turned in on herself. She curled up in the passenger seat, as though she was trying to take up as little room as possible.

"Where do you want to go? I'm done for the day."

"My car." She nearly whispered it.

They drove back to headquarters in silence, and he found her car in the lot. She still had Ohio plates on it and a bumper sticker from the Ohio Police Benevolent Society.

He turned to her. "I just don't understand. What was going on back there? If there's

357

something you need to tell me, then tell me."

She hesitated for a minute, as though she was weighing something, then she went to open the door. "No," she said. "I'm sorry. I won't let it . . ."

Quinn's cell phone rang. When he looked down, he saw it was Steve Kirschner and he put a hand up. "Hang on," he told Ellie, answering the phone, "Yeah. It's Quinn."

"Look, I found out something for you, I think. That guy, Naki Haruhito. We investigated him after the 1979 theft. There was word on the street that he had some of the Egyptian pieces that were taken from the Hapner. But we were never able to nail him. Here's the thing, though. A couple years ago, we did get a good lead on this guy Martin McMaster. He's from Belfast and he was supposed to have carried out this other thing and he's had some connections with Haruhito that we know about. He had two known associates in Boston, though. This guy Michael Fox and Fox's brother-in-law, guy named Vinnie Keefe, they didn't come up in 1980, but some intelligence we've gotten recently says they were involved."

"Yeah. Wait a minute. Did you say Keefe?"

"Yeah. Like the security guard."

"Do you think — ?"

"I know," Kirschner said. "He's Denny Keefe's cousin. We checked it out."

"He was the inside guy. What are you doing?"

"I'm on my way to the museum. Meet me there."

Quinn put the phone back in the glove compartment. There was a long silence, and then Ellie said, "I'm really sorry. I just . . ."

But Quinn had turned the Honda around and was heading back toward the university. "Later," he said. "We'll talk about it later." He stopped at a red light, then thought better of it and went through, sounding his horn as he went.

"But I . . ."

"Later," he said. "Listen. Remember in the file, when it said that the police were already on their way because of the silent alarm? Well, I just thought of something. Keefe wasn't behind the desk when he was attacked. So how'd he set off the alarm? The button's back there, hidden away, right? So how'd he set it off?" He looked at her. "He must have been in on it. We're going to the museum."

THIRTY

Tad Moran put down the box and went over to the window, taking a moment to get himself together before he finished packing up Willem's desk. He'd known he was going to have to do it, but seeing Willem's things, neatly organized in his desk drawers, had been so much sadder than he'd thought it would be. And then he'd come across the spare pair of running shoes that Willem had always kept in the bottom drawer. Standing in front of the window, Tad held the shoes for a moment, feeling the weight of them, smelling the new shoe scent. Willem had hated to have anything on his shoes and he had kept the spare pair in case he stepped in a puddle or something.

He had been a scrupulous person, Willem. Well, about some things, anyway. His clothes had always been perfectly pressed. It was the thing that had struck Tad about him the first time he'd seen him, teaching a class on museum exhibition during Tad's first year of graduate school. Willem's blue shirt was as pristine at the end of the four-hour class as it was at the beginning.

Tad had wondered how Willem kept from going crazy when he was in Egypt, where everything you wore ended up covered in layers of dust and dirt. But Willem had been a different Willem there. It was like he had found a way of not caring about the same things he cared about at home. In Egypt, Willem was looser, younger, more human. He stayed up late drinking on digs, he told stories and jokes and wrapped everyone up in his charismatic charm. He was warmer, more passionate, as though the hot desert sun did something to his personality.

It had been in Egypt that Tad had known he was in love, and it had been as much a surprise to discover that he was capable of this love as to realize that his love was for a man. It wasn't that he had never suspected this of himself, but in his twenty-three years he had kept it so far beneath the surface of his reality that it had felt genuinely shocking to realize the truth about himself. He had never imagined that he could fall so hard for someone who did not love him in return.

Nothing had happened on that first trip.

It was only later, when it suited Willem's purposes. That had always been the way. It had always been about Willem's purposes, Willem's needs, he saw now. If he had fooled himself into thinking that if his love was not returned, perhaps his affection was, he saw now that he had been wrong. Still, he couldn't fault Willem for deceiving him. Tad had allowed himself to be deceived for a long time. And then, at some point, he had accepted that what happened once a year and then once every three years or less, might never happen again, and it had been a strange kind of relief, not to wonder anymore, to be left only with his love, which burned as bright and as inevitable as the sun.

He thought of Egypt now, of that brutal sun and the way the endless sand had always smelled to him of dry leaves, old wood. It had been a long time since he had been over, and suddenly, for the first time, he saw what Willem's death meant. He was free. He had his Ph.D. He could get a teaching job now, move somewhere else. He was no longer chained to the museum.

But then he remembered his mother. How could he have forgotten her? She wouldn't want to move somewhere else, and he had the house to care for. When a lawyer had called him a couple of days after Willem's death and asked to speak to him, Tad had almost dared to hope that he'd been left something in the will. But as it turned out, Willem's considerable assets had been left to his estranged brother. Tad had been left a small limestone statue of a falcon that Willem had kept on his bookcase at home. It had held no particular significance and Tad couldn't begin to imagine why Willem had left it to him. It had been the final insult, really, the impersonal little piece of antiquity.

He turned the shoes over in his hands. He would give them to the Salvation Army, he decided, putting them aside. And then, turning away from the late-afternoon sun streaming in the window, he went back to work.

THIRTY-ONE

Sweeney drove out to Greenfield on Tuesday. She'd always liked this part of northern Massachusetts, with the little mill towns close up against the Vermont border, the way the landscape seemed to open up here and offer views beyond the green fields and pine forests, and as she drove, she reflected that while she was grateful for the Jetta's competence, she was still nostalgic for her old Rabbit's quirky charm. If she'd been driving the Rabbit, she knew, she'd be nervous the whole time about it breaking down, but this was the first adventure she'd been on without it and she allowed herself to feel a little sad.

After speaking to Susan Esterhaus, she wasn't sure she knew any more about Karen Philips than she had known before, and though she suspected that there was more to the apparent disappearance of the falcon collar than she yet knew, she didn't have any idea how to go about learning what it was.

All she knew was that she had talked to Willem about her suspicions and now Willem was dead. And so she had decided to see what she could learn about Karen in the place of her birth. Ever since she had learned about Jeanne's affair with Trevor Ferigni, Sweeney hadn't wanted to be in the museum. She wasn't sure if it was the memory of Trevor's desperate face, or the way Jeanne had broken down afterward, but she welcomed the chance to get far away from the university and out of the city heat.

The downtown consisted of a row of little gift shops and cafés, though she suspected they existed to serve the tourist population since she had seen a strip of big-box stores and large supermarkets on her way into town. She stopped at the first restaurant she came to, an authentically vintage little diner with a sign that read, BREAKFAST ALL DAY. Sweeney, who loved breakfast, checked her watch and decided that three P.M. wasn't too late for Belgian waffles. When the teenage waitress brought her food, Sweeney, not expecting much, said, "I'm in town looking for the Philips family. Do you know where I might find them?"

"There are a couple of Philipses in town.

Do you mean Harold or Charlie?" The girl's large green eyes were open, helpful.

"I don't know, actually," Sweeney said. "I'm looking for the parents of Karen Philips. She died when she was quite young, probably before you were even born, but I'm hoping I can talk to her parents."

The girl didn't bat an eye. "Oh, it's Harold you want. You're out of luck, then. They're both dead." Sweeney resisted an urge to ask her why she had offered Harold as an option if he was no longer around.

"Oh. Well, thanks anyway," she said.

She started on her waffles, trying not to feel too disappointed. She hadn't called ahead, so she wasn't sure why she should have felt any certainty about finding Karen Philips's family. She'd finish eating, then maybe ask around a bit. See if she could find anything.

She was up at the front counter paying for her meal when the waitress with the remarkable eyes came out from the kitchen and said, a little furtively, "You know, I was just thinking. There's Diana. She lives out on the County Road. You can't miss it, it's a big yellow farmhouse. Says Sturgeon on the mailbox."

"Oh, thank you," Sweeney said, adding to

her tip by a dollar. "Was she a friend of Karen's?"

The waitress looked at Sweeney like she was an idiot. "No, she's Karen's sister. That's the house where Karen grew up."

County Road wound its way out of town up a gently rising hill. At first the houses were built quite close together, a series of colonials and saltboxes interspersed with trailers. As she kept going, the houses were farther apart and there were more old barns and farmhouses. Finally she saw up ahead a large yellow house with a couple of barns around it and a large black mailbox that said STURGEON. Sweeney pulled in, and two graying black Labs came rushing out to meet her car, barking ferociously but wagging their tails. When she got out of the car, she looked up to find a large woman with short gray hair coming out of the house. She was wearing a long flowered skirt, ruffled at the bottom like a can-can dancer's petticoats.

"I'm so sorry to bother you," Sweeney started. "But I was hoping to talk to you about your sister."

"About Karen? Whatever for?" Diana Sturgeon didn't seem angry, just curious.

Sweeney nodded. She had come up with

a story in the car, one that wasn't strictly a lie if it came to it. "I teach at the university and I've gotten very interested in coeducation. I'm interested in stories of women at the university at various points in history. I'm sorry, my name's Sweeney St. George." She smiled in what she hoped was a reassuring way.

Diana Sturgeon smiled back, her face open and trusting in a way that made Sweeney feel just a little bit guilty. "I'm happy to talk about Karen," she said. "Why don't you come in where it's cool."

Sweeney followed her into the house, which was indeed cool and smelled of stones and wet dog. It was shabby and comfortable, with a number of colorful quilts hanging on the walls and draped over the couch and chairs.

"Are these yours?" The quilts filled the room with color, red and blue and yellow calicoes and ginghams.

"It's my hobby. I make them for friends and sell them at a few of the craft fairs." Without asking if Sweeney wanted it, she handed her a glass of ice water. Sweeney gulped it gratefully.

"Well, they're beautiful."

"So what did you want to know?" Diana asked. "It's funny, I was thinking about her today. It'll be the anniversary of her death in March."

Sweeney decided to go right for the meat of it. "It seems like she must have been under pressure of some kind, to do what she did. I talked to a woman who knew her, and she said that Karen seemed depressed in the months leading up to her suicide."

Sweeney decided that Diana Sturgeon was perhaps the most peaceful person she had ever met. She considered Sweeney placidly. "I'm not entirely convinced that it was suicide, to tell you the truth. We never were, Mom and Dad and me."

Sweeney sat up in her chair. "What do you mean?"

"It's so hard to explain. Maybe everyone feels like this when a family member commits suicide, but it just wasn't like her. I can't explain it any other way. It wasn't like her."

"Did you ever say anything, to the police?"

"No. I didn't have anything to go on, just what I knew about Karen, and whatever had happened, we knew it wasn't going to bring her back. It wasn't like we were Catholic or anything. I mean, suicide, if that's what it was, doesn't particularly bother me. I respect someone's right to choose how she goes out of this world. So I didn't feel like I had to set the record straight. If the record wasn't straight to begin with, that is." She smiled. "I didn't *know.* I just thought. I'm a big believer in intuition, in feeling things. But the legal system isn't. So there you go."

"What do you think happened to her?"

"I have no idea. Obviously it wasn't an accident, so it would have to be homicide. The reasons for homicide are fairly pedestrian, aren't they? Greed, jealousy, that kind of thing."

Sweeney wasn't quite sure what to do in the face of such matter-of-factness. "So you don't think she was under any kind of pressure?"

"Oh, I didn't say that. She was working very hard because she was hoping to go to graduate school for art history. She was worried about how she was going to pay for it. And I know her responsibilities at the museum were weighing on her mind and she hadn't been sleeping or eating well, because of the work, I suppose. Even when she was younger, Karen would have these periods where she would just get really stressed about things, a little depressed, I guess."

"When was the last time you saw her?"

"She came home for Christmas that year. I was still in high school and I remember that I was so happy to see her and then she slept for almost all of Christmas Eve. I remember that like it was yesterday. I was asleep when she arrived home, and the next morning I waited and waited and waited for her to get up. We had always been close, you see, and when she went away to college, I was absolutely destitute. I had been fantasizing for months about how she would come home and I would tell her about my first boyfriend." She laughed. "I don't even remember his last name now, but at the time it seemed so very important. When she finally woke up, she took a shower and went straight over to her best friend's house. I was so mad. I cried in my room for hours." She smiled. "You feel things so deeply at that age."

"Did she ever talk to you about what she was going through?"

"A little. She came to my room the day after Christmas and we talked for a long time, but it was mostly me telling her about my life. I think my mother had told Karen how upset I was and she was trying to make it up to me. She was good like that.

"I asked her if she had a boyfriend at college and I remember she told me that she didn't trust men anymore and that the last thing she wanted or needed was a boyfriend.

It surprised me, because Karen had always liked boys and usually had a couple she was interested in at any one time."

"Do you think she could have been depressed about a guy? That makes it sound like someone broke her heart."

"Yeah, except she was more angry than depressed about it. Those can be the same things, I know, but . . . I had the sense that her exhaustion was more about how much work she had to do. Our family wasn't . . . well, we weren't particularly academic. Karen's going to the university was a big deal, and I think she felt a lot of pressure to succeed there."

"Did she say that?"

Diana considered. "She was working on her thesis about Egyptian jewelry. And she had all these books with her that she was studying the whole time she was home. I remember being so resentful. I wasn't much of a student and I didn't understand."

"Do you know what she was studying?"

"Something about the tombs at Darfur or Darshur."

"Dahshur?"

"That's right. I guess there were these princesses buried there, and there was some wonderful jewelry found near their tombs. Karen had seen it when she was in Cairo that summer before her death. She tried to explain to us what it was that made these particular necklaces so special. They were pretty, but they didn't seem so, I don't know, *important* to me. But she said that they were the most beautiful things made in Egypt at the time. She said people had lost their lives digging for just this kind of treasure in the Egyptian desert. She said that things like the necklaces made people do bad things, dishonest things. I almost had the feeling she thought there was a kind of curse on the jewelry, but maybe I was imagining it."

"Did Karen talk to you about the robbery at the museum, that fall before she died?"

"She didn't want to talk much about it. We knew that she'd been tied up, but she seemed, I don't know, like she'd just blocked the whole thing out. It wasn't that important to her."

"So that wasn't why she was so upset?"

"I didn't think so at the time."

The dogs started barking madly, running to the window to look out at the road. "That's Joe, my husband," Diana said, going to the window. "We've been married for twenty years this Christmas." She turned to smile at Sweeney. "I still get fluttery when I hear his car in the driveway."

A tall, bearded man carrying a brown paper grocery bag under each arm came in through the front door, covered in the barking dogs. "Hi, darling," he said, looking quizzically at Sweeney. Diana introduced them, and Sweeney took that as her cue to say she needed to get going.

"Hey," she said. "I was just thinking. Maybe I could talk to Karen's best friend. The one who she went to see that last Christmas?"

"Gerry? I guess so. She lives just up the road." Diana gave her directions, and she and Joe walked Sweeney out to her car. Sweeney thanked her again.

"No problem. If there's anything else, just let me know."

As Sweeney pulled out of the driveway, she looked back to see the two of them standing there, arm in arm, the two bodies leaning toward each other and mirroring the trees leaning toward each other in the late-summer light.

Gerry Tiswell lived only a few houses up the road, and when Sweeney pulled into the driveway of the light blue Cape, a woman who had been sitting in a folding chair on the front lawn stood up to wave. Sweeney waved back, feeling the oppressive heat of the early evening easing just a little, the sun hanging low on the horizon.

"Are you Gerry Tiswell?" she called out, walking toward the porch.

"I am." She was a large woman, carrying a lot of weight on her small frame, with dark curly hair and very blue eyes. Sweeney introduced herself and explained what she wanted to know.

"Do you remember her coming home that Christmas?"

"Of course I do. It was the last time I saw her. So I remember perfectly."

"How was she? How did she seem to you?"

"She was different. She'd been different since going away to school in the first place, but it hadn't affected our friendship. Even though she was so smart and she was doing so well and had all these new friends with money and nice cars and all that, she was still the same. But that last Christmas, I felt like she didn't have time for me. She was so preoccupied with this project she was doing, this thing with a gold necklace, and she didn't want to talk about any of the things that we always talked about, boys, or what we were going to do with our lives." Gerry Tiswell paused. "That was why it hit me so hard, her killing herself. Because we didn't get along the last time I saw her." She choked on the words, turning her face away, and Sweeney let her get her composure back. When her eyes met Sweeney's again, they were full of tears. "I'm sorry. I try not to think about her too much."

"You said you usually talked about boys, things like that. Did she have a boyfriend?"

"No way. She told me that she hated all men and didn't ever want to date anyone again as long as she lived. She was going to just concentrate on her work and live like a nun. That's what she said. Like a nun. She said that men were — what was the word she used? — 'plunderers' and that they took things from people. She told me about how Egypt had lost all of its treasures due to 'old white men' stealing them. She had gotten really radical about it. She said she was rethinking her whole career choice because of what she'd learned about how people got these treasures from Egypt, how they just stole them and took them back to England or whatever."

"It sounds like someone had broken her heart."

"If he did, she didn't tell me." Gerry Tiswell's voice sounded impatient now, and Sweeney knew she'd outstayed her welcome.

She thanked her for her time and stood to go.

"The project she was doing," Sweeney said, almost as an afterthought. "Did she talk about that?"

"Yeah. She said there was a piece of jewelry at the museum that shouldn't have been there, that had been taken out of Egypt illegally. And she was going to prove it."

By now, it was what Sweeney had been expecting. "Did she talk about anyone else at the museum, anyone who might also have known about the jewelry?"

"No."

Sweeney let the silence surround them for a few minutes, and then she asked Gerry, "You said you were upset because you hadn't gotten along the last time you'd seen her. But were you surprised she killed herself?"

"It sounds weird, but not really. I can't explain it, but she just wasn't herself. It was like someone else had taken over her body and she looked the same and everything, but it wasn't her. She wrote this weird poetry. You should see if Diana has any of it anymore. She might have some of her research too." A group of boys on dirt bikes rode along the road, hollering at each other, and Sweeney and Gerry watched them until they were out of sight.

Sweeney said thank you and turned toward her car.

"It's funny," Gerry said. "I don't think I ever got over Karen's death. I don't know why, but it seems like nothing really worked out for me ever since then. You know what I mean?"

Sweeney nodded, wanting to get away from the sadness that seemed to surround Gerry Tiswell. "Take care," she said.

Diana didn't seem surprised to see Sweeney again. She led her up the narrow flight of stairs to the second floor and opened the door to a staircase leading to the attic. The heat assaulted them as they gained the stairs, filling Sweeney's nose and lungs with a warm mustiness.

"I know my parents saved some of Karen's things," she said, pulling the string on a bare lightbulb hanging from the rafters. "But I don't know about her poetry. My mother turned her room into a sewing room, and I think they gave most of her clothes and books to the Salvation Army. But I feel like I remember some of the papers and notebooks and posters and things from her room at school being up here. I had to go with one of my aunts and help pack up her room at school. My parents couldn't face it. And

I think those boxes just went right up in the attic."

Sweeney felt her spirits rise. Could her luck really be that good?

They both looked around at the piles and piles of boxes, lying in corners of the large space, in deep shadow. It was stifling hot and Sweeney could feel her shirt slowly being soaked with perspiration. Diana looked a little disturbed. "Well," she said. "I'm not sure where it would be, but let me just . . ." She started with the pile that was right in front of them, clearing a thick layer of dust off the top and opening the box. "That's books. Not Karen's, though." She closed it and tried another. "Hmmm. This seems to be baby clothes." She tried a few more as Sweeney looked on awkwardly, not sure if she should offer to help.

Having finished with the pile, she stood up and looked around. "The problem is, I'm not sure where it would be." She wiped her forehead. "God, it must be one hundred degrees up here."

"Can I help by looking in those over there?" Sweeney offered, pointing to a pile of cardboard boxes in the opposite corner.

"Sure. It should say 'Karen' on it. I remember marking it with a pen."

They searched for a half hour but came

up with nothing, and when Diana said that she was feeling a little faint, Sweeney knew it was her cue to say, "It seems like maybe it's going to be too hard to find it."

"Let me just look in one more place."

Seeing the sweat dripping down Diana's face, Sweeney felt suddenly guilty and said, "I want to tell you something. I'm not really doing a paper about women at the university. I'm an art historian. I was curating an exhibition, and on the opening night a few weeks ago, someone was murdered at the Hapner Museum. It was during a robbery and, well, I've been looking into the 1979 robbery and I'm wondering if Karen knew more about it than she told the police. Maybe that was the reason she killed herself, or she was killed because she knew something that someone didn't want revealed. I'm sorry. I just thought it might be easier to find out about her if I didn't tell you what I really thought about her death."

Diana Sturgeon smiled at her. "I figured you were hiding something. But I got a good feeling from you so I was willing to let it go." She stood for a moment, looking around at the boxes. "Wait a second. I feel like such an idiot. I think I know where it is. Follow me."

They went back down the stairs and Diana led the way into a small bedroom tucked under the eaves. When she turned on one of the old-fashioned bedside lamps, Sweeney could see the pink wallpaper, with its pattern of vines and roses.

"I don't know why I didn't think of it," she said. "This was Karen's room. I think my mother put the box in her closet." She opened the narrow closet door and came out with a cardboard box.

"This is it," she said, opening it and taking out a high school yearbook. "I'll leave you to go through it. I'll be getting dinner ready downstairs. Let me know if you need anything."

On top of the items piled in the box was a yellow scarf, hand-knit by a beginning knitter by the look of it. The yellow was a particularly unattractive shade, but it must have had sentimental value to have been saved. Underneath the scarf was a stack of photographs. They mostly showed Karen clowning around with some teenage girls. One of the girls in a number of the pictures was clearly a younger Gerry Tiswell. But they all seemed to have been taken in Greenfield. There weren't any from the university.

There was a stack of letters next, the envelopes held together with a rubber band,

and it took Sweeney a long time to go through them, removing each letter from its envelope and scanning it for any reference to the university or the museum. Again, most of the letters seemed to be artifacts of Karen's childhood and adolescence. There were girlish notes to friends, gossiping about other girls, and boys they liked, and later, letters from friends about what they had done over the summer. There was one from Gerry Tiswell describing her summer visit to her grandparents' house in Ohio, and then a few during Karen's freshman year at college describing her friends' own experiences in college. But, of course, there wasn't anything to indicate what was going on with Karen, save a few vague references to whether a party had ended up being fun or if a boy Karen was interested in had asked her out. In a manila envelope, she found a copy of the Women's Arts Collective's magazine, with a poem by Karen on page 14.

Lord Carnarvon

Who owns these old things
Dug up, the faces golden beneath the
   years of earth?
Who owns these princesses, imprisoned

in coffins and tombs?
They lie waiting in this dark room, waiting
    for him to come discover them, steal
    them, imprison them, take their bodies
    for his own.
These dark hallways hold all manner of
    sin. He cares about possession. He
    knows only how to own.
He makes of her a mummy, her heart
    inside a jar.
He takes her blood, her bones, her jaw.
He locks her in a tomb.
When the other men discover her, she's a
    dusty relic, just a box of bones.

Sweeney read the poem again. There was
something about it that she liked. The logic
was a little hard to pin down, but she
thought that Karen was writing about the
mummies discovered by adventurers like
Carnarvon. She was identifying with the
mummies, their organs gone, locked in
tombs. Her friends were right. She must
have been depressed to write a poem like
that. There was a kind of violence to it that
Sweeney couldn't quite get out of her mind,
even after she'd turned to the other items in
the box.

She browsed through postcards and a few
paperback novels and then found a thin

sketchbook at the bottom of the box, Karen's name on the front.

The first few sketches in the book were of a sleeping cat, followed by a nicely drawn hand and a portrait of a woman. They weren't bad, the angles of the hand nicely shaded and the woman — who Sweeney assumed must have been Diana and Karen's mother from their resemblance to her — well proportioned and pretty.

But it was the final few sketches that made Sweeney stand up and reach for her car keys. They showed a nude man, looking over one shoulder, his back muscles well defined, a faraway look on his face.

Though she'd captured the basics of the man's anatomy, Karen hadn't been good enough to make the muscles look real, but she was good enough so that Sweeney could recognize the man's face.

It was a much younger Fred Kauffman.

Thirty-Two

"Tell me about Martin McMaster," Quinn told Denny Keefe. "Tell me how he convinced you to do it."

Denny Keefe sat silently in the interview room, his hands in front of him on the table, his shoulders slumped. "I don't know what you're talking about," he said. "I don't know who Martin McMaster is. I never met him."

"You didn't need to meet him. Your cousin Vinnie Keefe was the go-between. All you had to do was tell him when the staff meeting was and arrange with him the details of the theft. Then McMaster's men would carry it out."

"I told you. I have no idea what you're talking about. I haven't seen Vinnie in years. We're not a close family. I got beat up, for Christ's sake. They almost killed me. You can't really think I was in on it, can you?" He was pleading with him, and for a moment Quinn wondered whether he'd gotten it wrong, but then he saw something in Keefe's eyes that made him see what must have happened.

"You did get beat up. I think the plan was that you would get beat up, so it would look authentic. It worked pretty well. Nobody suspected you because of how badly you got beat up. I don't think that part of it was according to plan. Not your plan, anyway. I think that either the guys who were carrying out the burglary went overboard, trying to keep up the charade, or more likely, they wanted to scare you. I think they wanted you to know that they held your life in their hands and if you ever told anyone about your role in the theft, they would finish the job." As he said the words, he knew he was right.

But Keefe, his eyes scared now, kept up the charade. "I'm telling you. I was working, and the last thing I remember is someone behind me. I must have gone into the booth first and pressed the silent alarm. I just don't remember. That happens with head injuries, you know." He looked from Quinn to Ellie, willing them to believe him.

"Denny, if you tell us everything that happened, any judge you come before is going to know that you cooperated. Your role in this was pretty small. What happened? Did

Olga see something all those years ago? Did she know who carried out the theft? Did she tell Willem? Did Vinnie and McMaster's friends have to kill them in order to keep it quiet?"

Now he just looked confused. Quinn's warning bells went off. He'd been on sure footing. He knew he had. But now Keefe seemed genuinely bewildered. He regrouped. "Or did McMaster's guys come back for another try? Did you tell them about the opening? Did you tell them that it would be a good time to hit the museum?"

"What? No."

Quinn looked deeply into Keefe's tired gray eyes. There was something there. He knew it. But it wasn't time yet. They would wait. He'd learned this over the years. Time was the best antidote to untruths. People eventually grew tired of lying. It was exhausting. He'd seen people kill themselves because they were so tired of lying. Hardened criminals had walked into headquarters and turned themselves in because they just couldn't stand to keep it up anymore. It was hard to live with a lie, he told himself. Eventually Denny Keefe would break down.

"Well, I've got lots of time," he told Keefe, standing up and nodding to Ellie. "I've got a lot of homework to do, actually. In fact, we have all the time in the world."

"They found Hutchinson," she said once they were out in the hall. "He says he left Keane at five-thirty or so. He was in town on business and Keane wanted to talk to him, to reassure him, Hutchinson says, that they were taking steps to make the museum even more secure in light of the attempted theft. They chatted. Hutchinson says he seemed as usual.

"Where was he? Why couldn't we get hold of him?"

"He and his wife decided to go up to their house in Westchester County. Their 'country house,' he called it." She raised her eyebrows. "La-di-da. He said they decided on the spur of the moment and they keep extra clothes up there, so they called the butler when they arrived."

"And the guys who interviewed him thought he was telling the truth?"

"I guess so. We could make him come up for questioning."

"I don't know. What do you think about Keefe in there?"

"He's lying. You can tell." She still looked miserable, and he knew they were going to have to talk about what had happened at Jason Fowler's apartment. But for now, he decided to pretend it had never happened.

"I think you're right. Well, it's true what I told him. We've got all the time in the world."

THIRTY-THREE

It wasn't until she'd pulled up in front of Fred's house that Sweeney realized how stupid it was to confront him this way. He'd been having an affair with Karen. He'd probably killed her and staged her suicide. He wasn't going to be particularly happy when Sweeney told him she knew.

She turned off her car and got her cell phone out of her bag, dialing Quinn's number and listening to the phone ring a few times before his voice came on, saying, "This is Tim Quinn. Please leave a message or a page." She hesitated for a moment, then clicked off the phone and looked up at the house. Lacey had heard the car and was standing in the kitchen window, looking out to see who it was. She looked so perfectly normal standing there that Sweeney felt a sudden surge of confidence. What could happen with Lacey there? She would tell Fred what she'd discovered and tell him she would drive him to turn himself in. If he got violent, she and Lacey together should be able to subdue him. Lacey could call the police. She got out of the car and, holding the sketchbook under one arm, she rang the doorbell. Lacey answered almost immediately.

"Sweeney? I was wondering who that was? Come on in." Sweeney stepped into the warm house, feeling again the utter normality of it. Lacey had brightly colored sweaters piled up on the table in the dining room and Sweeney could smell chicken roasting. "Do you want a glass of wine? I was just pouring for us."

"No, thanks. I was hoping I could talk to Fred."

Lacey studied her. There was something a little cold, a little suspicious in her eyes. "Sure. He's in his study. You sure you don't want anything?"

"No. I'm fine, Lacey. Thank you."

"Okay." There it was again. Her eyes narrowed a little and she said, "You know where he is, right? Down the hall on the right?"

"Yeah. I'll find it. Thanks." Sweeney went down the hall to Fred's study. He was sitting at his desk, reading, and when he looked up at her, she could see how tired he was, and how scared.

"Sweeney. Hi. What are you doing here?"

"Hi." She left the door open and stood in front of him, the sketchbook under her arm, and said, "I'm sorry, Fred. I know. I know what you did."

"What do you mean?" But he was bluffing. She could tell.

"Come on, Fred. I have proof."

He put his head in his hands, then pushed the papers aside, and when he looked up at her, she could see he had tears in his eyes.

"I knew it," he said. "I knew someone was going to find out. It's been awful the last few weeks. I can't sleep. I haven't been eating. I feel like I might jump out of my skin any minute. What are you going to do about it?"

"Does Lacey know?"

"I don't think so," Fred said. "Though she knows that something's wrong. She's been patient with me, but she knows something's going on."

"Fred?" Sweeney started and turned to find Lacey standing in the doorway, holding a knife. She'd been cooking. It made sense she'd have a knife, but something about the way she stood there made Sweeney nervous.

"Lacey, it's okay," Fred said. "We need to talk about something."

"What is that?" Lacey asked Sweeney. "Did you do that?" She gestured toward the sketchbook. One of the sketches of Fred was turned to the outside.

Sweeney looked at Fred, waiting for him to say something. But instead of explaining to Lacey about Karen and the sketch, Fred just looked confused. Then he stood up and came over to Sweeney, taking the sketchbook from her and looking through the sketches.

Sweeney saw confusion flash across his face. "What are these?"

"It's one of the sketches that Karen did of you," Sweeney said. "I know you were having an affair with her and I know that you killed her when she threatened to tell the university that you'd slept with a student. You had to make it look like suicide, didn't you?"

"What?" He was incredulous, staring at her.

"What is she talking about, Fred?" Lacey had taken the sketchbook from him and was looking through the pages.

Sweeney went on. "I think Olga and Willem must have found out about it somehow, and they must have also threatened to tell. Maybe you'd almost forgotten about it, maybe you'd hoped it would just go away.

Everyone had believed that she'd killed herself. No one looked too deeply into what she had been doing just before she died, no one looked into her relationships."

"Sweeney." Fred was still standing. "I have no idea what you're talking about. I didn't kill anyone." He took the book from Lacey and looked through it again, as though he was trying to figure out where he'd seen them before. "Oh, my God," he said finally. "Oh, my God." And then he started to laugh.

"I was a poor struggling grad student," he said. "And when one of my friends who was teaching studio art asked if I wanted to come in and pose for his life drawing class for a hundred bucks, I agreed. I dare say I wasn't the hunkiest model they ever had, but they seemed fairly happy with my work."

"So Karen must have taken the life drawing class," Sweeney said.

"I guess so. I think I remember her being in it. It's so long ago now."

Lacey was standing next to him, still looking at the sketches of her husband as a young man.

"Fred," Sweeney said, "I have to ask you. What did you think I was talking about?"

He sat down and took Lacey's hand in

his, caressing it and then rubbing it against his face. "Oh, love," he said, looking up at her. "I told you. It's something bad."

"What is it?" Sweeney watched the look that passed between them, not sure exactly what it represented.

Lacey put her hands on his shoulders, and after a moment she said firmly, "What? Tell me. I told you. Anything." Sweeney didn't know what she was talking about, but she watched Fred reach up to encircle her wrist with his fingers.

"I was in graduate school," he started. "I was working on my thesis on Potter. We had become friends in a way; he'd allowed me a lot of access, a lot of time. He knew about my thesis, but I went to see him one afternoon and told him I wanted to write his biography. We had spent a lot of time together and I think he had come to trust me, but he was very unwell at this point and his children were always around, waiting for him to die so they could get their hands on the estate. He had been a terrible father, and they all thought they were owed that at least.

"Anyway, I was telling him about how I wanted to write his biography, and he pointed to a cabinet in the corner of the room and said that I could have his journals.

I hadn't even known he kept journals, and I went over and looked and there were about fifty of them. He'd been writing since he was a kid. I'm sure you can imagine, I almost fainted. It was my book, right there. And I would be the only one to have it. It was . . . Well, Sweeney, you can imagine what it was like. So few biographers have access to anything like these journals. And he said I could have them. I promise you that. He told me they would be mine after he died. Well, he died a few weeks later. I got the call from one of his nurses who knew how close we'd become. I arrived before any of the children did, and the nurse told me that his oldest son, Garrison, hadn't even expressed sorrow about his father's death. He'd just told her and the housekeeper not to let any of his siblings remove anything from the house.

"A couple of days later, I tried to explain to one of his daughters about how I wanted to write his biography and how he had promised me the journals, but she didn't know about them and she just became very angry and said I had no right to poke around in her family's business. I realized that there was no way they were going to honor their father's word, so I said goodbye and went around to his studio and took them. I took all the journals. I want you to understand that. I knew what I was doing and I took them.

"Later, I got a call from one of his children, asking if I had taken anything, and I said that he'd given me a few notebooks but that was all. I thought I'd gotten away with it, but a couple of weeks ago, I got a letter from Garrison. He saw something about my book, about how it included information from Jennings's journals. He thought the journals had been lost, but he realized I'd taken them, and he threatened to call my publisher."

He put his head in his hands. "Garrison's going to make it public. The thing is, it's going to taint everything in the book. The book is good, I know it is. But because of the publicity about the journals, it's going to be ridiculed. I'm going to lose my job. Oh, honey." He reached up for Lacey, who put her arms around him. "I think he'd contacted Willem. Just before he was killed, Willem said he wanted to see me. He wanted to tell me something."

"Fred," Sweeney said, "what if you just explained to your publisher? As you say, you had a verbal agreement with Jennings. That's got to count for something."

"I don't know," Fred said. "It's such a

mess. I've been so afraid to tell you, Lace."
He looked up at her. "I've been so afraid
someone was going to find out." He looked
up at Sweeney. "But I don't understand.
You think Karen Philips's death had something to do with Olga and Willem's deaths?"

"I don't know," Sweeney said. "That's the
problem. I just don't know."

It wasn't until she was almost home that
Sweeney remembered the dinner. It was
Tuesday night and she had promised Ian
that she would meet him and Peter and
Lillie at the restaurant at six-thirty. It was
now eight. If they hadn't already finished
dinner, they must be pretty close. And if
she showed up at the restaurant now, she
knew that there would be a scene and it
would ruin the meal for everyone. Better to
try to explain what had happened when Ian
got home. Besides, Ian and Peter had a lot
to talk about. Probably they'd rather be on
their own, anyway.

She pottered around the apartment, organizing bills and drinking wine against her
nervousness. By eleven, she'd had four
glasses and decided that maybe it would be
better if she was in bed when he came
home. She found a *New Yorker* to read, but
it was only a couple of minutes before her

eyes started to close and she fell asleep.

She woke up to the sound of the toilet flushing, and she sat up, the magazine falling to the floor. Ian came out of the bathroom, barely looking at her.

"Hi," she said sleepily. "I tried to wait up, but I was really tired. I'm so sorry about tonight. I went out to Greenfield and I thought that I'd be back in time. How was dinner?"

For a minute he didn't say anything, and she watched him undress with the sinking feeling that it was much worse than she had thought it was going to be.

He got into bed and rolled away from her. "It was humiliating, actually," he said. "Peter had been looking forward to meeting you. But I don't want to talk about it tonight. We'll talk tomorrow night." He said it sternly, as though she was a naughty child.

"I'm sorry." In the dark room, she listened to him breathing, knowing he was still awake, and she wanted to cry, to tell him that she loved him, that she wanted to make it up to him. But she found that she didn't have it in her, that all she could do was to close her eyes and go to sleep.

THIRTY-FOUR

When Sweeney woke up the next morning, her head aching from the wine, Ian was already gone. He'd pulled the covers up on his side of the bed as though he'd never even slept there.

She groaned and caught sight of the General, sitting on the chair by the window and watching her. "Do you hate me too?" she asked him. "Come over here and show me you don't hate me too." But the cat just stared at her, then turned and was gone through her bedroom window.

Sweeney rolled over and went back to sleep. When she woke up again, it was nearly three and she was bathed in sweat, the sheets stuck to her skin, the air in the bedroom so oppressive she could barely haul herself out of bed. She stripped the sheets, picked up her dirty clothes strewn around the room, and went to take a shower. When she got out, she cleaned the apartment and checked her e-mail, then took the *Boston Globe* with her out onto the fire escape.

The first thing she saw was the headline, "Museum Security Guard Questioned About 1979 Art Heist." She read it twice. According to the story, Denny Keefe had been brought in for questioning after police received information that one of the two men who may have carried out the armed robbery of the museum was Denny Keefe's cousin. So Denny was the inside man on the 1979 robbery.

Had he been the inside person on the attempted theft of the canopic chest too?

If he had, that meant that Karen's death and her work on the collar were unconnected to the robberies. But what would drive a brilliant young woman, with a promising career and a passionate interest in art, to end her life? Perhaps it was as simple as a bout of depression. Sweeney now understood that her father had killed himself because of an illness that he'd never named, one that plagued him all his life. If he'd been born a little later, perhaps he would have found treatment, perhaps he would have conquered it. She wasn't sure.

Sweeney, more than most people, had had moments in her life where things seemed utterly hopeless. After Colm's death, she had been so overwhelmed by grief that she hadn't much wanted to feel it, hadn't much wanted to be around to experience that bone-crushing sorrow. But she had never reached the point where she could have done anything about it.

She couldn't shake her feeling that it was Karen's work on the collar that had led her to that point. It seemed clear to Sweeney that the falcon collar had in fact come from one of the tombs of the princesses at Dahshur and that Karen had figured it out.

But how had it led to her death? Sweeney's instinct told her that it was something about the collar, some secret that lay buried deep as the tomb it had been found in. She wished she knew more about Egyptian antiquities. If Willem was still alive, she could ask him, but of course he wasn't.

But Tad was, she realized. Everyone forgot that Tad had also been an Egyptologist. Apparently he had been quite gifted. She could ask Tad. It was almost five. He would still be at the museum and she could ask him and get home in time to talk to Ian. Not that she was looking forward to that.

As she got her things together, she noticed there was a message on her cell phone and she checked it, hearing Quinn's voice telling her that he wanted to ask her about something. She called him back but got his voice mail. "It's Sweeney," she said. "I'm just heading over to the museum to ask Tad about something, but you can try me later."

As she left the apartment, she caught sight of Ian's trench coat hanging behind the door. It seemed so out of place there, so lonely. She ran the soft fabric between her fingers, the expensive Burberry's weight of it, memorizing the way it felt, then went out the door.

Thirty-Five

"Whatcha reading?" Ellie asked Quinn, coming up behind him at his desk.

"*The Rime of the Ancient Mariner.*" He was halfway through and he'd been eyeing the clock, trying to figure out when he was going to give Denny Keefe another try. He'd come in early, thinking he'd get all his reading for class that night done before the day started. He also needed to figure out what he was going to do about Ellie. She had been out of control while they were questioning that kid, and he needed to find out why. He needed to find out if it was going to happen again.

" 'Water, water everywhere and not a drop to drink!" she announced dramatically.

"You read it?"

"Yeah, of course. I like to read." She stood awkwardly over him, as though she wanted to say something.

"You okay?" he asked finally.

"I'm okay." Her whole expression fell, her eyes full of regret and pain, and he wanted to scream at her, to tell her to control her emotions better, to keep hold of herself and not let everything show on her face. She was never going to be a cop if she couldn't do that at least. "I wanted to talk to you about that, about what happened at that kid's place."

Quinn looked up at the clock. It was almost nine. "Let's talk later. I want to get to him before he's too awake." She hesitated. "The lawyer's here. So come on."

He had Keefe brought into the interview room, and he gave him a casual glance. "Hey there," he said. "How are you?" The lawyer sat next to him at the table. With his new suit and shaggy hair, he looked even younger than Ellie.

Denny Keefe looked up, tried to seem nonchalant too, and shrugged his shoulders. "Okay," he said. But Quinn could tell he was scared.

"Anything you want to tell me?"

Keefe whispered something to his lawyer, then looked up at Quinn. "Nope." His eyes went up to the ceiling, then down to the table. His hands were shaking. He was getting close, Quinn knew it.

"Okay. You don't mind if I just sit here

and drink my coffee, do you?"

Denny Keefe shook his head. "Okay, good." Quinn had brought his book in and he read and hummed a little tune, waiting for Keefe to break. Ellie had a magazine and he gave her a glance to tell her she should read too. He took a piece of paper out of his pocket and made some notes on it. Ellie hummed a little. It was a nice touch. The lawyer looked annoyed. All the time, Quinn could feel Denny Keefe getting closer.

Still, he was completely taken aback when he finally looked up to see him sitting there with tears running down his cheeks. The lawyer looked just as surprised. "My client needs to take a break," he said, pushing a Kleenex over to Keefe, who ignored it.

"No. I want to tell. You said it just like it happened," he choked out. "They said they was just going to rough me up a little, just give me a black eye, something obvious so it would be believable. But they didn't do that. They called me a piece of shit. They yelled at me. They started kicking me. I remember, lying on the ground while they kicked me, and I screamed that I didn't want them to kill me. They did their job well. I wasn't going to say a word. They had me scared shitless. All these years, I've been waiting for those guys to come back and finish the job."

Quinn sat back. "Okay," he said. "Tell me how they came up with the idea."

"I was telling the truth. My cousin Vinnie and me weren't very close. I hardly ever saw him. But one day he came by my house and said he wanted to talk to me. He said he'd heard from our grandma that I was working at the museum. And he said he had some friends who were very interested in that information. It wouldn't cost me much, he said, just the kind of stuff that you dropped to people sometimes at a barbecue. He said since I was the security guard, I would know when people came and went, how the security system worked, that kind of thing. All I had to do was tell them some of this stuff and they would give me a lot of money. It was more money than I make in a year of working, two years. I had a lot of bills, a mortgage that stretched me right to the limit, a couple of kids and another on the way. I knew what they were talking about. I knew that they were going to take something. But the way I thought about it was that the insurance was going to pay for it, anyway. I knew about the insurance guys. They came and asked me questions about our security procedures, about how many times I walk around the museum, stuff like that, and I remember that I asked one of the other guards what would happen if someone took something from the museum, and he said that the insurance would just pay them, sometimes more money than the thing was even worth.

"That's when I decided. I figured out a day when I was on duty and there was a staff meeting. I figured that was the best way. No one would be around, there wouldn't be a lot of visitors. It made sense to do it that way. I knew who they were when they came in. There was something about them, even if they were dressed in business suits. I nodded at them and they walked around the museum. The plan was that they would hit the silent alarm, just before they left. I showed them where it was. But first they came up behind me and let me have it. That was that. It took me eight months to recover. I still have pain in my leg and I have a nightmare about it almost every night. What's going to happen to me?"

"We'll be asking for a plea," the lawyer said hurriedly, trying to make the best of it. "Mr. Keefe is cooperating fully."

"We'll have to see," Quinn said truthfully. "The FBI'll get involved now. If you're will-ing to testify about McMaster's involvement, you may be able to cut a deal for no jail time. If you can help locate the stolen works of art, things may even be better for you."

"He'll kill me."

"There's witness protection."

"Oh, hell. That's no kind of life." Keefe slumped even farther down in his seat and Quinn felt a pang of pity. But then he remembered Olga and Willem.

"What about the murders at the museum? You have anything to do with that?"

"The . . . What? No way. When Olga was killed I thought maybe it was McMaster's guys again. Sometimes, after I got better and came back to work, the way she looked at me sometimes, it was like she knew. I'm serious. I wouldn't put it past them."

Quinn stood up, ready to go. He didn't think there was anything in that. How would Olga have gotten in touch with McMaster? "Do you remember a girl who worked at the museum, back around the time of the theft? Karen Philips?"

"Uh-uh." He shook his head. "A lot of students have worked here over the years. I can't remember much about any of them."

"She was tied up during the robbery."

A horrified look came over Keefe's face. "I swear to God I didn't know she was going to be down there. They were all supposed to be up at the staff meeting. When I heard that there was a little girl down there, I almost told them. They didn't hurt her, though. They didn't hurt her like they hurt me."

Quinn stood up. "Okay," he said. "The FBI is going to have to take over now." And as he walked out of the room, he turned to look at Denny Keefe. "I'm sorry," he said, not sure why he'd said it.

It was only as he walked out of the room that he realized Denny Keefe reminded him of his father. How had he not seen it? One of his mother's cousins, visiting from Ireland and a real space shot, had once told him that she saw people as colors. Quinn for example, she'd said, was a combination of blue and red. Now he thought he knew what she meant. There had been a grayness about his da, a dark pit of sadness the color of smoke.

And when he looked at Denny Keefe, he saw the same bottomless grayness, the sense that his soul had died a long time ago, even if his body kept on going.

THIRTY-SIX

When she didn't find Tad in his office, Sweeney tried the museum. But he wasn't anywhere to be found, and finally she decided to stop by Harriet's desk before assuming that she'd missed him.

"Have you seen Tad?" she asked Harriet, who was tapping away at her computer with a manic intensity.

"He's in storage," Harriet said, then corrected herself. "He's in the storage *area.*"

"Thanks. I'm just going to go in and see if I can find him."

"You want a key?"

"Well, you could just let me in."

"Technically, anyone who wants to go into the storage area needs to sign out a key. That way, we know who's been in there."

"Everyone? Even Willem and Tad?"

Harriet nodded.

"Fine. I'll sign out a key." Sweeney signed Harriet's paper and took the passkey from her. She waved it in front of the door, punched in her password, and walked into the main storage room. It was cool in here and she stood for a minute, enjoying the feel of the temperature-and humidity-controlled air on her skin.

"Tad?" she called out. "Are you here?"

There was nothing but silence in the huge room. Against one wall, she could see baskets piled between two of the mobile storage units. On one row of shelves was a series of Roman busts. The shelves were filled with beautiful things.

"Tad?" she called out again. It was a moment before she heard his footsteps. "Where are you?" There was something slightly eerie about him not talking to her when she knew that he was there. "It's Sweeney. I just wanted to ask you something."

But the large room was silent as she walked along the storage units, catching glimpses of vases and silver and ceramic ware.

She found him sitting on the floor next to a tall rack that held paintings from the European and American collections. When he looked up at her, she could see that he'd been crying, though he tried to hide it, smiling at her and standing up.

"Tad, what's wrong?"

"Nothing, I'm just . . ." But he must have seen that she wasn't going to let him avoid the subject of his tears. "It's just . . . Willem." He said it lightly, as if to say that everyone was missing Willem, weren't they? "It's been a hard couple of weeks."

But when she looked at him, she saw something else entirely on his face. His eyes were haunted, bereft, the eyes of a despairing, heartbroken lover.

"Tad? Were you . . . ?" She couldn't think why she hadn't seen it. Neither Tad nor Willem had ever had relationships that she knew of. And it would explain why Tad had given up his own career to work with Willem so many years ago. "You were in love."

Tad inclined his head. There was nothing else to say. "I'm sorry. Did you need something?"

She waited a beat. She wanted to say she was sorry, to reach out and console him, but instead she said, "I wanted to talk to you about the falcon collar. I think it was misidentified when it was given by Arthur Maloof in 1979. It looks like it may have been on purpose, to disguise the fact that it had been taken out of Egypt illegally. But I think it's actually much more valuable than anyone thought, and I think Karen Philips figured that out. I don't know if it had anything to do with her death or not, but I'm just wondering how it happened. Wouldn't someone have noticed the discrepancy between what the file said and the actual piece? I mean, you and Willem both knew Egyptian stuff really well, right?"

Tad looked warily at her. "Willem wasn't particularly focused on the jewelry," he said. "Maloof gave it at the same time as the gold mummy mask, and that was the piece he really wanted. The jewelry was just Maloof's castoffs."

"Willem loved that mask, didn't he?" Sweeney said. "It's beautiful. Of course he would. And he loved the canopic chest too. I remember catching him staring at it a couple of days before the opening. It was like it was a child."

"He'd been courting Hutchinson for years," Tad said. "It was a real coup to get it."

Sweeney smiled. "He was so proud of it that night of the opening, showing it off to everyone." He *had* been proud. She found herself remembering the way he'd looked as he asked guests to come down to the basement to see it. Like a proud papa. When she'd realized that the stopper was gone, she remembered that one of her first thoughts had been that Willem would be devastated.

"It was amazing, actually," she said, thinking out loud. "I would have thought he would have been completely frantic, thinking that something had happened to the chest. But he wasn't, he was . . ."

In the quiet, semidark room, she saw the look on Tad's face. His eyes darted away in shame.

With a rising horror, Sweeney stared at him. "Wait, he didn't think something had happened to the chest, did he? He can't have, not Willem. If Willem had really thought that one of the stoppers from the chest had been stolen, he would have been freaking out. He would have been raging all over the place, demanding that they find it. But he wasn't. He was perfectly calm."

"Sweeney, this is . . . I need to go." He tried to squeeze past her, but she kept talking and he was obliged to hear the rest of what she had to say.

"Tad? Why did he . . . He knew it hadn't been taken. How did he know that? He must have . . ." It dawned on her, and she saw Tad see that she knew. "Because he put it there himself, didn't he? He knew where it was all along. But that means that he . . . that means that Willem killed Olga."

Tad nodded very slowly. "It was an accident," he said in an almost whisper. "It wasn't like he planned on it."

Sweeney stared at him. "But if he . . . If he killed Olga?" She stood up, wanting suddenly to run, to get away from him. His eyes told her everything she needed to know. "That means that you killed him."

Tad stood too, taking her arm and pulling her toward him so he could look very deeply into her eyes, as though he was trying to find something there. "You're right," he said, gripping Sweeney's arm so tightly she gasped. "You're right. I did."

THIRTY-SEVEN

It was nearly five by the time Quinn was ready to go home. He checked his cell phone, found a message from Sweeney, thought about trying her at the museum, and decided to wait until later. He was just about to leave when he saw the interview notes from the museum staff in his in-box. He'd wanted to double-check with Cyrus Hutchinson about the time he'd left the opening in order to pin down when he and Willem Keane had been walking down the stairs to the basement. He was wondering if maybe Keane had seen something that night, if he'd seen the person who'd killed Olga and therefore been a threat to that person.

He checked the notes, found Hutchinson's assertion that he'd left at six-thirty. It was possible that Willem had seen something as they'd walked back upstairs. Of course Willem couldn't tell Quinn that anymore, but Cyrus Hutchinson could. Perhaps it made sense to jog his memory a little.

He dialed the home number Hutchinson had given him and asked the woman who answered if he could speak to Mr. Hutchinson. He heard her call out, "Mr. Hutchinson. Telephone," and then Hutchinson came on the phone and said, "Yes?"

"Mr. Hutchinson, this is Detective Tim Quinn in Cambridge."

Hutchinson made a kind of snorting noise and Quinn could hear his fury across the phone lines. "Mr. Quinn, I was made to come back from my country house in the middle of the night, I was *subjected* to repeated questioning, as though I was a common criminal. I cannot imagine what motive you could possibly have for interrupting my dinner, but it had better be a good one."

Quinn took a deep breath. "Mr. Hutchinson, I know you're as eager as we are to find Willem Keane's killer, and I was hoping that we could go over some of what you told me about the night of the opening. You said you and Keane went down to the basement to look at the chest at about six-fifteen, is that right?"

"That's right. I wanted to see how he was

keeping it. I was satisfied with the security, though of course as it turned out I shouldn't have been."

"So you looked at the chest, and then he walked you out at six-thirty?"

"Well, I'd gone upstairs to his office so I could make a phone call," Hutchinson said. "I don't believe in these cell phone things, you know. Think they're silly. I made my call and then . . ."

"Wait a minute. You didn't say anything about this phone call when we talked to you before."

"Didn't I? I thought I did. Didn't Willem tell you?"

"No. So he stayed with you while you made the call?"

"No, that would have been rude. It was a private call. His assistant, Mr. Moran, showed me up to the office and waited for me while I made the call."

"Where was Mr. Keane? Do you know where he went?" Quinn felt his pulse quicken. Keane could have seen whoever it was who had killed Olga Levitch. But if he had, why hadn't he told the police? Was it possible he hadn't realized until later what it was he had seen? If that was the case, maybe he'd mentioned it to the killer and maybe that was why he himself had been killed.

"No, I don't. But when I was done, I met him out in the hall and he escorted me to the front entrance. I walked out to the street and caught a cab to the train station."

"Did he seem okay? He wasn't upset about anything?"

"No. He was as Willem Keane always was, calm, cool, and collected. Except for when he'd seen a piece he wanted. Then it was as though he was looking at a pretty girl."

"Thank you," Quinn said. "I appreciate your help. I'll let you know when there's some news."

He sat at his desk for a minute, thinking, then went back to the conference room and found the copies of the security tapes that he and Ellie had looked at already. He popped the relevant tape into the VCR, fast-forwarding to the right section. There were Hutchinson and Keane coming out of the museum, Keane carrying a trench coat elegantly slung over his arm. He watched Keane wave as Hutchinson walked away. Bingo. He had it. Keane had dumped the stopper, which meant that there hadn't been a robbery at all, which meant that Keane had killed Olga Levitch, which meant that someone else, someone at the museum, had killed Keane.

He jumped up, leaving all of his things on his desk and dialing Sweeney's cell phone number as he headed out to his car. When she didn't answer, he sped up, peeling out and disobeying every traffic rule as he tried to make his way through the rush-hour traffic on Mass. Ave.

"Come on," he yelled at the crush of cars and buses. "Come on!" He checked the time of Sweeney's message again. She'd left for the museum more than an hour ago. He might already be too late.

THIRTY-EIGHT

Sweeney stood with her back against one of the mobile storage units, the pain from Tad's grip on her arm making her dizzy.

"Please, let go of me," she whispered. "Just let go of me and we can talk."

"You have to understand," Tad was pleading with her. "I didn't mean to do it. We were . . . fighting. I told him I knew about Olga, and he hit me. I couldn't believe it. I don't know what happened. I think all those years of . . . of him keeping me hanging, using me when it suited his purposes, never telling me what was going to happen next. I think it all came out right then. I hit him back. We were up on the fourth floor, next to the balcony, and I couldn't stop hitting him. He was bent over the railing and he looked at me and the look was so ugly that I didn't care anymore, and I let him have it and he went over."

Tad took a deep breath. "I couldn't believe

no one heard him fall. The museum was closed to the public, so Denny or whoever must have been off doing something else. And the staff were all over in the annex, I suppose. I waited up there for almost an hour, waiting for someone to come and get me. Then I heard you and that cop down on the third floor, and I went back over to the annex and sat down in my office, and pretty soon I heard the sirens."

He had relaxed his grip as he talked, and Sweeney felt herself relax too as she understood what he was telling her.

"I don't understand," she said. "Why did Willem have to kill Olga? Was it related to Karen Philips?"

"In a way. You were right that Karen Philips knew about the falcon collar. But there was something else too. Willem raped her. I supposed that's the only word. If he didn't force her physically, he forced her all the same."

He saw the confused look on Sweeney's face and went on. "It started when we were in Egypt that summer before her death. Willem was leading a trip and I was along as his assistant. Karen and a couple of other students came along too. Egypt was where we . . . where he let me . . . where we were together sometimes. I think he allowed it to

423

happen there because we were away from everything familiar. He was somehow able to pretend he enjoyed it when we were there."

"So Willem wasn't gay?"

"No. He was mercenary about sexuality. He did whatever he needed to do to get what he wanted. He needed me. He knew that. In order to be a success as curator and then director of the museum, he needed me organizing things for him. He needed me to stay at the university. I'd had job offers at lots of places, but he convinced me to stay and work for him. He was amazing. He knew exactly when I had given up, when he needed to throw me a few scraps to keep me hanging. It was very . . . one-sided." He looked embarrassed.

"In Egypt, I could tell that he was going to force the issue with Karen. I knew him so well, I knew when he was in his predatory mode, but I didn't know how she would respond. There had been a lot of young women before her, and I have to say that most of them were willing participants. But with her it was different. I saw her one morning and I just knew. She looked . . . defeated. That's the only word I can think of. She looked like she'd had all the spirit beaten out of her."

"Why didn't she tell anyone?"

"Because she needed him too. Karen was from a working-class family. She needed fellowships if she was going to go to graduate school. She needed Willem and she knew it. I recognized the look on her face that morning. She was trapped. Just like I was trapped."

"Did the relationship continue once you were back at the university?"

"Yes. I think she probably did what she had to do to stay on Willem's good side. I caught them once, in his office. I'm still haunted by the look on her face." He shuddered.

"But then came this thing with the jewelry. Willem was so excited about the Arthur Maloof donation. The mask was going to put the museum's collection on the map. I suspected from the beginning that there was something wrong with the provenance, and I told him so, but Willem couldn't see past that golden face. It was like he was in love and wasn't willing to hear a bad word about his beloved. At some point I realized he didn't even care."

"So the piece was taken out of Egypt illegally?"

"Oh, yeah. Maloof had gotten it on the black market and created all these fake documents to make it look real. He was a publicity junkie. He loved having people hold him up as this great philanthropist, loved having galleries named after him. He was without a doubt the most arrogant man I've ever met in my life. Anyway, Willem thought everything was fine, but then Karen was researching the jewelry and she discovered that the falcon collar wasn't what the file said it was. It was a stupid mistake. Maloof must have gotten it mixed up, but she went to Willem and said that she had looked into the provenance and it was suspect. She said she thought they should look at all the other provenances again, including the paper trail on the mask. She was worried Maloof had been dealing on the black market."

"What did Willem say?"

"He told her that she couldn't say a word to anyone. That if she did, he would make sure she never went to graduate school. Ever." Tad grimaced. "He was actually proud of himself when he told me this. He thought he'd taken care of it."

Sweeney knew what had to come next. "So he killed her and made it look like suicide?"

Tad looked surprised. "No, it really was suicide. I think after she went to him about the collar and he reminded her that her entire future was dependent on him, she realized she really was *stuck*. I think she felt that there was no way for her to get out of the situation she found herself in. That's generally why people kill themselves, isn't it? They don't see any options." His eyes filled with tears. "I've always felt so guilty about that. I knew and I didn't tell anyone."

Sweeney couldn't argue with him. He'd had it in his power to save Karen Philips's life.

Tad gave her a small smile. "And then you came along. I think I'd forgotten all about the collar. When Karen died, Willem and I thought the questions would die too. But then there you were, asking me to go find the collar so you could put it on display. I told Willem, and of course he said there was no way we were going to risk exhibiting it. If someone else noticed the discrepancies in the file, they were going to start asking questions too and then questions might arise about the entire Maloof collection. So he told me to take the collar out of storage and hide it somewhere. We would just pretend that it had disappeared or been misplaced and hope you wouldn't ask too many questions."

It wouldn't have happened if it hadn't

been for her, Sweeney realized. It was her fault that Olga was dead. Willem too, when it came right down to it.

She was thinking about this when they heard voices from the other end of the storeroom and she looked up and saw Quinn standing there.

There was something about the look on his face that sealed it, that told her what she needed to know. She saw it in his half-stern, half-hopeful eyes. He was breathless, a hand on his holster, searching her face for a clue as to what was going on. He had thought something had happened to her. He was terrified that something was going to happen to her, Sweeney realized. *Oh, Tim, Oh, Tim.*

She smiled at him, seeing his face dissolve in relief, and her own heart rose a little. "You have to listen to him," she said, pointing to Tad. "You have to hear what he has to say."

THIRTY-NINE

Quinn sat down across from Tad Moran on the floor of the storage room to hear the rest of the story. Sweeney sat next to him, quiet and still. He was still reeling from the sense of relief he'd felt upon seeing she was okay, and he almost couldn't bear to look at her.

"She was a sharp old thing," Tad continued. "I always suspected it must have come from living in the USSR, from feeling always under surveillance. You would learn to be a spy of sorts yourself, wouldn't you? To observe and keep information that might help you later."

"Olga Levitch?" Quinn asked.

Tad nodded. "On the night of the opening, Willem was showing off the chest. He'd taken a few people down to look at it. Finally he took Cyrus Hutchinson down to see it, and he turned off the alarm and used his key to open the cabinet so Hutchinson could see all the security features. It was stupid. He knew it was stupid. But things like the . . . things like the chest made him kind of crazy. He wasn't himself. He wasn't thinking."

"Hutchinson went up to his office to make a phone call. You showed him in," Quinn said. "That's when it happened, right?"

"Yeah. Willem remembered that he hadn't locked the cabinet back up. As I say, he wasn't thinking straight. He was so consumed by the chest. So he went back downstairs and used the opportunity to look at it, alone. He picked up one of the stoppers to feel the alabaster. He had done this a hundred times, but he couldn't resist. He'd put on a pair of cotton gloves. And then Olga was there. She was supposed to be patrolling the museum, looking for litter or helping the caterers.

"She told him that she'd seen me taking something out of the storage room one morning and that she didn't want to go to the police, she just wanted to tell him.

"Willem thought she was trying to black-mail him. He said he panicked. He was holding the stopper and he just . . . he killed her. He said he was in a kind of dream as he did it. He looked down at the stopper, covered in blood, and it was as though someone else had done it and handed it to him. It was only later that he realized she wasn't trying to blackmail him at all. She was afraid of the police. She was telling him for his own good.

"Anyway, Willem left the cabinet unlocked and used his penknife to make it look like someone had broken in. He took off the gloves, turned them inside out, stuffed them in his pocket, and covered the stopper with his trench coat. Then he went to meet Hutchinson."

Quinn finished for him. "He walked Hutchinson out, turned his back to the security camera and bent over as if to tie his shoe, dropping the stopper into the garbage can. He knew it would be found. He knew all along that it would be found."

"That was the thing that made me think of him," Sweeney said. "If Willem had thought for a second that one of the stoppers had actually been stolen, he would have been beside himself. But he wasn't. I remember how calm he seemed. It was because he knew where it was. He knew it was okay."

"I didn't know right away, of course," Tad said. "It was after you asked me about the cabinet being unlocked. I realized that it must have been Willem. I came to talk to him. He was up on the fourth floor. There was no one around and I told him I thought he'd killed Olga. I knew as soon as I saw his eyes. He told me all of this. He said it wasn't his fault. He'd done what he had to do. I said I was going to have to tell someone. He swung at me. I'm not sure what he was thinking he was going to do. Perhaps he was going to kill me. I don't know. He was desperate. I ducked and swung at him. I got him on the cheek and he was so mad, he kept swinging. I shoved him against the balcony, and he kind of leaned back over it, trying to get his breath, I think. And then he said that he would say I had killed Karen Philips and I had killed Olga and that I would go to prison for the rest of my life. I punched him again and again and he . . . he just went over. I must have got him under the chin because he kind of went up in the air and then he was gone.

"He didn't scream. I don't know why he didn't scream. Maybe he wanted to . . . I don't know. But he didn't scream. I knew there weren't any security cameras out on the balconies, so I went back to my office and collected myself, combed my hair, changed out of the shirt I'd been wearing, and waited for someone to come tell me what had happened."

Quinn stood up. Suddenly, he was so tired he could barely keep his balance. "I don't understand why you were willing to cover up for him, why you didn't go to the police when you realized what had happened. Where did your loyalty come from?"

Sweeney looked into his eyes, as though she was pleading with him not to ask the question. Tad said nothing, and finally Sweeney looked up at Quinn with her green, green eyes and said, "He loved him."

Tad was crying again. "He could be . . . very kind. Sometimes. He could be very, very kind."

"I'll have to take you down so you can make a statement," Quinn said. "But I think there's an argument to be made that you struck out at Keane in self-defense. You may not even be charged."

Tad Moran didn't look relieved. He just looked sadly up at Quinn. "I'm so sorry," he said. "I'm so, so sorry."

Quinn thought of the same words he'd said to Denny Keefe and he thought about how he *was* sorry, how he sometimes felt as though he made things worse rather than better. He'd once had a dream in which he'd been invited into a room with perfect white carpeting. As he walked in, he realized that his shoes were covered with mud and he was tracking it in. He turned around, tried to go back, but everything he did only made it worse. He felt a little like that now.

The three of them waited together for Ellie to come with backup. They would have to hold Tad Moran until they'd had a chance to formally interview him, but he'd most likely go home tomorrow.

One of the uniformed cops cuffed him, and they led him downstairs and out onto the sidewalk, where the cars were waiting. Quinn held him loosely by the arm while they got everything organized. He'd meant what he'd said. If Tad Moran's story checked out, Quinn didn't think they'd charge him with anything other than being an accessory after the fact. Moran seemed more relaxed, standing there in the balmy summer air. It was dark now, and the night smells of cooking food and cigarette smoke and a sweet unknown smell, like perfume, wafted across the street.

Quinn watched Sweeney, standing alone by the sidewalk. She was staring out over the crowds of people, but beyond them, as though somewhere out there was a mountain range or an ocean, something only she could see. She was beautiful. He was in love with her. There, he'd said it. He'd said he loved her, if only to himself. But there was

Ian, and as he admitted his love to himself, a vision of Maura's face swam up in front of him, her small, feline prettiness, her tragic eyes, her sad, sad face. He had always known the state of her mind immediately on seeing her face. His last memory of her, lying dead in the bathtub, was of her face, expressive of pain even in death.

Students had gathered around the entrance to the museum and Ellie and some of the other guys tried to clear them away, speaking to them good-naturedly, pushing them back. Quinn watched her work. She was good. He had to admit it. She was good with people. She knew how to talk to them, how to read them, how to get them to do what she wanted them to do. And what was being a cop if not that?

Then suddenly he felt Tad Moran's arm slip away, and Sweeney was calling out, "No!" and he turned in time to see the tall, stooped figure dash into the traffic. There was a squeal of brakes, and he imagined the thud before he saw it happen.

And as everyone rushed forward and he saw Ellie raise her head and meet his eyes, and he knew that Tad Moran was dead, he found that it was Sweeney he searched for. And he reached for her, pressing her tearstained, horrified face to his chest and holding it there as she sobbed, and later he wasn't sure if he had kissed her eyelids or only imagined that he had, trying to take away the images of death she'd seen, trying to take away the awful finality of it all.

FORTY

They let Sweeney go at two A.M. There had been statements to give and things to approve, and as she drove home she tried not to think about what was waiting for her. She knew she should have called, knew she should have let Ian know what was happening, but there hadn't been an opportunity.

She'd explain, tell him that all she wanted was a drink and to go to bed and that they would talk in the morning. She didn't see his car in front of the house and wondered if he wasn't home yet. She had a sudden feeling of panic that she didn't stop to analyze, and by the time she reached the door, she knew. She didn't have to open the door and see his coat and shoes missing from the hallway, his books and papers gone from the dining room table, the empty half of the closet to know that he was gone. There wasn't a note. There wasn't anything. She went to the kitchen and poured herself a tumbler of whiskey, downing it in one big swallow and pouring another, and then she went through into the living room and sat down on the couch. The General came out of the bedroom and watched her from his post on the windowsill. She couldn't cry. She thought about calling Quinn. But instead she poured herself another drink.

It was a couple of days later that the weather turned. When Sweeney woke up, she knew there was something different, knew that fall had come again. That afternoon, she walked across the yard, wishing she had a sweater, and thought about how quickly it had gotten cold. She was getting into the car when the phone rang. It was Quinn.

"Hi," he said. "It's Tim. Tim Quinn."

She smiled. "Hi, Tim Quinn."

"I just wanted to see if you were okay."

"I'm okay. How about you?"

"Yeah. I guess so." There was a silence and then he whispered, "I'm still mad at myself for not keeping him under better restraint."

"He seemed really calm."

"I know, but . . ."

"It's not your fault." It was the only thing she knew to say.

"Yeah. Well, anyway, we've tied up some of the loose ends. I thought you might want to know about them. Do you think . . . I thought I might go to Flannery's tonight. Maybe, if you and Ian feel like a drink, you could head over."

Sweeney waited a minute. She didn't feel like going into it on the phone. "That sounds good. What time?"

"I'll probably be there from seven or so on."

"Okay, well, I'll see you there." She wondered if he'd noticed her use of "I," wondered what he thought about it.

We'll see, she told herself. *We'll just have to wait and see.*

He was sitting in a corner booth when she got there, with a pint of Guinness in front of him, listening to the musicians. She looked down and saw his foot tapping out the rhythm on the table leg. When he saw her, he smiled and waved.

"The music's good tonight," she said, sitting down across from him. "Have you been here a long time?"

"Ten minutes or so." He looked past her, then asked, "Where's Ian?"

"He left."

"To go back to London?"

"Maybe. I don't know where he is, actually. He may still be in Boston for all I know.

But he left . . . he left me."

"I'm sorry." He waited a beat. "So you're not going to London?"

"No. I'm not going to London."

He met her eyes across the table just as a waitress came up and asked Sweeney what she wanted. She asked for a scotch, straight up, and when the waitress had gone, she met Quinn's eyes again. He'd been about to say something. She could feel it still hanging there in the air. But instead, he turned to watch the musicians and told her, "I thought you'd like to know that Denny Keefe has agreed to testify against McMaster. We've brought in some of his associates, including one of the guys who roughed up Keefe. And the FBI has some really good leads on the paintings and artifacts taken in 1979. We may be able to recover some of them."

"That's great. What about Tad's mother? For some reason, I've been thinking about her."

"He'd taken out a life insurance policy. It explains why he did it the way he did it. Any other way and it would have been a clear-cut suicide, but this way it was that he escaped and was hit accidentally while trying to get away. She'll get the money. I hope it will provide for her care. But I can't stop kicking myself. I should have known."

"You couldn't have." She looked down at his hand on the table and wanted to reach out for it. "You've got to let yourself off the hook." He looked away and she changed the subject. "You know, I thought Jeanne Ortiz might have had something to do with it. Even after the thing with the kid."

"Oh, yeah, didn't you say something about her being around a lot around the time Karen Philips died?"

Sweeney nodded. "I asked her about it. Yesterday. It turns out she was having an affair with this woman Susan Esterhaus's boyfriend. Who's now her husband. She didn't want her to know, which is why she acted so strangely."

She sighed. There was something about it that just made her sad. "Well, congratulations," she told him. "On solving it. Although that doesn't seem like the right word."

"If I'd been on the ball from the beginning, we could have gotten Keane for Olga Levitch's murder. I don't know why, but I can't stop thinking about her. You should have seen this place where she lived. It was just so . . . sad. So empty. She had nothing to show for any of it, nothing at all."

They talked about the case for a bit, then

she asked him, "So how are things going with the new partner?"

"Better. I was giving her a hard time. It really freaked me out, having a woman partner. I think that's what it was. Anyway, I was kind of an asshole to her. But I think it'll be okay now." He looked so tired.

"I can't imagine you being an asshole to anybody." She tried to keep it light, but he looked up and his eyes were very, very serious, burning into hers before he cast them down again.

"Yeah, well . . ." He looked up again and Sweeney thought he was going to say something, but instead he drained his beer and looked miserably up at the clock behind the bar. "I guess I should get home. Patience was nice enough to stay late, but I shouldn't take advantage. Anyway, I just wanted to let you know what happened with Keefe."

"Okay. I'll walk out with you."

Outside, it was dark and cold. Sweeney had tied a sweatshirt around her waist and she put it on.

"Well, I'll be seeing you," he said, hunching down in his polo shirt, as though protecting himself from the cold.

"Wait, Tim." He stopped and turned, gratefully, she thought, but she wasn't sure. He stood there on the sidewalk, his blue eyes wide and somehow childlike. Sweeney suddenly had a glimpse of what he must have looked like as a little boy, his round head and short blond hair, his face open and curious and just a little apprehensive.

She strode up to him, emboldened now by that openness. "Are we going to talk about it?"

He just blinked at her.

"I don't know why you asked me for a drink if you were going to just act weird and then not say anything."

"I . . ."

The scotches had done their work. She didn't care anymore. "There's obviously something going on here. Ian knew it. He never came right out and said it, but I think he did. And Toby said something to me about it too. Apparently everybody's aware of it but us."

"What did Toby say?"

"He said that he thought we were attracted to each other."

Quinn stared at her. Then he did something that would haunt Sweeney for months afterward, whenever she thought about that night. He laughed.

"As though you'd . . . as though we'd ever . . . That's crazy." She watched his face as he said it and thought she detected something hopeful there. Was he saying it was crazy, or was he asking if she thought it was crazy? It was that little bit of hope in his face that gave her the courage to do what she did next.

One moment he was looking at her, his eyes dark in the late dusk. And then she was stepping toward him and she was kissing him, hard, as though kissing him could take away the silence between them, could say all the things they hadn't said. He kissed her back, his lips cool and dry and unfamiliar, then warm and moist. His arms had gone around her, and she took his face in her hands and kissed him some more, searching for him, trying to find something there that could consume her, subsume her. She wanted to lose herself in his face, his body.

Their hips knocked against each other, their bellies, their groins. Her lips were hot against his lips. She could feel her tongue against his.

"Sweeney," he whispered. She felt him step back, his hands on her shoulders. "Sweeney, just wait, just hold on a second." He pushed her back, away from him, and when she looked into his eyes, she saw confusion, and something else, something like disgust.

She could feel shame overtake her in a slow, burning flush. "I'm sorry, I shouldn't have . . ." She pulled away from him, his eyes burning her. "I had too many drinks. I should get going." She stumbled, wanting to get away from him but waiting to see what he was going to do. There was still something hanging there between them. But when she looked up at him, he looked only disappointed, and it was that disappointment that made her run.

She turned and felt her legs moving independently of her body, her arms pumping through the humid air. And suddenly she remembered something she'd long forgotten, a night, years ago, when she was only a child. She had been visiting her grandparents in Newport with her father, and they had gotten into an argument, about the way her father was living, she supposed, about the kind of father and son he was, about how much of a disappointment he'd been to his parents. Sweeney's grandmother never raised her voice, and she didn't raise it that night, but somehow Sweeney had known just how angry she was, and she had known that her father, who had a volatile temper, was about to lose it. She had jumped up from the dinner table and run out into the night. She could remember the sound of her sandaled feet on the pavement and the smell of the ocean as she'd run and run along the road, not knowing where she was going, just running and running, trying to get away from the voices, from the growing storm on her father's face, knowing that someone would have to come after her, knowing that her flight might stop the argument.

After a few minutes she had stopped, listening for the sound of footsteps behind her. But there had been only the silence of the night, and her loneliness, and feeling the same emptiness behind her tonight, she knew he hadn't followed her, and she didn't stop running until she was home.

FORTY-ONE

"It's cooler today," Ellie said. "I didn't think it would ever get cool again." She sipped her soda. "I'm really happy we got him," she said. "But it doesn't feel the same as if we'd broken him down, you know?"

The day before, she had come up to Quinn's desk holding a piece of paper and looking a little deflated. "We got him," she'd said dully. "The guy who killed Luz Ramirez. The computers came back with a match on the semen. He's a convicted sex offender. Aggravated rape. Got out over the summer. He was a ticking time bomb. We can go pick him up. I've got his address right here."

Quinn was already up and ready to go, checking his holster. "You don't seem very happy about it. He'll be locked up for the rest of his life now. He won't hurt anyone else."

"Yeah," Ellie said, looking out over the

lights from the buildings around the yard. "But we didn't do it. The computer did it."

"Be thankful for the computer," he said. "Years ago we never would have found a guy like that."

"Yeah, but . . ."

"I know what you mean," he'd said finally. "It's not as satisfying. But you know what? Most of these things, they get solved by chance. Someone mentioning something, some guy we already know about screwing up again." He'd given her a minute and then said, "You ready to go get him?"

They'd found him watching TV in his apartment and charged him, but Quinn knew what she meant. He hadn't felt all that great about it, either. After the outcome of the Hapner Museum case, it made Quinn feel like he didn't have a lot to show for the past few weeks of work.

Now, sitting at a table at an outdoor café around the corner from headquarters, Quinn studied Ellie's face. She seemed a little older today, her forehead drawn down in concentration. Or maybe it was him. Maybe he'd come to see her differently. Quinn didn't trust his own perceptions anymore. But no, he realized, she had her hair different today. That was it. She'd cut her hair. It was shorter, with bangs, and it was clean and shiny. It looked good.

She could tell he was staring at her, so he said, "You got your hair cut. It looks good."

"Oh." A hand flew up to her hair. "Thanks."

There was a silence, and he found that he knew what she was going to say before she said it.

"Look, when I went off on that guy, it was stupid. I shouldn't have done it. I'm sorry."

He hesitated. He could let it go, tell her it was okay. He was so tired, he almost didn't want to hear about anyone else's pain. But he knew she wanted to tell him, and so he said, "Why'd you do it?"

She took a sip of her soda, then leaned forward, squaring her shoulders, and looked him right in the eyes for a few seconds before looking away. "I figured Havrilek would've told you. I left Ohio because of something that happened out there. A guy, another cop, he asked me out and we went to the movies and his place and he, he . . . raped me. But because it was a date, you know the story. I went to the hospital, made them do a rape kit, had them hold the evidence. I didn't end up pressing charges because I couldn't do that to my parents, have it in the paper and everything, but everyone knew."

"I'm sorry," he said. "I'm really sorry."

"The thing is that I've said it so many times to victims, you shouldn't blame yourself. He had no right. But I do blame myself. I do." She picked up her soda again, but instead of taking another sip, she held it in both hands. Quinn recognized the gesture. It was what you did with a cup of hot coffee on a cold day, letting the warmth seep through the mug to your cold hands.

"They didn't fire you, did they?" He'd heard of cases where that happened, where a female cop got raped by another cop and they found a reason to let her go because she made everybody so damned uncomfortable.

"Nah. My lieutenant was pretty decent about it, actually. Gave me a really good reference. That's why I'm here." She smiled for a second before her face fell again. "You probably wondered about that. That's why I'm here. I got a kick-ass reference."

"You're here because you're good."

She looked up at him with eyes that he recognized for what they were. Maura's eyes, wounded eyes. He'd realized it standing there on the sidewalk in front of the museum, when he'd thought of Maura's face, when he'd realized he was in love with Sweeney.

Looking at her, he thought of Maura again. He would never forget the way she'd looked at him the last time he'd seen her alive, angry and accusing and sad. That was why Ellie irritated him so.

But Maura was dead. And Ellie wasn't Maura. She was his partner, a cop, a good cop, and she had had something bad happen to her. That was all.

"You shouldn't feel like it's your fault," he said gently.

"I know. But I do."

They watched a couple sit down at one of the other tables and lean in to touch hands across the table. The woman was younger than the man, very beautiful, wearing a halter dress that showed off her tanned shoulders. Quinn felt an ache, not desire exactly, but a kind of wanting.

"So what's the deal with you and Sweeney?" Ellie asked finally.

He decided not to lie to her. "God, I have no idea. I really have no idea."

"Does she know?"

Quinn didn't need to ask what she meant. But he didn't know what to say. He finally settled on, "No. Not exactly," because he was pretty sure that Sweeney didn't know that when she'd kissed him he'd been so surprised that he hadn't known what to do.

He'd thought about kissing her more often than he'd admitted to himself, but when it had actually happened he had wanted to slow it down, to stop and just . . . talk to her. Her hair had seemed to be everywhere, tendrils falling away from the barrette in which she'd pinned it up, and her long limbs had felt hot against his. Kissing her had been . . . different. That was all he could come up with. She had felt so different from Maura, so much more substantial against his body. From the first time he'd kissed Maura, the first time they'd made love, he'd always been careful with her, as though she would break under his weight. But with Sweeney, it was as though she was challenging him, with her lips and her body. He'd pushed her away, wanting to slow down and talk about whatever it was that was between them, wanting, he realized, to finish telling her about his class and about Megan and Patience. Over the last few months, he'd found himself saving up little stories to tell her, and there was a way his stories were still up there in his head, wanting to come out.

He had wanted to take her somewhere where they could stay up half the night, telling each other their stories. That was it, he saw. He wanted to know who her best friend had been in third grade, what her favorite movie was. What was the best vacation she'd even taken? He wanted to know what she ate for breakfast and whether she'd ever broken any bones. But she had misunderstood, and before he could explain, she was gone.

Why hadn't he gone after her, called her that night? All day yesterday, he'd kept taking out his phone and finding her number, but he hadn't known where to start.

Now he thought he did know.

"I have some things I should do," he said awkwardly to Ellie. "Do you mind if I take off before you finish your soda?"

"No, not at all. It's nice to just sit." She grinned at him. "Good luck."

He allowed a little smile. "Thanks. I'll see you tomorrow?"

"Yeah." She sat back in her chair, the late afternoon sun on her face, and Quinn left her there, looking like a cat curled up in a patch of light.

He tried Sweeney's cell phone, and when it went directly to voice mail, he sat there in the car for a moment, thinking about what to do. The waiting itself gave him courage, and the idea of going to her house became clearer the longer he sat there watching the traffic. He could almost see himself at her door, telling her that he'd made a mistake, that he'd just wanted to slow everything down, to talk to her, to know what it was she had meant when she had kissed him.

It didn't take long to get to Russell Street. He knew which apartment was hers, though he'd never been inside. He climbed the stairs and knocked on the door, his body suddenly full of a riotous energy. It zinged through his veins, zipping through his limbs like electricity. He knew what he was going to say. It was simple. Or perhaps he wouldn't say anything, perhaps he would just . . . take her in his arms and kiss her. It was what he wanted to do, he realized suddenly. It was his . . . he almost laughed as he said the word to himself . . . destiny.

He heard footsteps inside and then the door opening, and he took a deep breath and looked up into the eyes of a tall, dark-skinned man wearing white painter's pants and a blue undershirt. The smell of paint filled the hallway. Beyond him, Quinn could see the empty apartment, the stepladders and buckets, the sheets spread over the floor.

"Can I help you?" the guy asked.

It took Quinn a minute to say, "I'm a friend of Sweeney's. Is she . . . around?"

"She moved out a couple days ago," the guy said.

"Did she say where she was going?"

"Nah. She said she might be out of the country for a while, so I should send any mail to a post office box. You want it?" Quinn shook his head. "The guy who helped her move her stuff was this tall guy, dark hair. I saw him around a lot. Nice guy. She didn't tell you she was moving?"

"No, but that's okay. I'll just . . . I'll give her a call. I didn't realize she was moving."

"Hey, I think it was kind of a spur-of-the-moment thing." The man looked genuinely sorry. He must have seen something on Quinn's face that made him feel the need to soothe his ego. "I'm sure she was gonna tell you."

"Thanks," Quinn said, turning and stumbling a little as he headed back down the stairs. Behind him, he heard the door to the apartment close. Outside again, he felt suddenly dizzy. All that crazy energy he'd felt at the door was now just sitting in his stomach. He leaned over for a second, sure he was going to throw up.

That was it. She'd gotten back together with Ian, gone to London with him. Of course she had. The kiss had been just a stupid thing. She'd been drinking, hadn't she? That must have been it.

He got back in the Honda, started it up, then shut it down again and got out. His stomach still knotted up, he started walking toward Davis Square. He needed a drink. Before he could go home and face Patience, with her knowing eyes, before he could face Megan, he needed a beer. He took one last look up at the building, as though he might find Sweeney in one of the windows, then put his head down and started walking.

FORTY-TWO

Sweeney looked out the window of the airplane over the dry, beige landscape. She could see a patchwork of farmland every once in a while, and then long stretches of desert. There was something soothing about it, the land uncomplicated and laid bare, nothing hidden or obscured.

In Cambridge, it was already winter. An early frost had killed everything green and living, and a freak October snowstorm had covered everything in a virginal white layer of snow, then melted into a depressing slushy mess. On the way out to the airport that morning, she had watched the almost-bare trees and dirty snow flash by and finally felt her spirits lift at the thought of sun, of spicy food, of mariachi bands and beers with limes.

"We have a beautiful day for our flight to Oaxaca City," the pilot's voice came on the address system. Then he said something in

Spanish and Sweeney turned to her seatmate. "Did you hear what he said? What did he say?" The Spanish came again, fast and incomprehensible to her. She'd been listening to language tapes for a couple of weeks, but the pilot's voice was much harder to catch than the slower-speaking man and woman on her tapes.

Toby, who spoke nearly perfect Spanish, looked annoyed. "He just said the same thing he said in English, that we have a beautiful day for our flight to Oaxaca City."

"Okay, okay." She rearranged her magazines on her lap.

"Are you going to do this to me the whole trip?"

"No. I'm practicing. *Yo soy Sweeney. Donde esta el baño?*"

"Not bad." He grinned, then said, "You're still going to ask me to translate the whole trip, though, aren't you? I'm starting to regret this already."

"Look, if you and I and the General could live together for six weeks in your apartment without killing each other, I think you can handle me for a month in sunny Mexico."

"I suppose that's right." He went back to the book he was reading, but Sweeney touched his arm and he looked up again, squinting into the strangely angled sun coming through the window.

"Toby. Thanks for letting me stay with you. I don't think I really said that."

"Come on. You don't have to say it."

"I know, but . . ."

He reached across her and pulled down the shade on her window. "You still haven't talked to Ian?"

"No." She moved the magazines to the seat pocket, then took them out again.

"And what about the cop?"

"Quinn." She shook her head. "Uh-uh."

He smiled at her, searching her face for something, and she looked away as the flight attendant came around taking drink orders. Sweeney got her wallet out of her bag and waved her over.

"Let's get tequilas," she said to Toby. "Because of Mexico." She ordered two Cuervos and poured them out, the yellow liquid running silkily from the bottle.

"To the Day of the Dead," she said, touching her plastic cup to Toby's.

They came in low over the brown and arid-looking land.

"To Mexico," he said.

ABOUT THE AUTHOR

Sarah Stewart Taylor is the author of three previous Sweeney St. George mysteries, including the Agatha Award finalist *O' Artful Death.* She lives with her family in Vermont. Visit her online at www.sarah stewarttaylor.com.